Berkley Prime Crime titles by Christine Husom

SNOW WAY OUT
THE ICED PRINCESS

THE ICED PRINCESS

CHRISTINE HUSOM

BERKLEY PRIME CRIME, NEW YORK

**BERKLEY
PRIME
CRIME**

**An imprint of Penguin Random House LLC
375 Hudson Street, New York, New York 10014**

THE ICED PRINCESS

A Berkley Prime Crime Book / published by arrangement with the author

ISBN: 978-0-425-27081-3

PUBLISHING HISTORY
Berkley Prime Crime mass-market edition / December 2015

PRINTED IN THE UNITED STATES OF AMERICA

10 9 8 7 6 5 4 3 2 1

Cover illustration by Julia Green.
Cover design by Lesley Worrell.
Interior text design by Laura K. Corless.

**Penguin
Random
House**

*To my faithful readers who make it especially fun
for me to craft tales. And to my family and friends for their
unwavering love and support. I am truly blessed.*

ACKNOWLEDGMENTS

Once again, thank you to my agent, John Talbot; to Michelle Vega, senior editor at the Berkley Publishing Group, who is a delight to work with; to my proofreaders, Edie Peterson and Elizabeth Husom for all their help; to Timya Owen for going on a fact-finding trip for me; and Yvette Grant in Production, Marianne Grace my copyeditor, Julia Green for my lovely cover and Danielle Dill, the publicist for Berkley Prime Crime.

The idea for a story starts with the writer, but it takes a team to turn that story into a book. Thank you, thank you, thank you.

1

"Camryn Brooks, you and your antics cost me the election. My career is ruined." I envisioned the irate woman on the other end of the phone line, thankful she wasn't standing there in person. And if she was calling from Washington, D.C., it was a safe distance from where I was standing in Brooks Landing, Minnesota.

"Senator Zimmer, I—"

"Don't even try to give me one of your lame denials or excuses. I know exactly what happened. I saw it with my own eyes and in my own office. You had your hands all over my husband." That was true. I was doing my best to push him away from me, trying to find the most effective spot, which was difficult since I only had two hands and he seemed to have somewhere between six and ten.

"Senator Zimmer, I—"

"What everyone here in Washington and back home in Minnesota has been talking about is how I had no control over my staff and certainly could not be effective in the senate if they weren't doing their jobs. And they kept bringing up the whole moral issue besides. I did not do one single thing to deserve it." That was partly true. What the senator couldn't control was her husband's errant behavior. As far as I knew, everyone on her staff was professional, had high work standards, and did not cross ethical lines.

In my opinion, Ramona Zimmer should have known better than to marry a man who had suavely moved in and swept her off her feet after his previous wife had dumped him for two important reasons, infidelity and laziness. When he was courting her, Peter Zimmer somehow managed to land a good job that meant a transfer from Illinois to Minnesota.

But it wasn't long after Ramona was elected to the United States Senate that he quit his job to "spend quality time with his wife" in Washington, D.C. Ha. He must have laughed all the way to the bank when Ramona was elected. He had his sugar mama back where he liked her: gainfully employed. People had tried to warn Ramona about his character, or lack thereof, but she'd put her blinders on and earplugs in.

I felt a bit sorry for the woman. She had an inflated ego when it came to her political knowledge and negotiating skills but had little confidence in her personal relationships with men. She had trouble believing one would find her attractive, much less sexy. She was not homely by any means, and she looked pretty when she smiled. It was her large frame and the extra weight she carried that made her self-conscious. And her flat feet unfortunately caused her to walk with an awkward gait.

I'd first gone to work for her when I lived in Illinois, after I finished college at the University of Illinois in Chicago. I can't say that I regretted following her to Washington, D.C., to serve as her director of legislative affairs, exactly. But had I known the personal humiliation and career damage I would suffer because of her husband's inappropriate behavior, I would never have taken the job. My parents were called into question by the local townsfolk, and we learned in the fallout that people in small Midwestern towns took things to heart more than the big city folks in our nation's capital.

Everyone in Brooks Landing, Minnesota, had rooted for me when I'd landed the prestigious position, but it had all come crashing down a few short years later. I returned to my hometown the worse for wear. As it turned out, my mother had been diagnosed with a serious illness at around the same time, and I stepped in to run my parents' shop. Curio Finds wasn't where I'd planned to be at that stage of my life, but it was where I needed and wanted to be.

"Camryn Brooks, did you hang up on me?"

I wondered what else she might have said while I strolled down memory lane. "Of course not, Senator. You know me better than that."

"It wouldn't be the first time you did something I thought was out of character, am I not right?"

Not right, but there was no convincing the woman her sleazy husband had lied about the incident. I had tried to explain what really happened to no avail. And to top it off, she had a photo to support what she believed was true. Another senator had come into the room with her and snapped a picture of Peter and me with his cell phone. That senator later claimed he had no idea how the media had gotten their hands on it. But it was more than a little suspicious since he sat on the opposite side of the aisle from Senator Zimmer.

My friend and business neighbor Alice Nelson, whom we all called Pinky, stuck her head through the archway that divided our two shops. She mouthed the word "Senator?" and I nodded. That was enough to compel her to swoop in and plop down on the stool sitting next to me, behind the checkout counter. She leaned in close, and one of the feathers from her pink headband tickled my cheek. I held back a reflex chuckle and flicked a finger at the feather. Pinky took the hint and moved back.

"I'm sorry, Senator, but I need to get off the phone. Someone just came into my shop." I felt a slight touch of guilt leading her to believe it was a customer who needed my attention, but Pinky was someone and a special one at that. Plus, there was only so much tongue-lashing I would tolerate from her.

"Camryn, this is not settled. What am I going to do now? I *needed* that position."

"I can't talk right now, but call again, Senator, anytime. 'Bye for now." Why had I told her she could call anytime? I no longer worked for her, and we were barely on speaking terms. Old habits die hard, I guess.

Pinky took the phone from my hand and hung it up. "So that was that the soon-to-be-unseated Senator Ramona Zimmer?"

"It was."

"Honestly, Cami, I can't believe you're so nice to her after what she did to you."

"We were close friends for a long time, Pinky. I try to focus on that and our good years together, before she was bowled over by that creep, Peter."

"What did the fallen politician want?"

That made me smile. "Pinky, you are certainly full of all kinds of descriptive terms this morning."

She shrugged. "I guess. So what did the *senator* want? My snoopy side is dying of curiosity."

"She scolded me for costing her the election. I'm sure she's been stewing about it for the last six days since the results came in, and she finally reached her boiling point. She honestly thinks I'm to blame."

"As if. Did you tell her the guilty party is much closer to home?"

I shrugged. "You know I tried to back when the whole thing happened last spring. She wouldn't listen, and you can't beat a dead horse. Aside from all that, you know what bothers me almost as much?"

"What's that?"

"She acts like it was only her career that was ruined when her husband—who can do no wrong in her eyes—ruined my career, too."

"She should be begging your forgiveness for throwing you under the bus like that instead of blaming you and yammering on about it."

"That won't happen until Peter moves on to his next victim. And that's the main reason I don't want to completely shut the door on Ramona. She doesn't have all that many friends, and she'll need a shoulder to cry on."

"I think I'm going to be sick. I mean, really, Cami, you cannot be serious."

"It may sound a little goofy to you, but I can't help it. She meant a lot to me for a long time, starting back in Chicago when she was a state senator there. She hired me twice, after all. I believe the best thing to do when it comes to Ramona is to forgive and forget."

"I was taught the same thing growing up. But in this case none of us will ever forget what you went through."

I nodded. "I was working alone in the senator's office when Peter barged in. I should have run out the back door that connected our offices and locked it behind me. But I'd never been alone with him before, and I honestly did not expect him to do what he did."

Pinky snapped the dish towel she was holding. "You should have slapped him with a harassment suit from the get-go, long before he ever grabbed you."

"He didn't do anything glaringly obvious. He'd make little innuendos that I wasn't sure how to interpret. You know, a comment here and there, leaning in maybe a little too close when he talked to me. I was so focused on my job and doing it well that I didn't pay enough attention to the signs that said something was brewing and about to explode."

Pinky jumped up. "Brewing! That reminds me, I have more beans to grind before the coffee hour rush. We'll talk more about the senator later."

Her long, skinny legs carried her out of sight in seconds. I took an assessing look around the curio shop, trying to shift my attention back to what needed to be done in the present, not on what had happened in the past. The Christmas shopping season was right around the corner. Black Friday, the day after Thanksgiving, was the traditional start.

The explanation I'd heard growing up was that Black Friday was the day retailers started showing a profit for the year, moving from being in the red to the black. Personally, I'd avoided shopping on that day like it was the Black Plague since I'd had a bad experience years before. On that shopping day from hell, I was a young college student on a modest budget hoping to find some great deals on my family's Christmas gifts. I looked for a long time in a few stores for the perfect gift for my mom.

When I spotted a pale baby blue cashmere sweater at half price, I almost jumped for joy. I picked it up, envisioning what it would look like on my mom, and then someone snatched it out of my hands. My natural reaction was to grab it back. The woman actually pried my fingers loose from the sweater and took off with it. I stood there with my mouth open, stunned that anyone would be that aggressive over a good sweater deal. I went home and made a pact with myself that I would never shop on Black Friday again. So far, so good.

Now I was a retailer and needed to be open on the day after Thanksgiving. The downtown business association had been promoting a "shop locally" campaign and had encouraged all of us to offer sweet deals to bring in buyers. I had been mentally preparing myself, wondering how to gracefully handle rude shoppers, if it came to that. The citizens of Brooks Landing were, by and large, a nice, polite bunch of people, but there were some notable exceptions.

Curio Finds specialized in both new and used snow globes from around the world and other unusual, fun, one-of-a-kind items. In addition to online inquiries with their contacts around Europe, my parents also frequented auctions and garage sales where they collected any number of things people enjoyed. I personally loved the snow globes the most, and in moments when there was some free time, I'd pick one up, give it a shake, and watch the flakes float over the scene and settle on the ground.

When I heard Pinky's grinder, I went next door to offer my help. She had a large assortment of beans from North, South, and Central America and Hawaii. She whipped up creative concoctions and offered daily specials served with or without the variety of muffins and scones she baked.

There was a large open archway between her aptly named shop, Brew Ha-Ha, and Curio Finds, so my customers usually followed where their smellers begged them to go. And her clients often wandered into my place.

I headed to the back of Pinky's shop, on the other side of the tables where she did her grinding. "It seems like you've been selling more coffee lately," I said behind her.

She looked over her shoulder. "It always happens when the weather cools. It's going to be near freezing again tonight. And getting busier is what I wanted to talk to you about. I think we should hire some temporary help for the holidays."

"What for? We're managing."

"But we're both worn-out. At least I am. It's not always easy keeping both shops going with just the two of us."

"I don't know. It seems complicated, especially when it comes to finding the right person, someone we can trust."

Pinky handed me a can of freshly ground coffee. I took a whiff before I put the cover on it then carried it to her counter. She followed behind me. We both looked up when the bell on her entrance door dinged. It was Molly Dalton, one of our high school classmates. Molly had run with a different crowd than Pinky and I had.

Molly opened the top buttons of her stylish dark burgundy wool coat and smiled. "Good morning, girls. I just had to run over and get a cup of your Cin-ful Guatemalan, Pinky. I've been craving it since I woke up this morning. It was so yummy when I tried it for the first time last week."

I'd observed Molly during her visits to the coffee shop in the months since I'd returned to Brooks Landing and wondered who she really was, under the surface. It seemed that she was hiding her true self, whomever that may be, underneath her glamorous exterior.

Thinking back to our first three years of high school, Molly had been on the quiet side, serious and smart. She wore plain-looking clothes and kept mostly to herself. Then in our senior year she made a dramatic change. It was weird. We ended junior year with plain Molly and came back in the fall to a whole new model. Her stepfather had died that July, and there were all kinds of rumors going around the school.

One group figured she had gone off the deep end with grief. Another group thought her stepfather had been overly strict and hadn't allowed her to wear cute clothes and makeup. Still others thought she'd had a surprise makeover and liked the results. Her outside appearance was one thing, but what I couldn't figure out was the change in her personality. She'd gone from shy and studious to bubbly and ditzy. None of us had actually asked her what had prompted the change, so we just kept making up stories about what we thought it might be. Typical teenagers.

I smiled and Pinky said, "Have a seat, Molly, and I'll have your drink ready in a flash. You want it here or to go?"

"Here, thanks. I have nothing but time."

Pinky poured chocolate milk in a metal container, sprinkled a generous amount of cinnamon on top, then held it under her special mixer and turned it on. She whipped it until it was frothy then set it down while she filled a cup half full with her Guatemalan blend.

She added the milk mixture and set it on the counter in front of Molly. "Cami and I were just talking about the fact that we have none. Time, I mean. Yes, we have the same twenty-four hours a day like everyone else, but it seems like all we do is work. The hours we spend here are just part of it."

"Pinky gets up way before dawn to bake her muffins and scones," I said.

Molly took a sip and closed her eyes in obvious apprecia-tion. "Mmm." She looked at Pinky like what I said had finally registered. "Oh. My. That's too early."

Pinky picked up a towel and gave it a quick flick with her wrist. "I love the early morning, watching the sun come up—which it does eventually at this time of year. And I don't mean to complain, because I love what I do, but the extra long hours over the holidays wear on me. I think we should hire someone for the season, someone the two of us can share. But Cami here doesn't think it's such a good idea."

I held up my hand. "I have to admit it would be nice to have more flexibility, but I'm used to long hours. This is noth-ing compared to the work time I logged when I was in Wash-ington. I never even kept track."

"What she's worried about is finding someone we can trust." Pinky directed a puff of breath at a strand of hair that was touching her cheek.

Molly's eyebrows lifted. "You can trust me."

"What?" I said, a little worried about where this was going.

"Hire me. I promise to do a good job. And you can trust me."

Pinky jumped right in. "Molly, I mean no offense, but

you live in a huge house, and your husband makes about a gazillion dollars a year." We secretly called her "the princess" because of the charmed life we thought she led as the wife of a corporate attorney. One who came from old money besides.

Molly pushed her lips out in a pout. "Most people wouldn't believe that I'm bored and . . . lonely. There, I said it."

I looked at her, wondering how that was possible when she could do just about anything she wanted. "Why?" I said.

Molly did not hold back. "My husband is never home, and when he is, he's on the phone with some client or other attorney. I've tried different hobbies, but I've finally realized all I really want is the family I didn't have growing up." Maybe we'd find out what happened that summer between junior and senior year after all.

"Not so good?" I said.

"That doesn't matter now." Or maybe not. "But if I can't have children, I think a job would really help. It'd make me feel useful again."

"Molly, we can't pay very much. And you know, there are all kinds of volunteer jobs out there," I said.

"Yes, there are, and I've done a bunch of volunteering. But when people find out who my husband is, all they do is talk about what a famous attorney he is and how wonderful it must be to be married to him. They don't understand that he's almost always working. Don't get me wrong, when we are alone together, it's wonderful, but it doesn't happen often enough."

Listening to her story, I actually felt a little sorry for Princess Molly, surprisingly.

"Working here would be so much fun. Please give me a chance." She was not too proud to beg.

"Pinky and I will talk about it, and we'll let you know if we decide to hire someone, okay?" I felt Pinky's stare burning a hole in my forehead and did not dare look at her.

"Oh, thank you. I'll write down my phone numbers." Molly dug through the large Coach bag she'd set on the seat next to hers and came out with a flowery notepad and matching pen. She jotted her home and cell phone numbers on a sheet, tore it out, and gave it to me.

I finally braved a look at Pinky. She was staring at Molly with her mouth half open. I had a pretty good idea what she was thinking, but she had herself to blame for starting the whole discussion in the first place. I caught a glimpse of a customer in my store and pointed in that direction. "Gotta go."

Molly turned on her stool. "Ooh. Can I come with you, learn a little more about the cool things you sell?"

There wasn't a nice way to say no. Besides, she was a fairly regular customer. "You're always welcome in my shop," was my noncommittal answer.

She jumped up, and by the time I was on her side of the counter, she was already in my shop greeting Mrs. Emmy Anders, an older woman who often stopped by to browse. Emmy was alone and lonely and—it occurred to me— possibly a perfect match for Molly.

Molly moved to Emmy like there was a magnetic pull. "Hi."

"Hello." Emmy gave her a guarded look then glanced up at me.

"Emmy Anders, this is Molly Dalton . . . my uh . . . my friend. Molly, this is Emmy, another friend."

They nodded and smiled at each other.

"I might be applying for a job here," Molly spit out.

Emmy eyebrows lifted. "Oh?" She might have been thinking there was no way we could afford to pay Molly whatever she was used to earning, given the expensive way she was put together.

"Pinky thought maybe we should have some extra help between Thanksgiving and Christmas," I said.

"Oh. I'd be happy to help you out, too, on a strictly volunteer basis, of course."

Twenty minutes ago, I hadn't given a thought to bringing on more staff. And now we had two women who not only wanted the job, but were practically clamoring for it. Pinky and her big mouth.

"That's very nice of you to offer, Emmy."

"Of course, you'll have to teach me how to run that credit card machine of yours. We didn't have them back when I worked at the hardware store. I'm older, but I can still learn, and I know a fair amount about your merchandise." Yes, she did.

Molly put a hand on Emmy's arm. "And you wouldn't have to pay me, either." A little competition going on: two women vying for the same job at no pay—and one that hadn't been officially created yet.

I heard Pinky clear her throat and noticed her standing in the archway between our shops. "Cami and I will mull this over today, and we'll let you both know what we decide sometime tomorrow." She'd found her voice again.

"This is so exciting. I haven't had a job outside the home in years." Molly's face brightened.

"Nor have I," Emmy said. Her wrinkles deepened with a smile as big as I'd ever seen on her face.

After Molly and Emmy left, I helped Pinky serve her midmorning coffee break crowd. When the rush was over, I shook my finger at her in a lighthearted way. "Be careful what you wish for."

"What are you talking about?"

"Wanting to hire temporary help."

"Holy moly, Cami, I would never have brought it up in front of the princess if I'd had a clue she would practically get down on her knees and beg us to hire her."

"It threw me for a loop, I can tell you that much. And then Emmy. Golly, I wonder how many people out there might want to work for us."

"I don't even want to know. Look what happened when the two of them found out we were just considering it."

"It makes me think there are probably a lot of people who could use some extra money for Christmas gifts."

"Oh, I'm sure that's true. What I couldn't believe is how I let just a few words slip out, and a minute later we have two new possible employees. And at no cost."

"But you know very well we couldn't ask them to do that; we'd need to pay them."

She nodded. "For sure. I wouldn't feel right about it if we didn't. Hey, the good thing is they'd settle for minimum wage, right? So it sounds like you're coming around, thinking we should bring in some help after all."

"The more I think about it, the more it makes sense. I've been trying to be penny-wise, but maybe I've been pound-foolish." I filled a glass with water.

"What do you mean?"

"I wanted to save my parents' money by running this shop alone until my dad, at least, would be back at work."

"As long as your mom is home recovering, I don't think he wants to leave her side."

"That is true. It's worked pretty well with the arrangement you and I have helping each other out. But there are times we probably don't offer the best customer service when it gets really busy and people have to wait."

"You're right about that, which is why we need at least one more person. And you don't have to worry about your parents' finances. I think they have a nice nest egg built up."

"I know my dad has a sizable pension from all those years he worked for General Mills, but still."

"'But still' nothing. If you must know, it was your parents who told me I should figure out a way to make you hire someone in the first place." Pinky could only hold on to most information for so long, and then she was compelled to spit it out.

"All right, all right, let's do it. Should we put a sign in the window? Help wanted?"

"Cami, I don't want every Tom, Dick, and Harry, or their female versions, walking in and applying. No, let's keep this simple and hire Emmy—heaven help me for saying this—and Molly."

"Really? Sorry, but you have not always been kind in what you've said about Molly."

"Well maybe I'm a little jealous."

"I thought it was because she seems needy."

"No, that's what *you* thought. I hadn't picked up on that until you mentioned it a while back when we were looking through those old yearbooks."

I took a drink of water. "That's right. Now we know a little about why she's the way she is. And it sounds like we'll actually be doing her a favor by giving her something to do. She can donate her paychecks to whatever cause she wants to."

Pinky nodded. "And Emmy should be fine; maybe better in your shop than mine."

"True. If we're swamped and all she does is run the cash register, that'll be fine with me."

"Holy moly, we better talk to your folks and find out what we need to do, legally speaking, to hire people."

2

Schoolteacher Erin Vickerman and Brooks Landing police officer Mark Weston, our mutual friends from childhood, came into Pinky's coffee shop just after 4:00 p.m. Erin asked Pinky and me to join them and headed to the tables in the back area. Erin grabbed the back of a pink padded black metal chair, and Mark stood to her right behind a black padded one.

"Are you calling some sort of emergency meeting?" I said, noticing the way Erin's jaw was set and how her dark, almond-shaped eyes had narrowed.

Pinky fell in next to me.

Erin came around to our side of the table, reached her arms up high, and placed the inside of her wrists on Pinky's forehead and on mine. "When Pinky talked to Mark earlier and told him you were thinking of hiring the princess to help out here, I thought we'd better stop in and check to see if the both of you had spiked a fever."

"Very funny, Erin," I said then reached up and tapped her hand. She pulled her arms down and crossed them on her chest.

Pinky nodded up and down as she talked. "I hear you, my friend. Who knew?"

Mark was in uniform and stuck his thumbs into his duty belt. "The question I have is, how are you going to get rid of Molly when she doesn't work out?"

I felt an unexplained sense of loyalty to Molly. "Now, let's not jump the gun here. First off, we have not given her a job offer yet. And what ever happened to giving someone the benefit of the doubt?"

"Cami's right. I have to say the princess seemed really eager to work here in our shops. It was a big surprise to me, since she can go anywhere in the world and do anything she wants. She could buy her own store to run, for heaven's sake. It just goes to show you never know about some people," Pinky said.

"That is the truth. I find that out just about every day on the job," Mark said.

We sat down to finish our conversation.

Erin tapped her fingers on the table. "I know it's not up to us, and it'll only be a short time she'll be working here, but . . ."

"But what?" I asked.

"This is going to sound insulting to the two of you." Erin pointed at Pinky and me.

I couldn't imagine what she had to say. "Just spit it out. We're big girls."

"And I'm the biggest," Pinky said. She was, at that. At

five-ten, she had four inches over me, and we both measured over five foot—even Erin.

"Well, she's kind of high society. Since your businesses cater more to regular people, they might feel a little intimidated by Molly's appearance," Erin said.

Pinky frowned. "Do you think we should tell her to dress down?"

"No, I don't think you should bring her on at all. She is not exactly the brightest bulb on the Christmas tree," Erin said.

I lifted my palms up and then clapped my hands together. "Molly's not as dumb as she sometimes acts. Remember back in the earlier years of high school? She was super smart."

Mark reached over and bumped Erin's arm. "That's right. Back when she flew under the radar, she kept to herself and got good grades. I kind of forgot about that. She's been more on the flashy, uppity side for so long."

Erin nodded. "I forgot about that, too. When did the princess move to Brooks Landing? Was it in ninth or tenth grade?"

"Ninth," Pinky said.

"That's right. The first time I saw her at any after-school events was senior year. I'm a little ashamed to admit this, but I didn't really notice her before then. I never had a class with her."

"We had English and algebra together junior year. Mark, you were in our algebra class," I said.

Mark shook his head. "Don't remind me. Old man Fingen made me sit in the front row, and I got yelled at if I turned around. I don't think Molly and I said a word to each other all year."

"I talked to her senior year when she was suddenly more outgoing," I added.

"Maybe if we hire her, we'll find out what it was that made her change back then." Pinky loved prying into people's personal lives.

"Really, girls, there are plenty of folks who are looking for a job. And like Mark said, how are you going to get rid of her if she doesn't work out?" Erin said.

I gave Pinky a quick look. "Actually, we're thinking of hiring Emmy Anders, too."

Erin's eyebrow's shot up. "Emmy? She's like a hundred and four."

"Be nice, Erin," Pinky said.

"I know she isn't exactly young. I think she's somewhere in her seventies, maybe late sixties. But she's sharp and seems younger than that," I said.

Erin narrowed her eyes like she thought the opposite was true.

"We figured between Molly and Emmy, we'll get by with all the help we need," Pinky added.

"Emmy does not like me, I can tell you that much," Mark said.

That surprised me. "What do you mean?"

"Every time she sees me, she turns tail and runs."

"You must be imagining it," I said.

"Cami, I know that I'm not. Facts are facts. The first couple of times I thought it was a fluke. Then when you girls had that snow globe–making class last month, I tried talking to her and she acted like she didn't hear me."

"Maybe she didn't," Erin said with a smile.

"Or maybe she thinks you're cute and she's embarrassed, thinking that you might pick up on how she feels," Pinky said in a teasing tone.

Mark patted his chest and smiled. "It is a challenge I face almost every day."

Pinky, Erin, and I all groaned. There was no argument that Mark was tall and great looking and fit. Of the three of us, Erin was the only one who'd had romantic feelings for him. They'd dated in high school, but things had cooled between them and never really heated up again after they left for separate colleges. I knew Mark still loved Erin and would gladly rekindle their romance.

"Really, Mark, do you think you said something offhand that might have offended her?" Erin said.

Mark's shoulders hitched up. "No, not that I know of. Maybe I remind her of someone she has a problem with, or maybe it's because she just doesn't like cops."

"Why on earth wouldn't she like cops?" I said.

"Maybe I'll ask her what's up. If I can ever get her to look at me, that is."

"Well, if Emmy comes to work here, she'll be one of us in no time and will come to love you as much as we do." Pinky smiled then added, "We'll make her. Right, Cami?"

"Right."

Pinky leaned in. "And guess what else happened today? Cami got a not-very-nice phone call from her old boss, the soon-to-be-former senator."

Erin rolled her eyes then focused them on me. "What could she possibly want from you, a little more of your blood, maybe? She already put an end to your rising career."

"Now, Erin, technically it was the senator's husband who did that," Mark said.

"Technically, Mark, you are right. But it was up to the senator to give her guilty husband the boot. Instead, she gave it to

Cami, who was totally innocent. And Senator Zimmer is smart enough to know better," Erin said.

"You'd think," Pinky said.

I stood up. "You know what, my friends? I can't talk about this anymore. Pinky and I have work to do and people to hire."

"Cami—"

Erin's protest was interrupted by the ding of the bell on Pinky's shop door. Assistant police chief Clinton Lonsbury strolled in like he had a purpose. He nodded at Erin, Pinky, and me, then directed his words at Mark. "I saw your car parked outside so I figured it's just as easy to stop in and give you an update on the Harmon case." He raised his hand and waved in the direction of a back table. "If I can borrow Mark for a few minutes, girls?"

The way he asked us if he could borrow Mark made it sound like he was snatching him away from his fan club. The man was irritating, I'd give him that much. And the worst part was he was put together in a very attractive package. Pinky called him "eye candy." I secretly agreed with her.

I'd known Clint back when we were in high school, but I hadn't had any real contact with him until I discovered the dead body of the most unpopular man in Brooks Landing last month. I was thrown into the large mix of suspects in the murder investigation. All because I was in the wrong place at the wrong time and did the wrong thing when I saw a knife sticking out of the victim's back. Yes, it was stupid of me to grab the knife to see if it was really stuck, but it was an honest mistake, a natural reaction to a shocking situation, if you ask me. The police officials, however, did not see it that way. Eventually, it was all sorted out and the real killer was named. Sadly, it was our older friend, Archie Newberry, who under ordinary circumstances would not even hurt another human being.

Mark left our table, and he and Clint sat down at another. Erin, Pinky, and I took that as our cue to leave. We headed into Curio Finds together.

"Well, I have errands to run, so I'll catch you two later," Erin said.

"Adios, and don't worry your pretty little head about our short-term help," Pinky said to Erin's back as she went out the front door. Erin turned and waved.

"So we're good? Or did Erin and Mark going ballistic on us make you change your mind?" Pinky said.

"Their reaction kind of surprised me. And as much as I value their opinions, I say we give our two ladies a call and see if they still want a job."

"Okay, I'll call the princess—I can't believe I'm offering to do that—and you call Emmy. Let's see if they can start tomorrow so they're trained before Thanksgiving."

"Sounds good to me. And you need to get out of the habit of calling her the princess, my friend."

Pinky lifted her hands in the air and gave them a shake. "I suppose." Her shop phone rang and she left to answer it.

I was about to call Emmy when Mark and Clint popped their heads into the archway between the shops on their way out.

"Think about what Erin and I said," Mark said.

"Good-bye, Camryn," Clint said.

I'd legally changed my name from Cami to Camryn before I went to Washington because it sounded more professional. My family and oldest friends still called me Cami, but since

Clint and I had gotten off on the wrong foot, I stubbornly insisted he call me by my proper name. Maybe it was silly, or childish, but since he got under my skin so often, I felt compelled to do so.

"Have a good night, officers," I said, mildly curious about what they were working on. Police work intrigued me, but the thought of carrying a gun was enough to throw me into a mild panic attack. And driving fast with sirens blaring and lights flashing would be too far outside my comfort zone to even consider. Not to mention what I'd do if I had to run after a bad guy who was escaping. I was the slowest runner I knew, and I'd be the laughingstock of the town. According to Mark, police officers had to pass certain fitness standards. Although, looking at some of the out-of-shape people in uniform, it made me wonder what standards those departments had. But that was another matter.

I picked up the phone to call Emmy as Pinky poked her head in the archway. "Princess Molly will be here at ten o'clock tomorrow. And I told her to dress in normal clothes."

"Pinky, what did you say, exactly?"

"I was tactful, sort of. I suggested she make a trip to the secondhand store if she had time today to pick up something less expensive than she usually wears."

"You did not."

"That's pretty much what I said."

Oh Lord. Maybe I should have made the call. "Did she sound like you insulted her?"

"Insulted her? I don't think so. Maybe she sounded a little surprised when she said, 'Okay.'" The bell on her door dinged, so she left to wait on her customers.

Emmy answered the phone with more cheer in her voice

than usual. When I told her we'd love it if she would help us out over the holidays, a small squeal popped out of her mouth. "I will be there promptly at ten o'clock tomorrow morning when you open your shop, Camryn."

"Wonderful. And to let you know, Pinky and I decided to hire both you and the, um, I mean Molly Dalton."

Her balloon of enthusiasm instantly deflated. "Oh. Well, I'll do my best to get along with her."

"Emmy, do you have a problem with Molly?"

She hesitated. "No, no, not really. It'll be fine."

"All right then. We'll see you tomorrow."

"Yes, and thank you." Her voice had quieted, and I hoped it wasn't because she didn't want to work with Molly. They would be sharing a position, so they wouldn't be working together often, but there were times they would be.

I found Pinky behind her serving counter washing mugs. "I'm wondering if Erin and Mark were right. Maybe we should have advertised for help. You have to tell Molly what not to wear, and Emmy seems less than thrilled Molly will be her partner in crime."

"Cami, it will all work out. You know how fast time goes. Christmas will be here before you know it, then Molly and Emmy can go back to their normal routines, and we'll go back to ours."

"I suppose. How bad can it be?"

We had no idea it would go from bad to worse to worst.

I barely slept a wink that night wondering how the next day's training would go. Since Molly and Emmy would be working limited hours for less than six weeks, my parents suggested that we hire them on as contract workers to avoid all the extra paperwork required by the state for regular employees. They had both agreed to those terms, and neither cared what they got paid, or if they got paid at all.

I rolled out of bed wishing I had slept more than a few hours but hopeful things would go well. I showered and dressed and put on my usual light dose of makeup without trying to cover the light freckles that sprinkled my nose and cheekbones. A few people had told me they gave me a youthful look. I was thirty-seven and never really thought about how old I looked. And I had quit fretting about the generous curves I carried.

A final check in the mirror confirmed I was good to go in my flowing navy skirt and ivory blouse. My wardrobe was not in the same league as Molly's, but it was of good quality. I had a number of suits, both with pants and skirts, and I often combined a jacket with a nice pair of jeans, or a silk blouse with a skirt. Not too dressy, not overly casual. Just right for me.

When I got to work, Pinky was hustling around in her shop, cleaning up after her morning rush. "What are you doing here so early?" she said.

I glanced up at the Betty Boop "Boop-Oop-a-Doop" clock that hung on the wall behind her counter. "I thought I'd get a jump on the day, seeing how we've got some job training to do. I'm going to write down procedures, like how to run the cash register till, how to ring it out, things like that."

"Good idea. Cami, as long as you're here, would you mind covering for me while I run to the grocery store? I went through more milk and cream this morning than usual."

"With it getting colder, that makes perfect sense. My parents used to tell me we need to put a little meat on our bones for extra insulation during our long winters. I know I get hungrier when it gets colder."

"Yeah, I think they're right. Milk and cream definitely add calories." She grabbed her pocketbook from a cupboard under the counter. "I'll be back in a jiffy."

A minute later the bell on her door dinged. I tensed up a bit when I saw it was assistant police chief Clinton Lonsbury and wondered why he had that effect on me. Clint wore his usual serious look all the way to the counter. "Good morning. I didn't expect to see you here."

"I run the adjoining shop and make my way in here from time to time." As if he didn't know. My words came out with a heavy dose of sarcasm.

He nodded slowly. "Where's Pinky?"

"Running an errand. Do you need her?"

"Not specifically. I stopped in for a cup of coffee."

Be nice to the patrons, Cami. "I'm covering for Pinky. What can I get you?"

Clint glanced up at the menu. The featured brew of the day was the Gobbler, a dark blend with spices and cream. "I'll take the special, heavy on the cream."

My face broke out in a huge smile.

"What's funny?" he said.

"You just gave further support to my parents' theory that we need extra calories in the winter."

He shrugged. "I guess we do. Shivering in subzero temperatures burns 'em all off."

I turned and walked to the other side of the counter, keeping my back to him so he wouldn't notice how his comment tickled my funny bone. I served up his drink and set it down in front of him. He settled down on a seat at the counter and took a slurping sip that was so loud it sounded like he was wearing a microphone.

A shudder ran through me. "Honestly, Clint, with all the cream in there, your coffee cannot possibly be that hot."

He didn't care in the least. "Force of habit, I guess."

I considered making it my mission in life to break him of that annoying habit. There must be a guide out there somewhere with tips. There certainly were all kinds of them for things like quitting smoking and biting fingernails and cracking knuckles.

"I'd like a box of a dozen muffins and scones to take back to the station with me. We have a meeting later this morning."

"Sure. What kind do you want?"

"A mix, half muffins, half scones, is fine. Blueberry is a favorite, so put in a couple of those. And whatever else you pick will work. They'll all go."

It was nice to have an excuse to make a little noise myself to cover the sound of his slurps. I filled the box and added the extra muffin Pinky always insisted on with a larger order; a baker's dozen. "Here you go. Anything else?"

"Yes, if you could put this in a to-go cup." He slid his mug toward me.

Thank God, that meant he was going to leave. "Sure thing." He paid for his purchases and was out the door and on to other things in no time.

Another man came in a little while later, and when I saw who it was, I was too stunned to move. Peter Zimmer was walking toward me, in person. "Your shop door is locked," he said.

"Uh, um, we don't open until ten," I stammered until it hit me how angry I was that he had the audacity to come within ten miles of me. "Why are you here? And don't try to tell me something stupid, like you're looking for a gift to cheer up your wife."

A red flush crept up his neck and colored his face. "It would take more than that. You should have been smart enough to support her campaign. You would have if you planned on returning to D.C. Ramona knows enough people to prevent you from ever getting a job there."

"Ever? Peter, I cannot believe you are actually threatening me. You're the one who caused the whole fiasco in the first place."

He smiled and raised his eyebrows. "I'm willing to put any hard feelings aside if you want to get together to finish what we started."

I picked up a mug, drew it back like it was a baseball, but stopped before I pitched it at Peter's head. "You need to leave immediately, or I will call the police."

He glared at me, and a stab of fear pierced me. I wondered if he'd come after me. I wrapped my fingers around a knife Pinky used to cut muffins and scones. If the man took one step closer, I'd hold it up to show him I meant business. Whether I could actually use the knife, I wasn't sure. Even on Mr. Peter Zimmer, the lowest of the low.

Had he truly cared about his wife, or her career, he would not have acted as he did, time and time again. The Zimmers could cast blame on me until hell froze over, but I was not at fault, and the sooner they realized that, the sooner they could get on with their lives. Together or apart, it no longer mattered to me.

Peter turned to leave and literally ran into Pinky in the doorway. He stormed out, forcing her to step aside with her bag of groceries. I rushed over to help her regain her balance.

"Wowser, that guy is either in one big hurry or totally absorbed in something."

"You're right. He is totally absorbed in something all right: himself. That was Peter Zimmer."

"*No*. Oh my gosh, I didn't recognize him. In the pictures I saw of him, he was always smiling. He looked kind of scary just now with that scowl on his face. What was he doing here in Brooks Landing? Did he come to apologize to you, or what?"

"Not even close. He is stuck in the same old blame game crap, among other things."

"Of all the nerve."

"All I want is to forget about what happened and chalk it up as a life lesson I will never have to study again." I looked at the time. "We have Emmy and Molly due in a half hour, and I still have to write out those instructions."

"You're right. We have more important things to concentrate on." Pinky emptied her grocery bag, put the milk and cream in the refrigerator under her counter, and headed to the back room with the rest of her baking items.

Emmy reported for work at ten minutes to ten, wearing a shy smile, brown woolen pants, and a coordinating earth-toned sweater. Molly arrived a short time later, acting jumpy and dressed like a vagrant. I almost didn't recognize her. Emmy frowned and pursed her lips in disapproval.

Molly stared at my face, which I'm sure displayed total disbelief. "Isn't this okay?" she said.

"Uh, I'll be right back," I said. Pinky was in the back room, and I hustled to find her. "Wait 'til you see what the cat dragged in. Molly took you literally and I think did a little dumpster diving for clothes the secondhand stores discarded," I whispered.

"Cami, you must be exaggerating. How bad can it be?" She peeked around the corner for a glimpse at our new help. When she pulled her head back in, both her eyes and mouth were opened wide. "Oh my gosh. She can't serve customers in that getup. You're going to have to tell her." Her whisper was probably loud enough for Molly to hear.

I shook my head. "Me? You're the one who told her to buy some new used old clothes."

"Okay, okay."

We left our hiding place to face the music. Emmy and Molly were still glued to their spots, standing by Pinky's counter. They kept their eyes peeled on us as we walked toward them.

Pinky pointed at a menu. "Emmy, if you want to sit down at the counter here and read over all the coffee and drink specials we offer, that'd be great. Cami and Molly and I are going to get started in Curio Finds."

Emmy didn't ask any questions. She nodded, sat down, picked up a menu, and minded her own business. Or pretended to, at least. Pinky led the way, followed by Molly then me. She marched to the storeroom in the back of my shop. When we were all inside, I closed the door.

Molly's lips quivered, and it seemed tears would closely follow. "Am I in trouble already?" she said.

"No," I said.

"Not really," Pinky said.

"Not really?" Molly said.

Pinky put her hand to her nose. "It's your outfit. I mean, have you been storing it since high school in mothballs?"

Now that we were in a confined space with the door closed, the odor was strong and distinctive. Molly lifted her arm to her nose and inhaled deeply. "I don't have a very good sense of smell. Like I pretty much can't smell at all. I found this sweater and pants at the thrift store. There wasn't a lot in my size, and they were trying to close up for the day, so I didn't have enough time to shop."

"Molly, I'm sorry, this really isn't what I meant. I should have been more specific. Those old V-neck sweaters are supposed to be worn over a shirt, not without one. I know a lot of women wear low-cut tops, but it would be too much for our customers. If you bent over, we'd see everything. Even with that purple bandana thing tied around your neck," Pinky said.

"And, no offense, but the way you are stuffed into those gold metallic pants, I don't think you could bend over if you tried," I added.

Tears filled Molly's eyes then ran down her cheeks. "I was just trying to fit in. I mean, Pinky, you're always wearing pink, so I thought the turquoise top would be a good complement."

Pinky looked at the wall behind me and pointed. "Cami, what about that outfit? The one you keep here, in case?" Molly and I turned and assessed the outfit Pinky was talking about: a pair of gray pants, a pale gray button-down shirt, and a wool shrug. "You two are about the same size."

Molly looked at me. "I'm a couple of inches shorter, so the pants will be too long." Her voice bordered on whining, and I tried my best not to feel irritated.

"Cami, what if you put on the gray outfit and give Molly the one you're wearing? For today, until she can get herself something similar."

Heaven help me, I said I'd do it. Molly definitely could not work in our shops dressed as she was, and reeking of mothballs besides. There was a hesitant knock on the door. Pinky opened it to Emmy.

"I'm sorry, but there are a number of customers, and I won't be able to help them like you can, not yet, anyway," Emmy said.

"I'm on it." Pinky flew out to rescue Emmy.

"Okay, Molly, do you need some help peeling off those pants?" I closed the storeroom door for privacy.

She sniffled. "I can manage." She did, too, with quite a bit of effort.

I slipped out of my skirt and shirt and laid them on a chair for Molly. Then I put on the spare outfit I kept at Curio Finds in case I spilled coffee all over myself, or if I had to be somewhere after work but didn't have time to go home to change. I used my "in case" outfit every couple of weeks, it seemed.

Molly smelled better as soon as she was out of the thrift store clothes. She threw them in a heap on the floor. "Should I burn them?"

"If you wash them, you could use them for a retro costume."

"Oh well, I guess I could donate them back."

"Sure."

We were both dressed and ready to take on the next challenge. I left the storeroom first and was surprised by the crowd Pinky had in her shop. I went to help her, with Molly at my heels. It was a group of people on a bus trip that had stopped in Brooks Landing to do some antique shopping.

When a number of them wandered into Curio Finds, I left Molly and Emmy in Pinky's capable hands, which she later said was the worst thing I'd ever done to her. I didn't know what she meant until I worked with them myself. It seemed the pressure of having a number of customers to wait on before they were fully trained and the fact that neither one appeared to like the other played a part in their first-day woes.

Emmy came into my shop about five minutes later, looking flustered. "Pinky said if you could go help her, I should mind your store."

I excused myself from a customer I was helping. "All right. Well, answer whatever questions you can, and come get me if someone wants to buy something."

Emmy forced out a smile and nodded.

Pinky and Molly were behind the counter. Molly acted like it was the first time she had ever held a cup of coffee in her hands. Her hands were shaking, and the hot brew was spilling out over the top. Pinky was actually sweating. I excused myself through the line of customers and stepped between the two of them. "Molly, why don't you go help Emmy? I'll finish up in here."

She set the mug down without hesitation, wiped her hands on a towel, got around Pinky, and made her way into my shop without further disaster. Pinky shot me a look that would best be described as pleading. We'd worked her rushes together many times. I took orders from the next four people in line. Four specials coming right up.

3

'd barely finished making and ringing up the drinks when I heard a crash and a cry of, "Oh no!" coming from my shop. Pinky was waiting on the last two people in line, so I broke away without feeling like I was deserting her. Lying on the old enameled ceramic tile floor, in a snow-filled puddle of water, was Marilyn Monroe wearing a long, flowing, strapless turquoise gown. I often admired the collectible globe. Amazingly, the figure was still intact. The water had likely insulated it in the fall.

I looked up from Marilyn to Molly. She was standing with her palms up, as if a police officer had directed her to do so. Her body was shaking, and I thought she might collapse. Three women closed in behind her to survey the damage. But my eyes were drawn to the woman Emmy was following out the door. It was Senator Ramona Zimmer. What in the world was she doing there? Following her husband, or spying on me?

I ran over to the door, and Emmy turned to me, flustered as could be. "I tried to catch that woman. I think she was the one who broke the globe, but she wouldn't answer me. Should we call the police?"

Thoughts were spinning in my head so fast that it took me a minute to slow them down and process what was going on. Should we involve the police? I turned to the group standing close to Molly. "Looks like we had a little mishap," I said.

Molly pointed at the snow globe mess on the floor then to a shelf a few feet away. "I was over there helping these ladies and had my back turned when we heard the crash. I don't know what happened."

Emmy used her thumb to point at the door behind her. "That woman who just ran out was staring at Molly and the others right before the snow globe dropped. She looked like she was waiting for her, so I asked her if I could help her find something. She said she was just looking, so I was going to help someone else. The next thing I knew that snow globe was on the floor in pieces."

Molly nodded. "When I turned and looked at her the woman got the funniest look on her face, like she was surprised. I thought she was going to apologize for having an accident. I didn't know what had fallen, or if it was even broken. Instead of offering to pay, she headed for the door without a word."

The three customers agreed with Molly. Had Senator Zimmer come into my shop with the express goal of destroying some merchandise, or was the broken snow globe an accident, as Molly had supposed? It was freaky enough that Ramona had the guts to be there in the first place. Then to duck out after she had everyone's attention was even freakier.

Emmy walked to the counter and picked up the phone. "Should I call nine-one-one?"

"No, I happen to know that woman, and I'll get to the bottom of it," I said. If I needed to, that is. I'd think on it and decide if it was worth it. I would just as soon never talk to her again. Ramona had come into my shop the same morning her husband had paid me an unwelcome visit. I didn't believe it was a coincidence. They lived in a town about twenty miles away.

One of the customers said, "You know who that lady looked like? Senator Zimmer, the one who just lost the election."

"Oh yeah, she does," another agreed.

Ramona Zimmer may have tried to go incognito in her insulated long coat and animal print winter hat, but I'd recognized her immediately and was surprised the others didn't know who she was. Of course, I'd worked beside her for years, and they had likely never seen her in person. I kept my mouth shut, not ready to either confirm or deny Ramona's true identity.

After the commotion, the women left without making a purchase, and I picked up the pieces of the broken snow globe. I didn't want Molly or Emmy getting glass stuck in their hands. And with the way the day was going, that was sure to be the next mini crisis. The two of them stood in opposite corners of the store, looking like two boxers about to go against each other in the ring. For the tenth time that day, I kicked myself for not following Erin and Mark's advice. Had I known Molly would rub Emmy the wrong way, I would have suggested to Pinky that we hire Molly since she was the first to inquire. On the other hand, Molly was not proving to be overly capable.

I set Marilyn Monroe on a shelf then bent over to sweep up the glass with a small brush and dustpan I had brought from the storeroom. Lying on the floor next to the largest chunk of glass was a penny. I could have sworn it was not there a moment before. A penny from heaven, or specifically, a penny from my birth mother who, along with my birth father, went to heaven when I was five. I believed it was she who left me a penny once in a while. Sometimes it seemed like she was warning me about something, and sometimes it seemed like she was telling me things would be okay.

Thanks, Mama. Yes, my friends and family probably thought I was a bit loony and was imagining things more often than not. But the pennies had appeared out of nowhere when I was lonely or sad or in trouble or when something big was going on.

A second crash sent my eyes heavenward. "I'm so sorry," Molly said and dropped down to pick up a plate she had knocked off a shelf. It had miraculously landed on one of the small mats lying on the floor and was not broken.

"Oh my stars and garters," Emmy said and moved in from her corner.

I lifted my hands to form a T. "All right, ladies, let's all relax and get on with a brief training. There are instructions by both the cash register and credit card machine."

"You don't use a square? A lot of the small businesses do," Molly said.

"What are you talking about?" Emmy said in a near growl.

Molly drew her thumb and index finger together to indicate

its size. "It's a little square thingy that you connect to your smart phone, and then you can run customers' cards through that."

Emmy crossed her arms tightly against her waist. "What next."

The day went downhill from there. After the morning rush, there weren't too many customers, which enabled me to devote more time to training. Not that we got very far. I was relieved when it was lunchtime and Emmy took the meal she had packed over to a table on Pinky's side, and Molly left to get some soup and a sandwich at a nearby deli. Pinky's business had quieted, so I waved her over to have a heart-to-heart. We went behind the counter, and I talked as quietly as possible. Even though Emmy was out of earshot, sometimes voices carried in strange ways.

"Pinky, I'm starting to wonder if Molly isn't putting on an act after all. She's struggling, but maybe that'll ease as time goes on."

"But she's clumsy besides. That's not a good thing in a shop that's filled with glass items, or in my place where the main task is serving hot coffee." She tugged at her headband. "Short of murder, how *are* we going to get rid of her?"

"Now, now, we have a few more hours in the day, and it's the first day, after all. We'll do more training and see how it goes."

"I don't know if I'll make it. I'm not all that smart myself and even I can run a cash register."

"You are very smart, Pinky. But no matter; Molly's not the only one. Emmy's having problems, too, and she has been crabby—bordering on nasty—to Molly. Which of course makes Molly even more anxious."

"We'd be better off without either one of them working here, if you ask me."

"You convinced me we need help for the holidays, so let's not make a hasty decision here. Another day or two will tell us what we need to do. I'll keep them both with me for the rest of the day, and we'll do the coffee shop fifteen minutes at a time here and there until they are comfortable with running the till, at least." I tapped her arm. "Oh, and something else I've been waiting to share with you for over an hour. You won't believe it."

"Do tell." Pinky's eyes grew rounder. She loved hearing stories; the juicier the better.

"You know when we heard that crash earlier and I left to take care of it?"

She thought a second. "Oh yeah, toward the end of that mad rush."

"You will never in a million years guess who caused it."

"Justin Bieber."

"No. Worse. Ramona Zimmer. She dropped the Marilyn Monroe snow globe on the floor and broke it. And then she ran out without even apologizing."

"Get out of here."

"It's true. I saw her leave. And I think she did it on purpose. But how would I prove it?"

"That is cold. And downright mean. The fact that she ran out after breaking an item without offering to pay for it screams guilty. I bet you're right, that she did it on purpose."

"Talk about immature. I think losing the election has made her a little wacky."

The bell on Pinky's door dinged, and she went back to Brew Ha-Ha. I waited until Molly and Emmy came back from lunch and were each fairly comfortable with running the cash register and credit card machine then decided I needed a break myself. "Will you two be able to handle the shop while I pick up some lunch and take a walk? It shouldn't be more than thirty minutes."

Molly and Emmy both raised their eyebrows like they thought I was kidding.

"Don't worry. Pinky is here if you have any questions. Look at the shelves to familiarize yourself with what we have. Some people come in looking for specific things, like a snow globe with a barnyard scene in it. So the more you explore, the more you'll know. My parents have boxes of new things in the storeroom and at their house. Well, they're not all exactly new. Most of them are antique, one of a kind. We'll be adding them as we have room."

They glanced at the shelves, and as if by mutual agreement, Emmy went one way and Molly went the other. I grabbed my long wool coat from the storeroom, slipped out past Pinky, and told her I'd be back in a half hour.

Then I mouthed the words, "You're the referee," so her customer couldn't hear me. Pinky gave her head a little shake. "Do you want anything?" I asked.

"Nothing that money can buy."

I stopped by the Bread Man deli for a bowl of stuffed green pepper soup, one of my cold weather favorites. It was only forty-four degrees, but the sun was shining, so I opted to eat outside. I had my choice of any one of the twelve seats around the three small, round patio tables. The crisp air was refreshing compared to the heat created by the tension in our shops. I spooned soup into my mouth and considered how to make the new situation work. A person couldn't make another person like someone, but I would try to smooth things over between Emmy and Molly.

Although at that particular moment, I didn't care much for crabby Emmy or needy Molly. I preferred yelling over whining, but not by much. My adoptive mother had created a harmonious home, even with her Italian husband, who could be hotheaded at times. Harmony, that's what I longed for among family and friends. And employees. One of them would have to go if they couldn't be coaxed into getting along.

I finished my soup faster than normal, knowing the last thing Pinky wanted to be in life was a referee. When I got back to Curio Finds, Emmy was scowling, Molly was crying, and Pinky was hiding in her back room. My referee had left the game.

"I was just asking Emmy to show me how to use the credit card machine and she yelled at me," Molly said.

"Molly, I asked you to step back because you were pushing against me so tightly that I couldn't breathe," Emmy countered.

"I'm sorry, but I like being close to people."

"That's suffocating. I live alone and I'm not used to all this togetherness."

"Okay, Emmy, why don't you come with me? It's slow, so it's a good time for Pinky and me to show you how to make the most popular coffees. Molly, you can get familiar with the categories of items we have on the cash register buttons. And remember that you have to push the sales tax button on every item you sell."

Molly headed to the spot behind the counter, and Emmy followed me into Pinky's shop. "Read over some of the drinks, and you can decide what you want to practice making. Look in the fridge under the counter so you know where Pinky keeps the different items. She likes to keep things in the same spots. That way she can reach in without looking. I'll go get her."

When Pinky saw me, she pretended like she was banging her head against the wall. "Put me out of my misery."

Instead, I put my hands on her shoulders. "I've got Emmy making coffee. And Molly is working with my till. I think we need to show more confidence in the efforts the two of them are making. And we should keep them separated as much as possible. Emmy needs to lighten up, and Molly needs, well, she needs . . ."

Pinky pushed away from the wall and turned to me. "What she needs may not be something we can help her with."

The bell on Brew Ha-Ha's door dinged. Pinky straightened up like she was preparing to go into battle. "The afternoon rush is about to begin."

I checked to see how Molly was doing in Curio Finds. There were no customers milling around, and she was spending more time studying the merchandise on the shelves. I joined Pinky and Emmy behind the counter.

"Emmy, would you check to be sure the tables are all wiped off in the back?" Pinky said.

"I can do that." She picked up a damp cloth from the counter with one hand and a cup of coffee she'd made in the other. She headed into Curio Finds, and I thought she'd misunderstood what Pinky had asked. But a few seconds later, she reappeared minus the cup of coffee, still armed with the cleaning cloth, and went to check out Pinky's tables.

There were a number of people I didn't know, which was

unusual. More groups of antique shoppers, I learned. Many of them took their coffee and wandered into my shop. I kept an eye as best I could, but most of them seemed to be simply looking. Emmy wandered around, talking to customers in both shops, and it occurred to me that maybe that should be her main role. She could be the first line of defense, answering questions to the best of her ability and refilling coffee cups. Our very own customer service specialist.

Pinky focused on whipping up different drink combinations and serving muffins and scones. She seemed more relaxed than she had all day, giving me hope that the worst was behind us and we could make our new arrangement work for the next few weeks. I patted the penny in my pocket, taking it as encouragement that things were on an uphill trend after all.

Since Pinky opened her shop at 7:00 a.m., we did our best to get her out the door between 3:00 p.m. and 4:00 p.m., depending on what was going on. Both of our shops stayed open until 6:00 p.m., but it was unusual for either one of us to be overwhelmed with customers at that time of the day. With the Christmas shopping season approaching, that would likely change, and we'd need to extend our hours. It was a relief knowing we'd have two workers trained before long. Hopefully.

The afternoon rush was over by 3:15, and I told Pinky to take off. "Are you sure?" she said, sounding anything but.

"Yes, we will manage just fine. In fact, I'm going to send Emmy and Molly home pretty soon, too."

She blew some air out of her mouth. "Good idea. All right,

then, I'll go home and bake. That always makes me feel better."

Pinky gathered her things and was out the door in a flash. Not that she was in a hurry to get out of Dodge or anything. I went into my own shop and found Emmy frowning at a snow globe.

"Is everything okay?"

It took her some seconds to look at me. "What?"

"I was wondering how you're doing."

"Oh. Well, I hate to admit it, but I'm a little tired."

"That's understandable. The first day on the job is always tough. At least I think so."

Emmy nodded but kept her opinion of how tough she thought the day had been to herself.

"That's why I wanted to tell you and Molly to go on home for today. Where is she, anyway?"

"She went into the little ladies' room a while ago."

"Well you go ahead and take off. So we'll see you tomorrow?"

"If you and Pinky decide to keep me on."

"You plan on it, and we'll see you at ten."

Emmy raised her eyebrows slightly, and I wondered if she was weighing the pros and cons of sticking with the job or giving it up.

I spotted a to-go cup on the checkout counter and pointed. "Is that your coffee?"

Emmy barely glanced at it. "No, I think it's Molly's."

"All right, well enjoy the rest of your evening, Emmy."

She collected her coat and purse and slipped quietly out the shop door while I made sure no one was waiting for service in Pinky's shop. Every so often I looked over, although I didn't hear the bell on her door sound. Betty Boop's hands indicated it had been over five minutes since Emmy told me Molly had gone into the bathroom "a while ago." A feeling of unease grabbed hold of me. Was Molly really in the bathroom, or had something upset her so much that she'd left without telling anyone?

I went to the storeroom and saw her coat hanging on a hook. Hmm. Was she having a crying jag in the bathroom? I moved to the door and listened, but there was no sound, so I knocked. "Molly? Molly, are you in there?" There was no response. I tried the doorknob, but it didn't turn. It was locked. What in the world? "Molly! Answer me."

Maybe she wasn't in there after all, but why would she leave without her coat? Maybe the lock had accidentally been turned and latched when the door closed. I usually kept the door closed since it wasn't posted as a public restroom. It was a tiny space. If people needed to use it, they were welcome to, but few asked. It was four feet by five feet, and the joke in the family was telling someone, "Don't get lost in there," before they saw how compact the room really was. Most people laughed when they opened the door and gazed into the tiniest restroom they'd probably ever seen. The occasional person would close the door without even trying to squeeze into the room.

"Molly, really, if you're in there, you have to tell me. I'm getting worried." How could I get in without breaking down the door? And the door didn't push in, anyway; it pulled out. I assessed the situation and figured there were two options: pop out the pins on the hinges, or find out where the key was to unlock the door from the outside. That was the better option, but I had no idea if my parents even had a key. I'd never had reason to ask before, and they hadn't thought to tell me.

I went to the counter and used the store phone. My dad answered. "Hi, sweetheart. How are things there?"

"Hi, Dad. Well, I have a dilemma. The bathroom door is locked, and I'm wondering if there's a key."

"There is. Yes, it's on top of the doorframe in the store-room. Every so often a little one locks the door and shuts it. We put it up high so it doesn't get lost. I can reach it fine, but you'll need a stool."

"Thank you. I better run. Say hi to Mom. 'Bye."

"'Bye for now."

I mumbled a complaint about what my parents were think-ing when they picked their hiding spot for the key as I dragged a stool over to the storeroom door. I unhooked the key from its very secure spot and closed my hand around it like it was a piece of gold. One of the first things I'd do is get a spare made to keep in a more convenient place in case the door got locked again. I gave the door one last knock. "I'm coming in now," I said, no longer believing anyone was in the bathroom.

You have no idea how much I wished that were true. What was it my father said when I was little and wished for some-thing special? "If wishes were horses, beggars would ride." Chills traveled up my back like cold fingers as I turned the key in the lock then grabbed the knob and pulled open the door. Sitting on the toilet, with her head resting against the wall and looking very dead, was Molly Dalton. Her eyes were open and bulging. I jumped at least a foot in the air and two feet back. "Ahhhhhhh!" Then I froze to that spot for the longest time, staring at poor Princess Molly, who must have suf-fered a heart attack and died on the throne. That was the crazy and inappropriate thing that popped into my shell-shocked brain.

"Ahhhhh, ahhhhhh." Had she called out for help? But none of us had heard her. The walls, even those enclosing the bathroom, were very thick, and I had been in Pinky's shop for most of the past hour. And Emmy did not have the best hearing. But still.

Her vacant eyes seemed to be looking right at me and through me at the same time. They held me in place, making me think my feet were bonded to the floor with high-quality adhesive. I was scared witless. Molly had died in the bathroom of Curio Finds on her first day of work. How would we tell her husband? And the rest of her family?

My legs started to wobble back and forth, and the next thing I knew I was on the floor, crawling away from the bathroom. As fast as possible. Thank God the adhesive had let loose. I reached the archway between the shops the same time the bell on Pinky's door dinged. With great effort, I lifted my head high enough to see who it was. I should have been relieved and grateful it was assistant police chief Clinton Lonsbury, but all I could think was, *Great, just great. He's going to think I did something to cause the poor woman's death.*

"What are you doing, Miss Clean, sweeping the floor with your knees?"

He had to be the most infuriating man on the face of the planet. What kind of a policeman was he? He should have recognized something was wrong with me, that I was in distress. When I didn't answer, he rushed over and knelt down beside me. That earned him a number of points in my book. "Are you hurt, Camryn?"

I shook my head. "Molly died." Saying the words out loud choked me up, and tears filled my eyes.

Clint hooked one hand under my left arm, slid the other under my right hand, and guided me to my feet. Had I been completely rational, I wouldn't have thrown my body against his or my arms around him. I vaguely registered the equipment on the front of his duty belt poking into me, but that did not matter in the least. It was an immense relief not to be alone with Molly.

"You got bad news about a loved one?" Clint said.

I pushed away from him. "Worse. She's . . . here. It's . . . Molly Dalton."

His eyebrows came together. "What are you talking about?"

"Look in the bathroom." I turned toward my shop and pointed.

"Molly Dalton is deceased, in your bathroom? Is anyone else here?"

I shook my head.

Clint walked through the archway, looking right then left then forward. I imagined he was looking for anything that was out of place. He'd find that in the bathroom, all right.

He had done a sweep of Curio Finds about a month before during an investigation and knew where the bathroom was. Even if he hadn't, it was very easy to find in the back of the shop. I crept along behind him, hoping against hope I'd had a hallucination and Molly would not be in there after all.

"Ah," Clint said and stopped in front of the open door. He was silent as he surveyed the scene, then he turned to me. "Mark mentioned Molly Dalton was going to help out here through Christmas. So she worked today?"

I nodded.

"What happened?"

I told him everything I could remember from the time I

discovered the door was locked to the moment I opened the door and saw Molly sitting there.

"Did you go in there, touch her, or anything?"

"No, her staring like that scared the living daylights out of me. I collapsed and was heading for Pinky's phone to call nine-one-one when you came in."

"Your own shop phone is right over there." He pointed at the counter not eight feet away.

"That was too close to . . . *her*."

He gave a single nod, indicating he understood what I meant, then pulled out his cell phone and hit some numbers. After he was connected, he said, "This is Assistant Chief Lonsbury. I'm at Eighteen Central Avenue, here in Brooks Landing. I need the coroner and the on-call Buffalo County Sheriff's Office investigator. I'll be bringing my officers in as well. Thanks."

When the people of Brooks Landing called 911, the Buffalo County Sheriff's Dispatch answered and sent out the appropriate officers, medical personnel, or fire department members. Or the coroner. There were a total of three police departments in the larger cities of Buffalo County, and Brooks Landing, the county seat, had the largest. Mark had told me that police departments asked Buffalo County for mutual aid on the most serious cases, since the county had all the bells and whistles.

Clint called Officer Mark next, even though Mark was off duty. The two on-duty officers were both tied up on other calls. When he'd finished talking to Mark, he tipped his head to one side and then the other as he studied Molly's body.

"Did she tell you she was feeling ill?"

"No, not at all. She looked healthy and seemed fine. But I hadn't actually talked to her for a while."

"How long?"

"I'm not sure, maybe twenty minutes. I was helping Pinky."

"Was she alone in here for all that time? Were there customers around?"

"I don't think there were any customers when I was next door, but Emmy Anders was here with Molly. She started working for us today, too."

"You don't say." He pulled out a small notepad and pen and wrote something down. "We'll talk to her next."

I thought of what Mark had said about the way Emmy avoided him and wondered if she'd had a bad experience with a police officer at some point in her life.

"I've heard that sometimes when people are having a heart attack, they feel the need to use the bathroom and end up dying there," I said.

"If that was the case then Molly didn't get that far. The toilet seat is down and her skirt is in place."

Her skirt. It was *my* skirt. She'd died with my clothes on.

"I have my suspicions that Molly did not die a natural death," Clint continued.

"What else could it be?"

"We'll have to wait for the coroner, but it looks to me like she may have been poisoned."

4

My knees started wobbling again, and my heart pounded for the longest time after Clint dropped his bombshell. "Why would you think that?"

"Her deep pink skin tone is not natural. I've seen that once before on a guy that was accidentally poisoned at work."

I hadn't noticed her skin color until Clint mentioned it, but then again, I had only been able to look at her for a few seconds at a time, and my brain wasn't exactly sharp, given the circumstances.

"Had she been overexerting, moving heavy boxes?"

"No."

"And I'd say she's too young to be having hot flashes."

I braved another look. "I guess she is pretty flushed. Doesn't that happen when someone has a heart attack?"

"It can, but not always. It's a telltale sign of cyanide poisoning."

"Cyanide? The gas that they use as a chemical weapon?"

"Yup, that's the one you hear about, but it's also used in manufacturing, and for making pesticides, things like that."

I wanted to hold on to the belief that Molly had died a natural death, young as she was. I couldn't let myself think she was poisoned. If only she had let us know she wasn't feeling well, we would have called for medical help and she'd probably still be alive.

Mark Weston rushed in, looking a little flushed himself. He moved to Clint's side and stared at Molly. "I don't believe it. She seemed fine a few hours ago, when I stopped by for a cup of coffee. Did she tell you that she had any health problems, Cami?"

"No, but we didn't exactly do a formal job application process."

The bell on Brew Ha-Ha's door dinged. What time was it, anyway? "I'll take care of it," Clint said. I heard him talking to someone, saying we needed to close early. When he came back, he told us he'd locked the door and hung up the Closed sign.

"We've got to let Pinky know what's going on," I said. "And my parents."

Clint scratched his chin. "Yeah, people will be talking, especially when the rest of the troops arrive. Let's notify Molly's husband, then you can go ahead and call them. Did Molly give you his phone number, in case of an emergency?"

My throat tightened. "No, we didn't think to get that information."

Clint's eyes narrowed, and if I hadn't already felt awful, the way he was looking at me would have cinched it. "How about her cell phone? Do you know where that might be?"

I had to think if I'd even seen her with one. "No. Um, there are pockets in that skirt you could check. If it's not there, maybe it's in her coat. That's in the storeroom."

Clint barely fit in the small bathroom with all the equipment he had on his belt. I couldn't see what he was doing, but when he straightened up and backed out, he was empty-handed. "Not in her pockets."

"I'll check her coat," Mark said, and the two of us went to the storeroom.

Molly's mid-calf-length wool coat was hanging on a hook. As I stared at it, it struck me that I'd never see her walk into the shops again. Shivers danced up my spine and down my arms. My coat was hanging next to hers. "The brown one is Molly's."

Mark pulled a rhinestone-covered wallet and ring of keys from one pocket and the sought-after cell phone from the other. He put the keys back then went to the next room and handed the phone to Clint.

Clint nodded when he saw the wallet. "Go ahead and find her driver's license and write down her date of birth, address, et cetera." Mark followed Clint's instructions while Clint focused on the cell phone. He turned it on and pushed a couple of buttons. "Not a very long list of contacts. What's her husband's name?"

"Will," I said.

Clint scrolled down and found the information he needed. He jotted the number in his little notebook then set Molly's phone down on the counter and pulled his own from its holder. He shook his head. "This is the worst phone call an officer has to make, especially if foul play is suspected."

I still had trouble believing anyone would poison Molly. And where would a person get cyanide, anyway? Erin Vickerman's words, "How are you going to get rid of her?" played in my mind. That was now a moot issue. Molly was gone forever, rid of for good, and not the way Erin had meant at all.

"Buffalo County to five-oh-two." It was the 911 dispatch officer calling on the police radio.

Clint spoke into the radio microphone that was clipped onto his collar. "Lonsbury here, Buffalo County."

"The coroner will be arriving at your location in ten to fifteen minutes. And the county crime team should be right behind her."

"Copy that." He let go of his mic. "I'll see if I can reach Molly's husband. There's going to be a cluster of folks here in no time." He dialed then waited what seemed like forever before he said, "Will Dalton? . . . This is Assistant Chief Lonsbury with the Brooks Landing Police Department. Are you somewhere you can talk? . . . All right, I'll wait." Clint covered the phone and told us Will was going into another room.

He resumed his conversation. "Mr. Dalton, I'm at Curio Finds, and I'm sorry to tell you your wife was found unresponsive here a few minutes ago. Sadly, she's dead. . . . Mr. Dalton? Will? Are you still there? . . . I know it's tough to think right now, but can you tell me if your wife had any medical conditions you were aware of, like a heart problem? . . . No? Okay, well, we're waiting for the coroner, and she'll help us get to the bottom of it. . . . Where are you now? . . . Okay, well, I'd caution you about driving. We can send someone to pick you up. . . . If you're sure . . . All right, then, here's my number. . . . Yeah, it's the same one that showed up on caller ID. . . . We'll be waiting for you here."

Clint hung up. "He's at a meeting in St. Paul and is going to have his assistant drive him to Brooks Landing."

"What a shock for the poor guy. I'm glad he's got someone to drive him," I said.

Mark grimaced. "Clint, do you think it's a good idea for Molly's husband to see her like that?"

"No, I don't. It's going to take Mr. Dalton an hour to get here, at least, depending on traffic. The coroner will have her on a gurney by then."

Their discussion left me feeling weak. Finding Molly and being there with Clint and Mark was completely unreal. And then there was Will Dalton, who had just gotten the blow of a lifetime from the assistant police chief. He just received such horrible news, and being out of town made it seem worse. Poor Will Dalton. His wife had left for her first day of work that morning. Her first—and last—day of work.

"Is it okay to call my parents and Pinky now?" I hesitated to ask, but with the police cars sitting out front and the other emergency vehicles about to arrive, they would be hearing about it from someone else in no time flat.

"Yeah, go ahead, but tell them not to come in and to keep quiet about what's going on until we've sorted things out."

"Pinky might have trouble with that," Mark said.

I nodded. "That's a good point. Clint, if Pinky can at least tell Erin, it will help save her from exploding, trying to hold in the news."

"Erin is one of the Three Musketeers," Mark said.

Clint raised his eyebrows. "All right. It's only a matter

of time before the whole town knows. But I don't want her starting any gossip. You tell her that."

Yes, sir. I walked into Brew Ha-Ha pondering the best way to break the news to my parents. When I made the call and got connected, it was to their answering machine instead. "Hi, Mom and Dad, it's Cami. Call me when you get home. 'Bye." Dad hadn't mentioned plans of going anywhere when we'd talked earlier, but then again it was a very brief conversation. I decided not to try either of their cell phones. They didn't need to get that kind of call when they were out and about. My mother had been under medical care for months, and consequently, my parents didn't stay away from home for long.

I hung up and dialed Pinky's number, wondering how I was going to spring the news on her. No need to wonder— the words sprung out of my mouth with a life of their own. "Pinky, Molly died right here in my shop bathroom. Clint and Mark are here, and Clint thinks she got *poisoned.*"

Pinky screamed, and it started my eardrum pounding. I pushed the phone away, as far as my arm would reach. After she stopped screeching, I switched the phone to my other hand and held it up to the ear that was still capable of hearing.

Pinky's voice was shaky. "Cami, if that's a joke, it is not even a tiny bit funny."

"No, to both. It's not a joke, and it is not the least bit funny." I wandered back to the archway and leaned against the wall.

Pinky made a hiccup-like sound. "I can't believe it. Tell me again, and maybe it'll sink in."

I repeated myself, adding a few more details. "And Clint told me to tell you that you can let Erin know, but nobody else. Oh, and don't come down here." My shop door opened, and a woman I recognized stepped inside. "Sorry, I gotta go. The coroner is here," I told Pinky.

"Cami—" I heard Pinky say my name in a pleading way as I hung up, but I left it at that. We'd spend lots of time hashing out recent events later; that was a given.

I'd met Dr. Trudy Long the month before under circumstances that were almost as bad as these. I'd discovered the body of a man who had been killed in our town park. At least I hadn't known him personally. Not like Molly.

Clint walked over to meet Dr. Long. They exchanged a few words, then he led the way to the bathroom. The coroner stole a look at me when she passed. "Ms. Brooks," she said in a serious yet kind tone. I swallowed and nodded. It struck me that I'd been secretly hoping the doctor wouldn't recognize me from the first time we'd met.

The flow of adrenaline that had been running through me since I found Molly suddenly stopped, making me feel like I was going to drop. I felt a measure of responsibility for Molly's safety. After all, she was my employee and I was in the shop at the time she'd died. I inched my way to the checkout counter and sat down on the stool.

I caught a whiff of the to-go cup of coffee, partially full, sitting on the counter. Its distinct odor was unusual—similar to cherries or almond extract. I picked it up and leaned my face in for a closer smell. Very strange. Pinky had a recipe for almond syrup she made and used for one of her specials. But it hadn't been on the menu for days. Plus, this blend had a completely different smell than her standard one. It'd be easy enough to find out if she'd changed her recipe.

I heard Dr. Long say, "In addition to her bright pink skin

tone, I detect an odor associated with cyanide. It smells like almonds."

I got to my feet lickety-split and moved in behind Clint and Mark in the gap between their bodies. "Umm, Doctor?" I managed.

Dr. Long turned away from Molly. "Yes, Ms. Brooks?"

"Umm, call me Camryn. I may know how Molly got the poison. Well, not really how she got it, but I think I know where she got it. Well, not really where she got it, but—"

Mark and Clint both turned and stared at me. "What are you talking about, Camryn?" Clint said.

"Spit it out, already," Mark said.

"It might have been in her coffee, if that's her coffee cup on my checkout counter." I pointed back in that direction.

All three of them frowned at me. "What makes you think that?" the doctor said, and she took a few steps forward, filling the gap between us.

"I just heard you say cyanide smells like almonds and that Molly smells like almonds. Well, so does that cup of coffee."

They all cautiously crept over to the counter like they were approaching the enemy. Maybe they were concerned about spilling it. Clint and Mark pulled on fresh vinyl gloves.

"Pinky's new to-go cups have a nice, smooth surface, so the crime lab should have no problem pulling prints," Mark said.

How could I tell them? "Sorry, but mine will be on there, too."

Clint's frown crease deepened. "Explain."

"When I got a whiff of the coffee there, it smelled kind of weird, almondy, but not like Pinky's normal almond syrup. I picked up the cup to see if I could identify it. She has that Almond Joy special with chocolate and coconut and almond syrups, and I wondered if it was that for a second. Then Doctor Long said she smelled almonds on Molly."

Clint blew out a big puff of air.

"Cami had no way of knowing she was tampering with possible evidence," Mark said.

When Clint didn't answer right away, I had a feeling he was counting to ten. "I know," he said.

Dr. Long was the first to bend over the cup to smell the contents. "I'd be confident saying this is the source, all right; the vehicle of delivery for the cyanide. The cup is about two-thirds full. Our victim likely ingested a lethal dose of poison in the first few sips." She lifted her head and backed away.

"But where and how she got it in the first place is what we have to figure out." Clint turned to me. "Do you or Pinky have a supply of cyanide in your shops?"

"No, of course not."

"I asked so we could positively rule out accidental ingestion as the manner of death."

Mark nodded. "And you can rule out natural, because what happened here is anything but. That leaves us with either a suicide or a homicide." He stepped behind the counter and took a sniff. "I don't smell almonds. It smells like coffee to me. One of Pinky's medium blends is what my smeller is telling me."

"That is the challenge of relying on the scent of almonds to diagnose cyanide poisoning, because only forty percent of people can actually smell it," Dr. Long said.

Mark leaned over and took a second sniff. "Really?"

Dr. Long went on, "It's genetic. Either you can or you can't. I've only had a few cases of cyanide poisoning over the course of my career, but the ability to detect the odor has proved helpful each time. I've been called to assist other jurisdictions outside of Buffalo County."

"Well, I didn't notice the odor on Molly's body, which I should have in that confined space." Clint stepped in and did his own sniff test on the coffee. "Nope, I'm with Mark. Coffee is all I can smell."

The bell on Pinky's door dinged. I thought it'd be the Buffalo County guys until Pinky and Erin came storming in through the archway. Then I remembered Clint had locked that door, anyway.

Clint lifted his arm and pointed for them to halt right where they were. "You can't come in here. We're investigating a crime scene. Mark, get some tape from your car to cordon it off."

Mark left to take care of it.

Pinky's curls bounced around her headband with a life of their own when she and Erin stopped in their tracks. "Then what is Cami doing in there?"

"She found the victim and has been helping us. But you make a good point." He turned to me. "Camryn, if you'll go wait in the coffee shop until we're ready to talk to you some more." Clint switched his attention to Pinky. "And you, too. Hang tight until we get back to you."

I was abruptly excused from being in the thick of things. And I had to admit it was intriguing watching how the officials worked to get to the bottom of it all. Once I got past the fact that Molly had died, and that someone had probably killed her. Molly and I had not been close friends by any stretch of the imagination, but I didn't think she would have poisoned herself. It was obvious she was needy, but she hadn't given any indication she was depressed enough to kill herself. She'd even mentioned wanting to start a family.

Mark returned with a roll of crime scene tape, and the next thing I knew I was being nudged into Brew Ha-Ha to join the other two Musketeers. Mark secured the tape to one wall then stretched it across the open span and taped it to the wall on the other side. Pinky, Erin, and I stood back, just far enough.

"Thanks a lot for ratting me out, Pink."

"Well?"

"If you had kept your mouth zipped shut, at least one of us would have had a front-row seat to watch what was happening," I said in a whisper.

Pinky flicked her hand at a loose curl by her ear. "It just came out. I wasn't thinking that far ahead."

"I don't blame you, really. It's not easy to process something like this," I said.

Pinky pointed into Curio Finds. "Could there be anything more awful?"

"As awful as this is, we all know there are a lot of things that could be worse," I said.

Pinky, Erin, and I hovered in the archway. Erin was in the middle and reached over and grabbed my hand then reached for Pinky's with her other hand. Two Buffalo County deputies wearing black polo shirts with "Crime Scene Team" embroidered above their hearts came through my shop door. One was a man around fifty, and the other was a woman somewhere in her early thirties. The man had a black duffel bag, and the woman was carrying a camera. They glanced up at us, no doubt wondering who we were and why we were there. We must have been a sight. Little five-foot-nothing Erin standing between Pinky, who was almost a foot taller, and me, who was a half a foot taller. I was a little surprised myself that we hadn't been told to wait somewhere out of the way.

The crime scene team went about their business. Clint pointed out the coffee cup with its questionable contents. They took pictures of everything, it seemed, and put the coffee cup in a container to take back to their lab. Pinky, Erin, and I whispered back and forth.

"Pinky, I didn't tell you this yet, but that's the cup. They think someone put cyanide in Molly's coffee," I said.

"Oh my God! I don't even remember her getting a cup of coffee from me," she whispered back.

Erin squeezed my hand even tighter. "You're cutting off my circulation," I said.

"Mine, too," Pinky said.

"Sorry," Erin said. She eased her grip then dropped our hands altogether.

Mark walked over to the archway. "The deputies went to get the gurney from the medical examiner's van, so Clint wants you girls to back away, maybe sit down at Pinky's counter. Molly's husband will be here before long, and he'll have enough to deal with without gawkers, besides. Then we'll talk to you and you." He nodded at Pinky and me.

"I don't know anything, I swear," Pinky said.

"You might not think you do," Mark said, then he turned around to get back to work.

We backed up and watched as the crime scene team came in, rolling the gurney. We heard bits and pieces of what the officials were saying then saw Clint and Mark carry Molly's body out of the bathroom and lay it on the gurney.

Erin and Pinky each put an arm around me. We made

sounds but couldn't form words, not knowing how to adequately express ourselves. Seeing Molly the way she was now, not looking like the Molly we knew, was dreadful. Pinky and Erin were getting their first view of her since she'd passed on.

"The way her mouth is wide open, it looks like she was gasping for air," the female deputy said.

"That would support my theory that she died from cyanide poisoning. Her body was crying for oxygen while she was asphyxiating," Dr. Long said.

"Why didn't she tell someone she needed help instead of going into the bathroom?" the male deputy said.

"Once it's ingested, cyanide works very quickly. The victim probably felt dizzy, like she might faint. She may have headed to the bathroom because she was nauseated and thought she was going to be sick. She didn't know she was in real trouble until it was too late, and she wasn't able to call for help."

Dr. Long's details of what Molly had suffered through made it even worse. I nudged my friends. "Emmy and I were both here and had no clue. Golly, I feel bad for every negative thought I had and every not very nice word I said about Molly," I quietly said.

"Me, too," Pinky said as a tear rolled down her cheek.

"Even when you're not the best of friends with someone, you still like having them around. And you surely don't want them to get poisoned to death, that's for darn sure," Erin said.

"Pinky, can you think of anybody who acted suspicious around here this afternoon?" I said.

She shrugged. "When we were swamped, half the people could have been acting suspicious and I wouldn't have noticed. Wait a minute. There was a guy who stopped by looking for you when you were out on your break. He seemed a little odd. And he described you, instead of asking for you by name."

"Really? What did he say?"

"He asked if the blonde who worked here was around."

"The blonde, huh? What did you tell him?"

"I said, 'Oh, you must be talking about the manager of Curio Finds.' And he sort of shrugged and said, 'Yeah,' and I said you were out but would be back later."

"What did he look like?"

"Holy moly, let me think. He was a little taller than me. He had a stocking cap on. I think it was brown. He must have been pretty normal looking, because I can't think of a good way to describe him."

"Big nose? Small nose? Beard? No beard? Glasses? No glasses? Pale looking, or not so much?"

"He was a white guy, but he did not strike me as overly pale. I didn't notice that his nose was overly big or especially small. No beard. Sorry."

"Don't worry about it. He might have been someone I helped in the past who didn't know my name. He should have asked Molly or Emmy if he was looking for something."

"Maybe he did and they had no clue how to help him. That's why he asked Pinky," Erin said.

"Maybe."

Will Dalton, a man we had never met, knocked on the Curio Finds door. Mark let him in. Will literally burst into the room and filled the whole shop with his presence. And it wasn't because of his size. He was around five-ten and on the slim side. He had a worn-out look that added years to his face. A youngish, petite redheaded woman crept in behind him.

"What in the hell happened to my wife?" He seemed angry more than anything else. The way he said "my wife" sounded like she was his possession, not his partner in life like my mother was to my father.

Pinky started to visibly twitch and shake. The man's tone had clearly frightened her. Maybe she thought the murder weapon, poisoned coffee from her shop, would come back to haunt her in the form of a lawsuit or worse. That's what popped into my head listening to the man, a well-known, powerful attorney who was demanding to know how his wife had died.

I put my hand around Pinky's waist for support, and we moved closer to the archway for a better view. I felt Erin's shoulder touch the back of my arm as she settled into a spot behind me.

Molly looked like she was sleeping. The display area of the shop was better lit than the bathroom, making it more obvious her face was indeed an unnatural shade of pinkish red.

Will Dalton dropped to his knees by the gurney. It looked like he was about to dive headfirst into Molly's stomach when Clint put a hand on his shoulder. "Sorry, but we need to keep contamination to a minimum."

Will turned and stared at Clint. "What?"

"This is an official crime scene. Every one of us has any number of particles on our persons that we leave behind here and there. Until we get to the bottom of what caused your wife's death, it'd be best if you didn't add to the mix."

Will thought about that for a minute while he stared at

Molly's body. He stood, and tears finally formed in his eyes. My first impression of the man was that I was not impressed. There was something about him I didn't like. Maybe it was the way he put everything else ahead of Molly, according to what she'd said, anyway. Maybe it was that he reminded me of the power-crazed people I'd met in Washington.

And something about the young woman with him, his assistant, struck me as off. She looked like a Hollywood star with her flowing red hair and professional model body. Why on earth had she come into the shop with her boss? If I was in her place, I would definitely have waited outside out of respect for poor dead Molly. She had enough people studying her, including Pinky and Erin and me. But we had a stake in the tragedy and a good reason to be there. The officials wanted to question Pinky and me. Erin was there for moral support.

Okay, I'd give the assistant the benefit of the doubt. Will Dalton may have made her come into the shop with him. She looked like the proverbial deer in the headlights, unsure of what to do or which way to go. She hung back and then seemed to notice she was surrounded by snow globes. She picked one up, gave it a shake, then set it down and watched it snow. A distraction for her, and for me also as I watched her. My imagination was probably playing tricks on me, but it seemed I'd seen her somewhere before.

Dr. Long's voice plucked me out of my daydreaming. "—and we'll notify you as soon as we're ready to release your wife's body."

"Release her?" Will said.

"For burial or cremation, whatever you choose. It'll most likely be later tomorrow, after the medical examiner has completed the autopsy."

Will looked a little dazed. "Autopsy?"

Dr. Long handed Will a card. "And after the exam and the tests, we should be able to positively pinpoint the cause of death."

Clint cleared his throat and took out his notepad and pen. "In the meantime, Mr. Dalton, can you tell me, did your wife mention having any kind of trouble with anyone, or had she received any threats?"

He looked down then shook his head. "No."

"If you find out anything different, let us know right away."

Will nodded.

Mark stepped in closer to Will. "Molly's mother. Do you want us to tell her?"

"I'll do it," he said, then he left without saying another word. His assistant followed him out the door. Out of curiosity, I scooted over to Pinky's door and opened it a crack to watch where they went, but they were already out of sight. And what business of mine was it, anyway? Both sides of the street were lined with idling parked cars. With the number of official vehicles there, the town was anxiously waiting for the story of what had happened in Curio Finds. And the medical examiner's van made it clear to all passersby that someone had died.

5

The team finished processing the scene, and Dr. Long left with Molly's body. Clint and Mark each took down an end of the crime scene tape that spanned the archway between Curio Finds and Brew Ha-Ha and rolled it up. They joined Pinky, Erin, and me, who were sitting silently at the coffee shop serving counter. Each of us was lost in our own thoughts.

Mark sat down next to me on the third seat from the end. I had been thinking about Molly's coat and cell phone and keys and wallet. "You forgot to send Molly's things with her husband. And what about her car?"

Clint moved in behind Mark. "We didn't forget."

All part of the investigation, I supposed.

"Pinky, let's go back to one of your tables where we can talk," Clint said.

"Just Pinky?" I said.

"Yup, just Pinky. But you're next, so don't you run away, Camryn."

I couldn't run if I tried. "I will be right here."

Pinky and Clint disappeared to the back area.

"Do either of you want something to eat or drink?" I asked Erin and Mark.

"Nah," Mark said and leaned his arms on the counter.

Erin lowered her voice. "Don't tell Pinky this, but drinking a cup of coffee seems downright scary to me after what happened to Molly. And I have no appetite whatsoever."

"I know what you mean." I glanced up at Betty Boop's hands. "Golly, it's after six o'clock. Time flies even when you're not having fun."

"You know what I've been thinking that is really terrible?" Erin said

Mark leaned closer to me, and I leaned closer to Erin. "What?"

"That as bad as I feel about Molly's death and the way it happened, I can't help comparing it to the shock I felt when my father died. It's not even close."

"Of course it's not, and that's not terrible at all," I said. Like my own parents' death when I was only five years old. Nothing could ever compare to that awful day if I lived to be one hundred. Thinking about them reminded me of the penny I'd found earlier, the one I believed my mother had left for me. At the time I'd hoped it was to reassure me that things would get better. *Mama, I guess you were warning me that time, weren't you?*

Pinky rejoined us some minutes later. She bent over and whispered in my ear, "Your turn with Officer Eye Candy."

"Do not even go there," I mumbled back. I cringed when

she said it, even though it was true. And if I was asked under oath if I found him to be a good-looking man, I'd have to answer, "Yes."

Clint's five-o'clock shadow was right on schedule and gave him a more human look. He looked up at me like he was seeing me for the first time. Although we were not bosom buddies, we had gotten to know each other during the course of a previous murder investigation.

"You know, we really should quit meeting like this," I said.

His lips tugged ever so slightly upward. "That would be fine by me. Sit down."

If Clint worked harder on his bedside manner, it was possible I might grow to like him.

He had his pen and notepad at the ready. "I know we went over some of this already, but tell me everything you remember from the time Molly arrived at your shop this morning to the time you found her body."

I filled him in on as many details as I could. I started with how Molly arrived at work in hideous clothes and how I'd given her my spare outfit to change into. I highlighted the challenge of training both her and Emmy, and about how irritated Emmy was with Molly all day. As an afterthought, I included the part about Ramona Zimmer being in Curio Finds and breaking one of my snow globes—probably on purpose—and then racing out of the shop without so much as an apology.

"And to top off the terrible behavior shown by the senator, her husband had actually been in earlier this morning. He had the nerve to stop by to see me." I waved my hand in the air. "Never mind about his visit, since it was before Molly started work and wouldn't count."

Clint narrowed his eyes, and I suspected he was trying his

best to read my thoughts behind what I'd said about the Zimmers. I'm sure he'd heard as much about that scandal as everyone else in the country who was tuned in to any kind of media source. And I was the hometown girl, so most people in Brooks Landing thought they had a personal stake in the whole mess.

"The visit does count, but not in this particular investigation. Unless he came back later and bought a cup of coffee and laced it with poison," Clint said.

His words caused nerve endings to prickle on the back of my neck. With all the people in the shops during the afternoon rush, it was a possibility Peter Zimmer had been back. Not likely, but it was remotely possible he had mixed in unnoticed with the crowd. Even if he had returned, what motive would he have had to kill Molly? None, as far as I knew.

Clint placed his left forearm on the table and leaned into it. "Tell me what you know about Emmy Anders."

"I'm guessing her given name is Emma, but I've heard her tell people to just call her Emmy. I met her when I returned to Brooks Landing last spring. She stops by here often. I got the impression she hasn't been in town for long, but I haven't really talked to her about it. She isn't the kind who talks much about herself."

Clint looked up from his writing. "I'll be interviewing her later. Go on."

"Okay. Well, I've always thought of Emmy as a lonely, kind older woman. But she wasn't overly kind to Molly today. The two of them did not hit it off at all."

"You don't say."

"It's not that they hate each other or anything. I mean, why would they? But Emmy acted like she was irritated with Molly from the get-go."

"You don't say."

The way he was concentrating on me made me more and more nervous by the second. "I mean what possible reason would Emmy even have to poison Molly, if that's what you're thinking."

"That's not what I'm thinking, nor am I putting words in your mouth."

He was right; I was the one who was blabbing on and on about dear old Emmy. If he'd just quit looking at me like that. We were way too close for comfort, so I leaned back in my chair.

"Pinky told me you helped her out here in the coffee shop for quite a while during the afternoon rush. During that time your two new employees, Emmy and Molly, were alone in your shop, correct?"

"Yes, that's correct."

"Did you notice anything unusual going on between the two of them when you returned?"

You mean how Emmy looked like she was ready to seriously injure Molly at any given moment? "Well, to be honest, things were tense between them. But you have to remember it was their first day on the job, and they were trying to learn as much as they could about Pinky's business and my business. I'm sure you understand how hard that would be. Emmy hasn't worked for years, and it doesn't sound like Molly had an outside job during most, maybe all, of her marriage."

Clint nodded. "Regarding the cup of coffee Molly allegedly drank from, did you see anyone deliver it to her? Did she get it herself?"

"No, I saw Emmy carry a cup from Pinky's shop to mine, but I didn't see what she did with it."

"We've collected the trash bags from the two shops, so we have any discarded cups if we need to check DNA."

Clint impressed me from time to time.

The bell on Pinky's door dinged, then Mark's voice rose in volume like he was addressing a crowd. Apparently he was talking to someone outside. "Sorry, but I'm not authorized to release the name of the victim just yet. We're doing an investigation to cover all the bases, and we'll let you know as soon as we can." The door's bell dinged again followed by the click of the dead bolt lock.

Clint let out a sigh. "We'll have to get a statement together for our friends at the newspapers and radio stations. The waiting public needs to be informed before any number of rumors start circulating."

I nodded. "And that reminds me, I left a message for my parents earlier and I'm surprised they haven't called me back."

"We'll wrap this up for now, but you will call if you think of anything else, right?"

"Right. Can I ask what you meant when you said you didn't forget to give Molly's things to her husband?"

He put his pen and pad in his pocket. "We want to check her phone and her car to see if there is any evidence that someone had threatened her."

"Oh." Police had to think of everything.

We returned to the serving counter where Pinky, Erin, and Mark were all swiveling right and left on their counter seats. Clint lifted his thumb when Mark looked at him. "Let's shove off, partner."

"Ten-four, boss. An evening of report writing ahead of us, huh?"

"Yup, after we pay a visit to Emmy Anders."

"See you girls when the sun is shining again and we all feel better," Mark said, then he followed Clint out the door.

Pinky jumped up to lock it behind them. "You better check your door, too, Cami."

I wanted to call Emmy to tell her about Molly and let her know the police were on their way. But what good would that really do? Police were trained to deliver all kinds of upsetting news.

Pinky, Erin, and I slowly wandered into Curio Finds. I tried the door, and it was indeed locked. I sighed as I turned back to my friends. "Golly, what should we do now?"

"I don't think I can do any baking tonight. Maybe we should go somewhere and hash this all out."

Erin looked around the shop. "I've read that sometimes ghosts don't know they're dead and they hang around in the place where they met their untimely death. Cami, you have that psychic thing of yours going on. Do you think Molly is going to haunt this place?"

"I'm not an expert on ghosts, but no, I don't." My friends gave me more credit for understanding the spirit world than I did. Yes, I sensed my biological mother's—and even my biological father's—presence at times, but I was not psychic. Plus, I believed everyone had times when they instinctively knew what to do or what to avoid or felt like they were being guided. Some people called it having a sixth sense; some called it extrasensory perception. I was just more in tune with it than others, that's all.

Pinky reached over and gave Erin's shoulder a small shake. "Stop that, Erin. It's dark out, and the way the wind is howling and banging against these old shop windows makes it feel eerie enough. We don't need any ghost stories."

That was for sure. On to more practical matters. "How are we ever going to be able to use that bathroom again?" My voice had a whiny ring to it.

"Do you think you should close it down until you can get professionals in to clean it, or what?" Pinky said.

"I don't know."

"Cami is like a professional cleaner. Who could do a better job than she can?" Erin said.

"True," Pinky agreed.

I'd think about it when I could do so more clearly. "Let's get out of here. If you two want to do something, go on ahead without me. I need to tell my parents the news before they hear it from anyone else."

"I hope your dad doesn't blow a gasket," Pinky said.

"Maybe we should go with you," Erin said.

I put a hand on each of their shoulders. "Dad has mellowed a lot in his older age. It'll be good to spend some time with them; it helps keep me grounded. Then, if it's not too late, I'll stop by Emmy's house. She'll be upset by her police visit, I'm sure."

The cars parked outside our shops, filled with curious onlookers, had all left at some point, and the main street through town was deserted. The sun went down early in mid-November, about 4:45 p.m., making it seem much later than 7:20. Pinky had picked Erin up on the way to the shops and parked in the back lot next to my car. We took the path between our building and the one north of it, momentarily protected from the cold wind. The streetlamp on Central

Avenue shed some light, and it was comforting to have my friends alongside me. If it wasn't bad enough Molly had died in Curio Finds, Erin's ghost talk had taken it to a scarier level. I'd never seen a ghost before, and it was a trend I planned to continue for the rest of my life.

"We'll be at Erin's for a while, if you want to stop by," Pinky said.

"Thanks. I'll let you know."

We all got in our vehicles, and I drove to my parents' house and let myself in through the side door of their attached garage. I knew they were gone, because all the lights were off except the one over the kitchen sink. They kept that on twenty-four hours a day for a reason I had yet to find out. I'd asked my mother about it one time, but instead of giving me an answer, she only smiled like she was keeping a secret. "Hello?" I said out of habit, knowing there would be no reply. I stepped into the kitchen and flipped on the switch, pushing out the darkness.

The red light on the answering machine was blinking, indicating my message hadn't been heard. It was possible my parents had gone out for dinner, but the best bet was that they were at the home of one of my four siblings. I picked up the phone and tried each of them, but not one of them answered. I leaned against the counter, wondering if I should try their cell phones next. I gave my dad's cell phone a try. It went straight to voicemail, which meant it was probably turned off. My mom's did the same thing. No one had called to tell me anything was wrong with anyone, so that was good. When my family members heard about Molly's untimely death in Mom and Dad's shop, the phone lines would be burning. I wrote them a note to say I'd stopped by and to please call me the minute they got home.

I hadn't been to Emmy's house, but I knew where she lived. It was in an older part of town, not far from my own neighborhood. I parked on the street in front of the small rambler instead of pulling into her driveway. The branches on the trees and bushes in people's yards were being pushed this way and that by the wind, making them look like living creatures in the poorly lit area. I was not the bravest person in the world and tried not to let my imagination run wild when I got out of my car and made the maddest dash possible to Emmy's front door.

The curtains were drawn, but a lamp near the window shone through. I rang the doorbell then called out, "Emmy, it's me, Camryn."

I heard movement then a thump and put my ear closer to the door, wondering if Emmy was all right.

"I'll be right there, Camryn," she called out.

Emmy opened the door. She glanced up at me then looked down. "Come in. The police were here with the news about Molly and left not ten minutes ago."

I touched her shoulder. "It's a big shock, all right." We went into the living room. Her bedroom door was open, and I noticed a suitcase on the bed.

"Did you stop by to talk about Molly?" She pointed at a chair for me to sit on.

"I wanted to see how you were doing and if you felt up to coming back to work. It was kind of a rough day, and then with Molly . . . well, I'm going to have trouble going back there myself." I took my seat, and Emmy sat down on a rocker by the window.

"Well, dearie, as it turns out, I was going to call you because of something that's come up. I just got off the phone with a friend of mine who asked if I might be able stay with her awhile, and I just couldn't say no."

There was something in her words that didn't ring true somehow. Maybe it was the timing, the suddenness of it. "Oh, well—"

"I'll be leaving in the morning. And Camryn, I'm sorry for you, what with that awful fright you had today. Is there anything special we should do for Molly's family?"

Golly. Molly's family. "I'm not sure, but I can let you know. Do you have a cell phone number?"

"No, sorry, but I'll be sure to call you soon."

"Emmy, I'm sure the police asked you this, but did you see how Molly got that cup of coffee with the poison in it?"

Emmy shook her head, looked down, and watched her folded hands twist to the right then the left. "I didn't notice. I saw her drinking from a cup shortly before you told me we were done for the day. Molly had disappeared, and the bathroom door was closed, so I thought that's where she'd gone."

"You didn't see her go into the bathroom?"

"No."

"She didn't say anything to you about feeling sick?"

"Not a word."

"Was there anyone in the shop today who you thought acted nervous or suspicious?"

"No one special that I can think of. But there were quite a few people throughout the day."

I nodded. "Pinky told me someone had been in her shop

asking for me. Actually, he was looking for 'the blonde.' He was wearing a stocking cap and was about Pinky's height. Do you remember anyone like that?"

She looked up at me. "Sorry, dearie, but I don't."

"Okay. He might have nothing to do with anything, but it had me curious." I stood up. "I hope your friend is better soon and you can get back home."

Her smile was weak. "Thank you." She rocked forward then used her hands to push herself out of the chair.

I gave Emmy a hug and slipped out to leave her to her packing. I briefly considered stopping by Erin's house but didn't think I had the energy to rehash the afternoon and evening events with them. Emmy's comment about doing something special for Molly's family sparked the idea to drive by her house to see how many people had gathered there to support her husband. Call it morbid curiosity.

The Daltons lived in a newer upper-scale section on the outskirts of the city. I'd heard the lots were two acres each, and the average value of each property was over a million dollars. There was a small lake in the middle of the community. The original owner had plotted the land so the backyard of each lot ran down to the lake. If my ancestors who'd founded Brooks Landing a century before could come back today and see the monster homes in their fair city, they would not believe it. For them, living on a lake meant having easier access to fishing, not a place to take a pontoon or speedboat ride.

I turned onto the street that wound in an oblong around the lake. It was a drive I'd taken a number of times, mainly because I admired the beautifully kept properties. I dreamed about how I might landscape my own yard someday. If I ever bought a house, that is.

The Daltons' house was on the west side of the oblong, so I veered left. There were four houses on each side and one on each end. Theirs was the second one in. When my dad's unmarried brother died some years back, we must have had eighty or ninety people crowd into our house when the poor man's body was still warm. I had no idea how many friends and relatives the Daltons had, but I certainly expected a large number of cars in their circular driveway and out on the street.

There was not a vehicle in sight. If there were any on the property, they were tucked away in one of the four stalls of their attached garage. There were security lights outside the house, and there may have been some on inside the home, but none were evident. I did one loop around the neighborhood and then another. It had been a couple of hours since Will Dalton left Curio Finds. Was he alone in there drowning his sorrows, or had he gone to a relative's house—maybe Molly's mother's, or his own parents'—to grieve with loved ones?

Pinky had been afraid of Will Dalton when he was in my shop demanding to know what had happened to Molly. Would he file a lawsuit against Pinky or my parents because of what happened to Molly? I'd read about people suing over wrongful deaths all the time. And unless Molly herself had put the poison in that cup of coffee, her death was about as wrongful as they came. Not that I was more concerned about getting sued than Molly losing her life, but a lawsuit would devastate my parents and Pinky. Not to mention that it would also likely destroy the businesses they had worked so diligently to build.

Molly had mentioned that her mother still lived in the same home as when she was a teenager, which Molly found a little embarrassing. I drove there next. At some point in the very near future, Pinky and I would have to pay her a visit and extend our sympathies. Oh my, how did a person talk to a parent about something that tragic? Will Dalton had said he'd inform the family, and I was glad for that. Mrs. Ryland lived in a very old, fairly well-kept two-story home. It was one that would look haunted if ivy had been allowed to grow across the windows. There were a few cars parked outside, and the inside of the house appeared to have lights on in every room. Good, Mrs. Ryland was not alone; she had someone to share her grief with.

I'd done enough snooping on Molly's family. It was time to concentrate on my own. It had been a few hours since I'd left the original message for my parents and an hour since I'd written the note. If they'd gone to a movie, they would have chosen an early show, either the four o'clock or six o'clock one. When I got home and saw I had six new messages on my answering machine, I pulled my cell phone out of my pocket. It was deader than a doornail. Oops.

The first two messages were telemarketing calls, and the last four had all come in the past six minutes. One was from Pinky. "Erin and I are checking to see how you're doing. Did you turn your cell phone off?" The next one was the local newspaper's star reporter and town gossip. "Camryn, it's Sandy Gibbons. I just heard that someone died under mysterious circumstances in your shop this afternoon. No one is there to talk to about it, and the police haven't returned my call. Call me. Right away, please." The next was Pinky again. "Sandy Gibbons is hot on your trail, so you'd better turn off your lights. She saw my car at Erin's and had the nerve to stop here to try to get all the juicy details. I told her to talk to the police." The last and most welcomed message was from my mom. "Hi, Cami. We were at your nephew's basketball game over in Sibley and just got home. Call when you can."

I dialed them right away. Unfortunately, Sandy Gibbons had phoned them a minute before, and my mom hung up on her to take my call. "Cami, I can't believe what Sandy just told me."

"It was horrible, Mom. That's why I called Dad earlier and asked about the bathroom key because it was locked from the inside. I didn't know why Molly wasn't answering, or if she was even in there for sure." I sniffed. "Molly Dalton got poisoned in our shop, and died in the bathroom. And I was the one who found her."

"We'll be right over."

I knew my mom would be exhausted from their outing. "No, really, Mom, I'm okay. I'll stop over tomorrow and we'll talk about it."

"How would she get into poison?"

"Someone put it in her coffee. No idea why. I mean, who would hate her enough to do that?"

"Oh dear me, are you saying someone deliberately poisoned Molly?"

"It looks that way, and the police are investigating, of course. None of it seems real. And if Sandy Gibbons keeps bugging you, tell her the police put a gag order on us for now."

"Cami, this is a horrible thing. For you, for her family . . ."

"And for Molly, especially."

"Of course. I don't know her mother very well, but we'll be sure to send her a nice bouquet of flowers. We'll order one for Molly's husband, too."

"That's thoughtful." It was not the time to bring up my fear that her husband might file a lawsuit against us. He didn't get high up on the corporate attorney ladder on good looks alone. If we sent him flowers, would he take it as a kind gesture or an admission of guilt?

Mom asked me more about Molly's death, and I filled her in, leaving out some of the upsetting details. And she didn't need to hear that both Mr. and Senator Zimmer had darkened the shops' doorways at different times that morning. "Oh, and our other employee, Emmy, is already taking a leave of absence to go stay with a friend in need."

"Goodness me. Well, if you need your dad to fill in, I'm sure he'd be happy to help you out."

"Thanks, I will let you know."

"And you get some sleep tonight, Cami. All right?"

"All right." But nothing was all right, not by any stretch of the imagination.

We'd barely said our good-byes when the front doorbell rang. I braced myself, thinking it would be Clint wanting to ask me more questions. I peeked around the drape that covered the living room picture window. I had zero desire to see Sandy Gibbons, but there she was, standing on my front step with her brown hair flying straight up in the wind. I opened the door so she wouldn't try to pump my parents for information they didn't have. And she did look cold.

"Cami, if it weren't for bad luck, you wouldn't have any at all. That's certainly been true lately, at least." Sandy was not known for her tact. She was missing the filtering gene that stopped most of us from saying things that might offend others. "Brrr, that north wind is brutal tonight." She stepped inside, and her hair fell back down and formed an unusual hairdo. Not unlike what mine looked like when I crawled out of bed in the morning.

"I've had a couple of bad—okay, really bad—things happen in the last month or so, but I don't know if it has anything to do with luck."

Sandy waved her hand in the air as if she were dispelling my words. "Can we sit down for a few minutes? I've been running all over town, and I'm not exactly a spring chicken, you know." She had seemed about the same age, sixtyish, for as far back as I could remember. She was likely nearing seventy by now.

"Let's sit at the kitchen table." I led the way. She plopped her large purse on the table then fished inside of it and came out with a notebook and laid it on the table. Then, as she lowered her body onto a chair, she slipped off her coat and let it drop on the seat behind her. She reached into the front of her shirt and pulled a pen from heaven knows where, ready to write.

Sandy sucked in a giant breath and looked me squarely in the eyes. "All right. I know someone died in your shop and that it's being investigated as a homicide."

"How do you know all that?" I said and sunk down on a chair myself.

Because I heard the Buffalo County dispatcher call for the major crimes investigators to go to your shop address, over my police scanner. I got down there as soon as I could. The shop doors were locked, and I saw the coroner and the Buffalo County crime team there, a sure sign it was a homicide.

"I was afraid you or Pinky had been robbed and killed

CHRISTINE HUSOM

on top of it all, but then I saw you through the window before
they closed your blinds. Pinky's were left open, and I was
relieved to see Erin and Pinky were safe and sound, too."
Sandy admitted she had been one of the snoopers sitting in
a vehicle outside. Not a bit surprising.

"Sandy, since the police won't tell you anything, what
makes you think I can?"

She brushed at something on her notepad. "Cami, the
police left your shop a couple of hours ago and said they'd
be releasing a statement soon. Were they just saying that to
get me to leave?"

Maybe they were. "The police need to talk to everyone in
the family before they talk to the media and the rest of the
world."

"It's the same old thing every time something big breaks.
We have to practically beg, borrow, and steal to find out any
details."

"But in the end you always get your story, right?"

"Well, back to your comment about everyone in the victim's family. Are you saying this person comes from a large
family?"

I smiled. "No, it was just an observation."

She leaned closer. "Is it someone you know?"

"Yes, Sandy, it is, but that is absolutely the last thing I can
say about it until the police tell me—" The ringing of my home
phone cut me off. I jumped up and saw it was Mark calling.

"Oh, you are home. You weren't answering your cell," he
said.

"It's on the charger. What's up?"

"Clint just released Molly's name to the major media

channels and said her death was under investigation. It'll be on the ten o'clock news."

That would make it seem more official. "Oh. I don't think I'll be able to watch it." I glanced over at Sandy, who was obviously eavesdropping. "And how about our local media?"

"Sandy Gibbons was chomping at the bit for the info, but she's been MIA for the last ten or fifteen minutes."

"Consider her found. You want me to tell her?"

"Yeah, go ahead, but no details yet."

"I understand. And how are things going there?"

"So-so. Hey, I'll catch you later."

By the time I hung up, Sandy's body had turned around in her chair. "My ears are burning."

"It was Mark Weston, and he said I can tell you that it was Molly Dalton who died, and that her death is being investigated."

Sandy almost toppled out of her chair. "Molly Dalton! Oh my God, I would not want to be the guy that killed her. Her husband will make sure he gets the gas chamber."

"You're jumping to conclusions. First of all, we don't know that she was killed. For sure. And even if she was, we don't have the death penalty in Minnesota."

"Oh, of course. But William Dalton and his family can probably move the trial to a state that does."

"Sandy, it doesn't work that way."

"Not for regular folks, it doesn't."

Thinking about what Will Dalton might do to hurt Pinky's and my parents' businesses was scaring me more and more by the minute.

6

The phone rang first thing the next morning. I reached over and lifted the cordless out of its cradle and managed to get it right side up. "Yes?"

It was Pinky talking in a quiet voice. "Cami, I hate to ask you this, but do you think you can come in early today? I am freaking out being here alone. That darn Erin and her ghost talk. And I don't even believe in ghosts."

I hadn't slept much all night. Between Molly's face with her unseeing eyes being front and center in my thoughts, and then worrying about her husband's reaction to the tragedy, I tossed and turned until after three o'clock. I rolled onto my side and looked at the clock: 7:20 a.m. It would have been dark outside when her shop opened at 7:00, since the sun came up just a little before that.

"No customers?"

·

"Not right now. The early crowd came and went, and I'm hoping the next wave will start soon, but in the meantime, here I am alone with my scary thoughts. The lights are off in your shop, and I keep seeing all kinds of shadows that seem to be moving whenever I look that way."

"It's going to take me twenty minutes to get there. Hang on 'til then."

"Oh, there's a customer coming in now, thank the good Lord!"

I hung up, and my body fought me every inch of the way as I got out of bed and waddled to the bathroom. I washed and brushed my hair and teeth and put on some light makeup then walked with less of a waddle to my bedroom closet. I threw on a peachy pink knitted pullover and gray pants, fluffed my hair, and stuck a silver necklace and earrings in my pocket to put on later. With my coat on and purse in hand, I was at the shops in fifteen minutes.

Pinky smiled from ear to ear when I walked through the door. She ran to meet me and threw her arms around me in a bear hug. "Wow, that was fast. Thanks for coming in and for wearing my color. I feel better already."

"That's what friends are for." I hadn't chosen Pinky's favorite color on purpose when I'd put on the sweater. Or maybe I had, after all. "I'll go turn on my shop lights, and that should dispel any scary thoughts you're having." *If only it were that easy.* I crept into Curio Finds, trying to ignore the moving shadows Pinky had referred to. I knew they were from cars passing by outside, but shadows had taken on a whole new meaning since yesterday.

I turned on the lights but kept the shop door locked. We wouldn't be open for over two hours. Pinky had another few customers to wait on, or I would have asked her to stand beside me as I checked out the place where Molly had died. I flipped on the bathroom light switch and took in every detail of the nondescript space. Toilet, sink, toilet paper holder, mirror, paper towel holder, and a picture of multicolored snow globes on the wall. Everything looked normal. I wondered how long it would take before it felt normal again.

When Pinky was free, I called for her to join me.

"Busy," she called back.

"Doing what?"

"Just busy."

I went into her shop, and when I saw she was standing there, not busy, I took her hand and led her to the bathroom door. She threw her free arm over her eyes. "I can't look."

"Pinky, there is really nothing to see. That's what I needed to see, too; that Molly really isn't still there."

She lowered her arm and opened her eyes. "Same old bathroom, but I'll never go in there again."

"Remember what they say about never saying never?"

"Yeah, yeah, yeah."

The bell on Brew Ha-Ha's door dinged, and we returned to the coffee shop. In walked Assistant Chief Clinton Lonsbury, of all people. Officer Mark Weston came in seconds later. Mark's expression was almost as solemn as Clint's. "What?" I said.

Clint cleared his throat. "Just how much do you know about Emmy Anders?"

Pinky and I looked at each other and shrugged. "Like what? Where she lives? Where she goes to church?" I said.

"More like her history, her life before she moved to Brooks Landing," Clint said.

"Before she moved here? Next to nothing," I said.

"I have to go along with Cami. Emmy started coming in here more the last six months or so but didn't like to talk about herself. And you know me; I tried to get her to open up more."

Mark nodded. "We have a pretty good idea of why she didn't say much."

Pinky and I were drawn in by his words and took a step closer to the officers.

"Do you know where she moved here from?" Clint said.

"The metro area," Pinky said.

I agreed. "Yes, it was Minneapolis."

"About three years ago, a man named Howard Andersohn was poisoned. His wife was arrested, charged, tried, and acquitted by a jury of her peers for lack of conclusive evidence."

"Why are you telling us this? Was it similar to what happened to Molly, or what?"

"There could be a common denominator," Mark said.

"We did an abbreviated background investigation on Emmy Anders and came up with some troubling information."

My heart started pounding. "No."

"Emmy Anders's real name is Emaline Andersohn."

Pinky clasped her hands and drew them to her chest. "I remember that name. But it can't be our Emmy."

"Unfortunately, Emaline and Emmy are one and the same. Her husband was poisoned, and just about everyone thought she'd done it. The problem was, they could not prove it beyond a shadow of a doubt in a court of law."

"I wasn't around here three years ago, I don't remember hearing about that case, and I have trouble believing Emmy would hurt anyone."

"Whether you do or don't isn't the issue now, is it? Most

people back then did. I'd say she changed her name and moved to our fair city to escape those who believed she was guilty." Clint looked at his watch. "We stopped by her house to talk to her before we came here, but it was dark. Do you have her scheduled to work today?"

"Actually, no. She told me last night that she had to leave early this morning to go stay with a friend who needed her."

Pinky's mouth dropped open. "Cami—"

"Sorry, Pinky, I meant to tell you, but I was thinking about Molly, and it slipped my mind."

Clint leaned closer. "Do you have her friend's name, her address?"

"No, I—"

"How about a phone number?"

"No, when I asked Emmy for her cell number she said she didn't have one and that she'd call me."

Clint narrowed his eyes. "Did it seem at all suspicious to you that she was leaving so abruptly?"

"A little, but I had no reason to think that—"

Clint turned to Mark. "It looks like our number one suspect has flown the coop."

Pinky reached over and grabbed my hand. Hers was shaking as much as mine was.

Clint moved in close to me and held up a finger in front of my face. "If Emmy calls, find out where she is and then get ahold of me right away. Understand?"

"Yes. Sir."

With that, Clint and Mark left without so much as a cup of coffee or even a good-bye.

Pinky swung her body around so we were face-to-face,

and she put both of her hands on my shoulders. "That man can be so intense at times."

"Tell me about it. I was the one three inches away from him. The irises of his eyes got so dark they were nearly black."

"Under different circumstances, I wouldn't mind one little bit if he looked into my eyes with that much passion. But seriously, this is scary stuff, and it sure doesn't look good for Emmy. I mean, she poisoned her husband and now Molly got poisoned when Emmy was with her. It seems like too much of a coincidence if you ask me."

"First of all, Clint said there was not enough evidence against Emmy, and second, why would she kill Molly?"

"She got away with it once, so she did it again."

"But why?"

"I don't know. Why do people do bad things?"

helped Pinky with a flurry of customers until after eight o'clock then headed into Curio Finds. "Hey, Pinky, since the sun is out now and you're feeling better, I'm going to turn off my overhead lights so people don't think the shop is open and wonder why the doors are locked. I'm going to use the time to get some bookwork and stocking done."

"Hey, you're the one in there, not me. Go for it." She went back to cleaning off her serving area.

I sat down at my checkout counter and looked around at the shelves filled with snow globes and other unique items. Yesterday, Molly and Emmy had been there, dusting and getting familiarized with the merchandise, and now they were both gone. Emmy certainly had not done herself any favors by disappearing, as far as the police were concerned. It was understandable that her checkered past had raised red flags for them. Clint was right; I had known something was off when I saw the suitcase on Emmy's bed and she said she was leaving to help a friend. She'd acted strangely, and I thought it was because the police had just dropped the bad news bomb about Molly, and because Emmy was torn about leaving town. Now it seemed like there might be a different reason altogether.

I went into the storeroom, and the first thing I noticed was the small pile of trashy clothes Molly had taken off and left on the floor. The sight of them caught me off guard and stopped me in my tracks. I grabbed one of our sales bags, picked up the items, and dropped them in it. Dressing down had a very different meaning for Molly than it did for Pinky and me. I set the bag on a shelf and decided to ask the police what to do with it. Molly had the clothes for less than a day, so her husband wouldn't want them. He'd be more shocked than the rest of us if he'd known she had shown up for work in that outfit.

I heard a noise in the shop and left the storeroom to see what it was. A woman was standing at the checkout counter with an envelope in her gloved hand. She was wearing a quilted black jacket and a black stocking cap pulled down to cover all but her mouth, nose, eyes, chin, and a little of her cheeks. Sunglasses completed the disguise. It took me a second to realize who it was. "Senator, what are you doing?"

Her eyes were somewhat visible behind the glasses and opened wider than I'd ever seen them. Her jaw dropped, and the envelope fell out of her hand. "Camryn, why are you here?"

"That's a silly question."

"Well, I mean your shop isn't open. And the morning

news said a woman died here yesterday, so I thought . . . I mean . . ."

"What are you getting at, and what possible reason brought you back after what you did here yesterday?"

"You saw me?" She pursed her lips.

"I sure did."

She picked up the envelope. "I wanted to give you this." And with that she dropped the envelope on the counter then scurried through the archway and out Brew Ha-Ha's door.

It took me a minute before I was able to utter a sound or move any part of my body. "Pinky!"

She came running in, holding a knife in her hand. "What is it?"

"Didn't you see who just ran out of my shop and out your door?"

"No, I didn't. I was washing dishes and had my back to the archway. When I heard the ding, I looked that way, but all I saw was a woman's back."

"It was Ramona Zimmer."

"No. What in the heck was she up to this time?"

I walked to the counter. "She delivered this." I pointed at the envelope.

Pinky dropped her knife-wielding hand to her side and stepped in beside me. We both stared at the suspicious object. "Are you going to open it?" she asked.

"I don't know. I'm a little worried."

"You're right. I would be, too. It might have, um, what is the name of that powdered poison that senators were getting in their letters a while back?"

"Anthrax, but some got letters laced with ricin, too."

"That's right. And we did have a poisoning here yesterday." She took a step back from the counter.

"Now you've really got me nervous." I stepped away, too.

"I think you better call nine-one-one and ask them about it."

"You think so? It might be better if we called the police department instead. Maybe Mark would check it out for us."

"We can do that."

"Do you want to call?"

"The letter is on your counter, left by your former employer for you."

"Maybe it'd be safer to go into your shop and make the call."

We looked like our sides were glued together as we turned and slowly walked into Pinky's shop. When we got to the counter, she stepped ahead, picked up her phone, and handed it to me. I shook my head. "My cell phone is in my pocket, and I have Mark on speed dial."

"Take it out."

"What?"

"Your cell phone. Cami, you are acting like a space cadet."

"I can't help it. I just thought of something bad."

"Like what?"

"I can't talk about it right now, so I'll tell you later when I can."

"Cami, you're scaring me."

"Pinky, I'm scaring *me*."

"Do you want me to call Mark?"

"Yes. Please."

Pinky broke the spell by hitting numbers on her cordless phone. "Mark, it's Pinky and Cami. Can you come down here, as soon as possible, like right now? . . . You're never going to believe this, but Senator Ramona Zimmer was here and left an envelope on Cami's counter, and we want to make sure there's no ricin or anthrax in it. . . . Okay, thanks." She pushed the off button. "He's on his way from the station."

"Good."

"So tell me your bad thought."

"I have to process it awhile first."

"You know I am way too snoopy and can't stand the suspense."

"I do know that. And you know that I need to think about big things for a while before I can talk about them."

Pinky lifted her hand up. "Truce?"

"Truce."

She smiled, lightening the mood a little bit. "But hurry up thinking through whatever it is, will you please?"

I smiled back. "I will try. Oh, and when Mark gets here, remind me to give him Molly's bag of clothes."

Pinky frowned. "You mean her trampy outfit? Why give them to him?"

"It's up to the police to decide what to do with them, not me. I'm actually surprised they didn't take them yesterday. They must have looked through them when they were doing all their searching around here."

"You'd think. Cami, I hate to ask you this, but are you going to try to get your clothes back, the ones Molly was wearing?"

I shook my head. "And you know what I realized during the night when I couldn't sleep? It was the same outfit I was wearing when Ramona Zimmer came in and found her sleazy husband's hands all over it."

"*No.*"

"I should have given it away then."

"Holy moly, that is one bad-luck outfit. You wore it and lost your job. Molly wore it and lost her life."

My heart felt like it dropped to my stomach. "Pinky, I felt guilty enough before."

"Sorry."

The bell on Brew Ha-Ha's door dinged, and both Mark and Clint rushed in like they were on a lifesaving mission. And maybe they were if the envelope in question contained a deadly ingredient. They were carrying vinyl gloves and pulled them on.

"Where is it?" Clint asked.

We went into the curio shop then stopped a few feet back from the counter and I pointed. Mark pulled a plastic bag marked "Evidence" from his back pocket. Clint moved up to the counter. "Camryn, you saw the senator lay this here?"

"I did."

"What did she say? Did she explain herself?"

"No. She was surprised I was here, because she knew what time our shop opens. She must have been watching Pinky and snuck in when she was in her back area. Or maybe the senator came in with other people. She was dressed so she wouldn't be recognized."

"Was she wearing gloves?"

I envisioned Ramona's hands. "Actually, she did have black leather gloves on."

Clint picked up the envelope. "It's addressed to you, Camryn."

I knew that.

"Mark, open that evidence bag, will you?" When Mark

did so, Clint dropped the envelope in. "We'll get this over to Buffalo County and see if their crime lab can do an analysis. If not, they'll send it to the Minnesota Bureau of Criminal Apprehension."

The nightmare continued.

"Are you going to arrest Senator Zimmer for trying to poison Cami?" Pinky said.

"First we have to find out what's in that envelope," Clint said.

"You could arrest her for breaking one of the snow globes in here and not paying for it," Pinky said.

Clint focused on me. "You mentioned that last night, Camryn. What was the value of the snow globe?"

"Around fifty dollars. It wasn't one of the older, more expensive ones."

Clint looked at Pinky. "No, we wouldn't arrest the senator on a petty misdemeanor charge. I could issue her a citation, however."

I held up my hands and shook my head. "No, please don't. It's not worth it. I'm much more interested in what the crime lab people find in that envelope."

"Cami's right. If there is poison in it, she will be in serious trouble, and we'll slap a list of felony charges against her," Mark said.

"Let's get this over to the county," Clint said. He started for the door then stopped and turned around. "I guess you know this, but as a reminder, keep on the lookout for any more unusual activity."

Mark nodded his agreement.

I raised my hand. "Before you leave, we have something of Molly's to give you."

"That's right, I was supposed to remind you about that, Cami."

Clint frowned. "What is it?"

"The outfit she wore here to work."

"But it was bad, and Cami gave Molly one of her own spare outfits to wear instead," Pinky said.

"We didn't know what to do with it," I said.

"We'll take it and check for possible evidence," Mark said.

I retrieved the pants and top from the store room, and handed them to Clint. His nose twitched, no doubt due to the mothball smell that clung to the clothes, but he didn't comment.

They said a final good-bye and left with Mark carrying the questionable envelope, and Clint carrying the discarded clothes.

"I can't handle any more unusual activity." Pinky's body straightened and stiffened like she was a missile ready for takeoff.

Her visible tension helped me to refocus. "Pinky, look at me. Hey, remember what we did when we were kids and got scared, or thought we were in trouble?"

"Yeesss."

"Okay. First let's shake our hands." We backed away from each other to avoid accidental slaps and shook away. "Now our feet." We circled one foot then the other. "All together now." We sang a little song as we moved: "Head, shoulders, knees and toes, knees and toes. Head, shoulders, knees and toes, knees and toes. And eyes and ears and mouth and nose. Head, shoulders, knees and toes, knees and toes."

When we stood up, there were two older women standing in the archway staring at us. Pinky's headband had slipped down to her eyebrows. "Oh, um, just getting in some exercise between customers." She fixed her clothes and pushed her band higher, gaining some control over her wild curls.

One of the women smiled slightly, but her companion wore a pained expression. I had to wonder if they were thinking Brew Ha-Ha put less emphasis on "brew" and more importance on "ha-ha." No matter. With Pinky running the show, that was often true. Pinky left to help her customers. When I heard one of them order a muffin, my stomach groaned, reminding me I hadn't had breakfast. I went to the serving counter for a cup of coffee and a raspberry scone.

Our teacher friend Erin stopped by after school ended. "What a day it was with my fourth graders. Even the kids who are usually angels had ants in their pants. I only had time to think about Molly about a hundred times." She blew out a breath of air and sat down at Pinky's counter. She looked at me then at Pinky. "How are you guys doing? You both have funny looks on your faces. And where is Emmy— was she too freaked out to come back to work?"

"Golly, Erin, you will not, not, not believe what I am about to tell you." I sat down beside her. Pinky stayed behind the counter and served Erin a decaf with milk.

Erin's mouth hung open through the entire account of Emmy's past—and how she had gotten out of town just before the law caught up to her.

"Sweet little old Emmy? I can't believe she's been living a secret life right here in Brooks Landing under an assumed name. Oh my gosh."

Then Pinky launched into the story of how Senator

Zimmer had left an envelope addressed to me, and how we were waiting to find out about the lab results.

Erin grabbed my hand. "Forget about what I said about my day. It was a breeze compared to what you've been going through."

There was no one else in either shop, so it was a good time to tell Pinky and Erin what had me on edge all day. "Do you want to hear what I think might have happened to Molly?"

"What?" they said in unison.

I looked around to confirm no one had come in. "This is really bad. And if it's true, I don't know how I'll ever make it up to Molly's husband."

"What in the world are you talking about?" Erin said.

"I think it was the Zimmers."

"The Zimmers what?"

I lowered my voice. "I think it was the Zimmers who poisoned Molly."

"Cami, you are not making sense," Pinky said.

"The Zimmers knew Molly?" Erin said.

"No, not that I know of."

Erin raised her palms. "Then why would they kill her?"

"Okay, I'll back up. I don't think they actually did it themselves. I think they hired someone and he got the wrong woman."

"A hit man? You're talking about a hit man?" Erin said.

"In Brooks Landing? Holy moly." Pinky came around the counter and sat down next to me.

"You are not saying what I think you are, are you?" Erin said.

I shrugged. "Pinky, when we talked about it earlier, I told you it was bad. Think about it, first Peter Zimmer stops by for a visit. Actually, he wanted more, but that's too disgusting to talk about right now. Then Ramona Zimmer shows up at Curio Finds and has an evil eye on Molly.

"Molly was helping a customer with her back to Ramona. I think she thought Molly was really me. On top of it all, Molly was wearing my clothes. Ramona's mad at me and loses it for a minute. She creates a little scene—maybe accidentally, maybe on purpose—and then takes off before anyone can stop her. The senator is no sprinter by any means, but she knows I can't run to save my soul. So once she was out of the store, she was home free."

"Cami, I hate to say it, but Molly did look a lot like you yesterday, especially after she'd changed into your spare outfit. I did a double take a few times thinking it was you, but it was really Molly," Pinky said.

"Really?" Erin sounded like she was trying to envision it.

Pinky nodded. "I wasn't going to bring it up, but it was kind of freaky. It's not that Cami's and Molly's features are that much alike, but their hair color and style, their height, and the way they're built is very similar."

"I'll have to think about that some more," Erin said.

Pinky shifted. "Cami, tell Erin about the outfit, what you told me earlier."

"It was the same one I was wearing when Ramona found Peter and me together."

"Oh my gosh. No wonder she flipped."

"I know. And I can see how if someone didn't know Molly or me very well, or was looking at us from the back, they might mistake us. I've certainly gotten people confused before." I let that sink in a second. "Back to the other thing that happened yesterday; there was that guy in here asking about the blonde that worked in Curio Finds, and I don't think he was looking for snow globes."

"That's right. He only said he was looking for the blonde," Pinky said.

"And then early this morning Ramona Zimmer snuck in via the coffee shop and was blown away when she saw me. That's when I put two and two together."

"You need to tell the police about your suspicions," Erin said.

"They have the envelope and are going to have it tested. We'll see what the results are first. Besides, they're really focused on finding Emmy right now. She seems to be their prime suspect."

"But you're looking at the Zimmers and you don't think Emmy is the guilty one?" Erin said.

I shrugged. "I would have said positively no yesterday, but I have to admit, her past has got me wondering."

"For sure. What surprised me about Emmy was the other side of her that Molly brought out. The catty side." Pinky lifted her hands, formed claws, and said, "Grrr."

"Catty is a good word. When Emmy was picking on Molly about little things—okay, annoying things—if Molly had stood up for herself and told Emmy to stop it, we may have had a catfight. I was planning on having a talk with Emmy about it to ask her to be nicer to Molly."

"I was thinking I should do the same," Pinky said.

"Are you planning to hire someone else?" Erin said.

Pinky and I stared at each other, trying to read the other's thoughts. I shrugged, then Pinky shrugged.

Erin put her elbow on the counter and rested her head on her hand. "Hey, I want to throw it out there that I'm available to help you on the weekends, even after school. Not every day and every weekend, but maybe a Saturday one week and a Sunday the next."

"Erin, that's more than generous, but we wouldn't want to burn you out. Plus you've got parent-teacher conferences coming up soon," I said.

Erin lifted her shoulders in a small shrug. "I'm nearly done with the students' reports. And the conferences are two of the evenings I couldn't work here."

"You do know a lot about both our shops." Pinky touched my shoulder. "Cami, we know Erin's really smart. And fast. She's helped me whip up my coffee delights before when I've been swamped. We wouldn't have to get all stressed out teaching her the basics."

I reached out and grabbed Pinky's hand on one side and Erin's hand on the other. "I think it's a great idea. And Mom said my dad can help in a pinch, too. But I don't want to count on that yet. Erin, how about we give you our master calendar and you can write down the dates and times you're available? That will give us an idea of whether or not we'll need to look for another part-timer." We gave our hands a final squeeze then released them.

Pinky swung around on her stool and stood up. "I'll get the calendar."

She went into her back room, and Erin leaned closer to me. "Cami, I know you too well. Don't put yourself in danger like last time, when you tried to find out who'd killed Jerrell Powers."

"I was not in danger, contrary to the popular belief held by you and Pinky. And a few others." Like Clint and Mark and my parents and . . . well, the list was fairly long. "And that is all water over the dam, or under the bridge, or whichever way it happens to flow."

Pinky returned with the calendar and handed it to Erin, who pulled out her phone and came up with some dates she'd be available. A day here and there would help ease our stress and give our customers better service.

While Erin worked on her project of finding dates she could help out, Pinky waited on new customers, and I went back into Curio Finds to sort through the rest of the merchandise my parents had delivered a few days before. They had ordered some new merchandise, but most of the stock—outside of the extensive and ever-changing snow globes from around the world—were unique items they found at auctions, estate and garage sales, and the want ads. Their scouting and scavenging had slowed during Mom's illness and treatment, but Dad got out on his own occasionally, as long as he didn't have to leave Mom alone for long.

I had started paying more attention to special finds myself, looking for things that would strike the fancy of our customers. People called the shop to tell us they had spotted things we might be in the market for at flea markets or other sales. Although I had never aspired to manage Curio Finds, it was the best place for me to be for the time being, and I had grown to appreciate working in the shop among the valuable and rare items, as well as the fun ones. But the best part was being near my family and forever friends again.

I walked over to the spot where the snow globe depicting Marilyn Monroe in her long silk dress had sat for several weeks. I'd strongly considered buying it because I'd gone to a number of costume parties dressed as the actress. I was amazed at how I could be transformed by the right clothes, makeup, and hairstyle. If Marilyn had been wearing the same outfit in the snow globe that I used for my costume—the white dress from *The Seven Year Itch*—I would surely have bought it. After Pinky and I had hosted a snow globe–making class the previous month when we'd hired a teacher and actually learned to make them, I thought about using my newfound skills to create another globe for Marilyn Monroe to pose in.

Ramona Zimmer had been holding the Marilyn Monroe snow globe and looking at Molly Dalton when she dropped it. There were two questions that kept churning around in my brain. One, did Ramona think it was me standing there helping a customer? Molly had her back to Ramona, and Ramona did act surprised when I said I had seen her in the shop. And two, had she deliberately smashed the snow globe out of uncontrolled anger, or was it just because she was clumsy?

She'd seen me in the Marilyn costume at least twice, maybe three times, over the years, and maybe the snow globe reminded her of that and had set her off. I'd seen her lose her temper with staffers before, and each time I'd thought she'd overreacted. She was under stress much of the time and didn't always manage it very well.

Ramona may have thought she'd found a way to get rid of me for good, but then the plan had failed when the wrong woman died. So she returned with a deadly poison in an envelope addressed to me. She may have thought I'd blindly open the envelope and become incapacitated and die on the spot. I wouldn't be able to name or identify her if I was dead. All she'd have to do was to sneak out Brew Ha-Ha's door without being seen or recognized.

Would she be so bold? Considering the possibility she could be that calculating and cold made me tremble.

7

Peter and Ramona Zimmer lived in Orten, a town twenty miles southeast of Brooks Landing. I had driven by the road leading to the mostly bedroom community more than a hundred times in my life because it was on the main route to Minneapolis. I'd also given the senator a ride home from the airport when we'd taken the same flight from Washington to Minneapolis the past Christmas.

As I drove down Highway 44, I wondered why I felt compelled to pass their house. I don't know what I was looking for and what I'd do if anything seemed suspicious. If their garage door was open and I saw a container labeled "Poison" on their shelves, maybe I'd snap some pictures.

If I was really lucky, Ramona would be out in the yard, standing over a large iron kettle set on a roaring wood fire. Ha. I imagined her as one of the witches in Shakespeare's

Macbeth, adding deadly ingredients and stirring them in. We'd read the tragedy in English class my senior year in high school, and I'd memorized the first witch's lines. "Round about the cauldron go; / In the poisoned entrails throw. / Toad, that under cold stone / Days and nights has thirty-one / Sweltered venom sleeping got, / Boil thou first in the charmèd pot." And then the other two witches joined the first in the familiar chorus, "Double, double toil and trouble; / Fire burn, and cauldron bubble."

Even though I knew the story was a product of William Shakespeare's imagination, envisioning those witches attending to their nasty deeds, uttering those ominous words, had scared me twenty years ago, and still had the power to send a chill through me now. In my wildest teen-aged dreams I could never have imagined that a real-life incident would someday trigger memories of *Macbeth*'s evil-minded witches.

The moon and stars were hidden by clouds, and the sky was darker than dark that November night. It added to my unsettled feelings about the Zimmers' possible connection to Molly's death. Had the poison that killed her come from them and been meant for me after all?

I'd bought my Subaru after I moved back to Brooks Landing, and I felt fairly anonymous in it, knowing Ramona and Peter would not recognize the vehicle if they saw me drive by. When I got to their neighborhood, I made one slow pass by their house then drove around the block for another look. The first time by it was difficult to tell if anyone was home. As I approached the house for the second time, I met a car. My heart almost stopped when the Zimmers' garage door went up and the car turned into their driveway and drove into the attached garage. I pulled into the driveway of the house across the street and turned off the ignition.

I was directly across from the Zimmers' and swiveled around in my seat for a good view of what was stored in their garage. From what I could see, it was bare of shelves. No obvious containers marked "Cyanide" or "Anthrax" or "Ricin." Of course there weren't. Ramona and Peter Zimmer were very daring people in different ways, but neither one of them was stupid. The car's trunk popped open, and my heart pounded in anticipation of what was in there and was about to be removed.

I had to blink twice when Senator Ramona Zimmer got out of the car on the driver's side and a strange man who was not her husband got out of the passenger side. Jiminy Cricket. Ramona's was the only car in the garage. Where was Peter, and who was Ramona bringing into their home when her husband was not there?

Ramona and the man met at the trunk of the car. He reached in and pulled out a suitcase. A *suitcase*. Peter was gone, and Ramona came home with a man and a suitcase. Unbelievable. They headed to the door that led to her house, and Ramona reached up and pushed a button that closed the garage door and ended my snooping.

My cell phone rang, startling me. I fumbled with the phone until I finally pushed the right button. "Hello."

Erin didn't bother saying hello back. "Cami, where are you?"

There was no good reason to tell her the truth and upset her over the phone. Call it self-preservation. "Just out for a drive."

"You don't go for a drive for no good reason."

"You are right; as if I could fool you. I'll tell you all about it when I see you."

"Pinky and I are at your house, and since you didn't say you had plans tonight we got worried. Very worried, after all the things you told us about the Zimmers this afternoon. Promise us you're safe."

"I promise. And I'll be home in about twenty minutes. Are you inside or outside my house?"

"Out."

"If you want to wait for me, go on in and make yourselves at home." They knew where I kept the spare key.

I heard Erin ask Pinky what she wanted to do, then she said, "Okay, we'll be here when you get home."

"See you then."

I backed out of the driveway then took a last look at Ramona's house and shook my head. Who was that man she'd come home with? It was no one I recognized from my time working in her office; that I was certain of. On the drive home, I went over everything that had happened since yesterday morning.

What if the Zimmers were not the ones responsible for the poison after all? What if some demented person had chosen Curio Finds or Brew Ha-Ha to randomly carry out his dastardly deeds? If that were the case, even our customers would be in danger and we'd be forced to shut down. That possibility was not in the probable realm, however. I also knew going forward I would do a smell test on every beverage I served, checking for that unique almond aroma.

And I worried that Molly's husband would file a lawsuit against the shops. My parents and Pinky would lose their businesses, and probably their life savings. In Pinky's case, that wasn't much, but it was still money she had worked hard to put away for her retirement.

Erin and Pinky were sitting at my kitchen table, drinking water and munching on pretzels when I walked in. They both got up and gave me a hug. "Don't go disappearing on us like that," Pinky said.

"We thought maybe somebody had nabbed you," Erin said.

I wasn't the only one having wild thoughts. "Nabbed me?"

Erin gave me a light push. "Kidnapped, abducted, stolen away, whatever you want to call it. Cami, you never know how dangerous some people can be."

That brought me back to my fears about the Zimmers. "I do know that. What I don't know how is I'll make it up to Molly's family if it turns out the poison was meant for me."

Pinky guided me over to a kitchen chair and sat me down. "That is nonsense talk. You are in no way, shape, or form responsible for what someone else did."

Erin sat down next to me. "But if Emmy is the guilty one, then you and Pinky will have to work through your feelings on that."

"Thanks a lot, Erin," Pinky said, and she plopped onto a chair on my other side.

Erin lifted a hand chest high and waved it back and forth. "I didn't mean it like that."

Emmy was a concern, but what Ramona Zimmer was up to was more immediate. "Girls, you are not going to believe what you are about to hear."

When I told them where I'd been, Erin gave my arm a

nudge. "Cami Brooks, what on earth were you thinking driving down there? Ramona Zimmer may be getting charged with a crime against you at any time, just as soon as the police are done testing that envelope she left."

"So?"

"So, I don't know. But if the police heard you were scouting out her house, you might be in some kind of trouble."

"I'm already in some kind of trouble."

"Then I don't think you should be asking for more."

Pinky leaned forward. "Erin's right. But go on with your story. I want to hear what you saw." Juicy news was a daily staple of Pinky's diet, and she always looked forward to a bit of gossip from one of her many sources.

I picked up where I'd left off, and when I got to the part about Ramona and the man and the suitcase, Erin and Pinky both gasped.

"You always said she was faithful, almost to a fault," Erin said.

"That is so wrong. Tell me more. What does he look like?" Pinky said.

"Tall. The senator is five-eight, and he was this much taller than her . . ." I lifted my hand about five inches from the table. "What does that make him?"

"Five inches would make him six-one." Erin was the fastest math calculator among us.

"What else?" Pinky said.

"I wasn't close enough to pick up details, like his eye color or anything. And the lighting in the garage wasn't very bright, but I'd describe him as nice looking. Very short hair, like military-cut short. His face was cleanly shaven and on the rounder side. The thing that struck me was his sober expression. I mean very somber, like he was on his way to prison or a funeral or something."

"Or into Ramona Zimmer's house," Erin said with a grin that made me smile, too.

Pinky's eyes opened wide. "Holy moly, Cami. That's the way I would have described the guy who was looking for you yesterday; you know, the one that asked for the blonde. But I didn't see his hair with his stocking cap on."

I grabbed her arm. "The man with the senator looks like the guy who asked for me, the one who might have poisoned Molly?"

Pinky started nervously flapping her hands then pushed her chair back and jumped up. "I don't know. I can't be sure."

Erin and I got up, too. And when Pinky started walking around the table, Erin and I joined her. If someone saw us, they'd think we were playing musical chairs. We made a few laps, then Pinky stopped without warning. I piled into her, and Erin piled into me.

"Jeepers creepers, Pink," I said.

"We need to calm down and think about what to do next," Erin said.

Pinky put her hands on the back of a chair and leaned into it. "Got any good ideas?"

Erin nodded. "I have one. Pinky, you saw that man up close when he asked you about Cami. I think you should talk to Mark, or maybe Clint would be better, and see if he can get you in with the Buffalo County sketch artist to come up with a drawing. Then Cami can look at it and see if it's the same guy she saw tonight."

Pinky gave her head a shake, which caused her curls to

dance for a second. "I've never done anything like that before, so I'm not sure how it would work."

"It's worth a try," Erin said.

"The biggest hurdle would be convincing Mark, and especially Clint, why they should do it in the first place," I said.

"After you tell them everything you've told us, Cami, why wouldn't they?"

Why wouldn't they? Well, we'd find out the answer to that question before long.

When Pinky and Erin left for their own homes, I realized that I was beyond tired; I was exhausted. Between not getting enough sleep the night before and dealing with the worst of the worst the last two days, the best thing I could do was drink a hot cocoa and climb into bed. And that's what I did. But I could not shut off all the thoughts swirling around in my brain. After about twenty minutes, I got back up and went to the bookshelf in the living room to pick out the most boring read there. There were a few books I'd tried to read but had given up on because they were so dull. I'd hoped one day they would appeal to me, but that day had not yet come.

I scanned over the one hundred or so books and came across *The Comedies and Tragedies of Shakespeare, In Four Volumes*, a collection I'd forgotten all about. My parents had found the set at an estate sale and gave it to me one Christmas. I was living and working in Washington, D.C., then and barely had time to do the required reading for my job. The books were in a cardboard box with an open front so the jackets were visible. I'd never even slid one of the volumes out of the holder. So it was about time.

The first and second books were tragedies; the third and fourth were comedies. I picked up the first volume and, paging through it, discovered that *Macbeth* was the last play in the book. A glossary and notes at the end of the second volume explained archaic words and phrases. I didn't remember reading any of Shakespeare's work since high school. No author, especially one with his great talent, would like to hear I chose his work to help me fall asleep. I carried the book back to bed, hoping the ancient language would lull me into dreamland.

I'd forgotten the details of the story and the whole cast of characters until I began reading. Note to self: witchcraft, murder, madness, crazed sleepwalking, and ghosts do not make for a calming rest or a dreamless sleep. But I got caught up in the tragedy and Shakespeare's way with words and read to the end. I closed the book, shut off the lamp on my nightstand, and fell asleep thinking about Molly.

A few hours later I woke up with my heart hammering in my chest. Molly's ghost paid me a visit in a vivid dream. I was at Curio Finds, and the place was packed with people, some I knew, and some were strangers. They were all interested in snow globes and were picking them up and shaking them. I was trying to wait on people but couldn't keep up. Then Molly was there, and I was relieved for a split second that she was there to help until I noticed her skin was pale and had a luminescent glow to it. She was dressed in a white flowing gossamer gown. No one else in the room paid any attention to her, which struck me as odd, since she stood out from the rest of the crowd. Molly looked at me and spoke, except there was no sound to her words. I had to read her lips. "My killers are in the shop." I looked around hoping to spot them, but everyone's face was blurry.

The sheer terror of it all woke me. I sat up in bed gasping for breath and thanking God my nightmare was just a dream and not really happening. I got out of bed and went to the kitchen to pour a glass of milk. My heart pounded for another minute, at least. I opened the refrigerator, and the light spilling from it fell on something shiny on the floor. I bent over, picked up the penny, and wrapped it in one hand while I pulled the milk carton out with the other. I got a glass out of the cupboard and poured a few ounces into it.

After putting the carton back, I downed the milk in a long drink then headed to the living room where I dropped the penny in the blue and brown ceramic dish filled with the other pennies from heaven I'd found over the years. Why I'd saved them was a good question I didn't have a good answer for. But finding this one helped calm my fears, and I went back to bed, got under the covers, and gratefully fell into a dreamless sleep.

When I awoke bright and early Thursday morning, the first thing that came to mind was the frightening image of Molly from my nightmare. I stared at the ceiling a minute then closed my eyes to imagine the soundless words she had uttered. I'd thought she'd mouthed, "My killers are in the shop," meaning there was more than one. That didn't make sense if the man Pinky had seen turned out to be the culprit. Unless she meant the person who put him up to it. Maybe Molly had really said, "My killer is in the shop."

I squeezed my eyes tighter and tried my darnedest to make out even one face in the crowded shop, but there was not a clear, identifiable one in the bunch. I opened my eyes and stared at the ceiling again, chiding myself for acting like Molly's words were real. It was only a dream, my brain trying to work out what had happened and why. We hadn't even gotten the official report on her cause of death. Although, it seemed clear the officials thought she'd been poisoned, which backed up what Clint surmised as soon as he noticed her red skin tone.

That got me to thinking about Emmy Anders, the person the Brooks Landing Police Department was most interested in. And that triggered the memory of one of the faceless people in my dream: a small, gray-haired woman who was wearing the outfit Emmy had on that fateful day. A feeling of doom spread through me and settled like a giant lump in the pit of my stomach. *Emmy, the longer you stay away, the worse it looks.* And if she never came back, it would certainly help convince Pinky and me that she'd done the deed, after all.

I phoned Pinky at her shop. "How are you doing there this morning? You need me to come in early?"

"I'm okay. Mark was here when I opened and hung around awhile. He just left, after checking every square inch of your shop and mine. No one hiding out, and no weird-looking envelopes or packages addressed to you. Or to me."

"Good. All right then, I have some errands to run before I open, but I'll keep my cell phone with me in case you need me."

"Okay, thanks. Gotta run. My faithful usuals are here."

"'Bye."

I looked at the outdoor thermometer, attached to the kitchen window by Sandra McClarity. She was the dear woman who'd lived here until she died, shortly before I returned to Brooks Landing. Sandra had been a childhood friend of Berta, my biological mother, so I'd enjoyed our visits when I was home on college break or taking a few days' vacation from my job. I was thrilled when her family offered me her place to rent until they decided to sell it.

It was 35 degrees Fahrenheit, only three degrees above freezing, so I'd need a long coat for extra warmth on my fact-finding adventure. Forty minutes later, I'd eaten, gotten ready, and was out the door. The home I rented was a smaller rambler with a detached garage in the back. I kept a second automatic garage door opener in my purse to avoid punching in the code on the door. And as the days got colder, I would appreciate the spare opener even more. I climbed into my tan Subaru, started it up, and eased onto the alley then turned left on my way to Emmy's neighborhood.

I didn't know who any of Emmy's neighbors were. I hoped to recognize at least one or find someone willing to talk to me. I rang the doorbells on four houses before a man, about Emmy's—and my parents'—age opened his door. He looked kindly enough, but I patted the Mace in my pocket, just in case. Overall, I felt quite safe in Brooks Landing, but I kept it despite Clint's warning that I needed to take a class on the proper use of the stuff. I'd been meaning to spray a small amount near my face to see how I'd react, but I never got around to it.

I smiled, hoping to look harmless. "Hi, I'm Camryn Brooks."

"I know who you are." The more I studied the man, the more familiar he looked. "I'm Lester Susag."

"Of course. Golly, it's been a few years." He'd lost most of his hair and put on at least fifty pounds in the last eighteen years. He'd owned a gas station in town when I was growing up.

He scratched his chin. "I'd say so. What can I do for you?"

"I have some questions about Emmy Anders if you don't mind letting me in for a few minutes."

He drew his eyebrows into a single line frown. "I don't mind at all. Come right in."

His house was the reverse floor plan of Emmy's. The living room was in the center of both houses, but Emmy's kitchen was off to the right, and Lester's was off to the left. He led me to the living room. "Can I take your coat?"

"Oh, no, thanks." I sat down on the side chair he pointed to, and he sat on the one opposite it.

"That was quite the ordeal you had at your parents' store day before yesterday, and I was real sorry to hear Molly Dalton had died. She was a regular customer of mine back before I sold my station. But I sure can't say the same for her husband. He was kind of snooty, if you ask me. I'd see him go to the fancier place across the street that had a car wash. But never mind about that now. You're here about Emmy."

"Yes, thank you. She had just started working for Alice Nelson and me, helping us for the holiday season. She and Molly started the same day, in fact. But then Molly died and Emmy got called away to help someone. I was wondering if you might know where she went, where it is her sick friend lives?"

Lester's face wrinkled up when he squinted. "Emmy went off somewhere?"

"Yes, she said she was leaving early yesterday morning."

"Lo and behold. No, she didn't mention it to me. I noticed her living room lamp was on last night when I got home from my bowling league, about ten or so."

"Would she leave her lamp on when she's gone?"

"I wouldn't think so."

"Did she talk about a friend who has been having health problems, one who might need Emmy to drop everything at a moment's notice?"

"No, I can't say she's talked about anyone like that. Have you tried her cell phone?"

"I didn't know she had one." She told me she didn't.

"Sure she does, like most of us seniors in this day and age." Lester patted his pocket. "It's comforting to know that help is just a phone call away."

I smiled. "Do you have her number?"

"No. I know she called my house from her cell phone once or twice, but I never thought to write the number down. I have her home number, though."

I nodded. "I don't mean to pry, but have you gotten to know Emmy?"

Lester smiled. "Well, as a matter of fact, we have stepped out a time or two, for dinner or what have you. I lost my wife four years ago, and it's been nice to have someone to do things with once in a while. And neither one of us is interested in anything serious, so it works out just dandy."

I wasn't there to hear the details about their relationship, but it seemed like I was talking to the right guy, after all. "I'm so sorry about your wife."

He drew his lips into a thin line and nodded. "I still miss her like the dickens, but I can't bring her back."

"No." I paused for a second. "But it's good to know you've found a friend in Emmy. And don't take this wrong, but she's always seemed a little lonely to me. I wasn't sure if she had any real friends around here."

"You're right about Emmy being lonely, but she mostly keeps to herself anyway. I think she got real hurt, probably when her husband died. And I wouldn't be surprised if she's afraid she'll get hurt again. I've been there myself."

"Did her husband die suddenly?" I felt a twinge of guilt asking that.

"I just don't know. When I asked her about him, she said she just couldn't talk about it. It struck me as kind of strange, because after my wife passed on, that's all I could talk about for a long, long time."

"I guess each one of us handles things a little differently, huh?"

"I guess so."

"I wonder why Emmy moved to Brooks Landing at this stage in her life, with no family here or anything."

"That I do know. She was downsizing from a bigger home in Minneapolis. She used to drive through Brooks Landing on her way to a vacation spot up north, and she thought our small town was quaint."

The word "quaint" sounded funny coming out of Lester's mouth and made me smile. "Okay. Well, I better get to work and let you get on with your day." I stood up. "It was good seeing you again."

"The pleasure was all mine, Cami. It seems to me you must be looking for Emmy for a particular reason, like you're worried about her."

"Lester, between you and me, I am a little worried, because she left so suddenly and didn't tell me where she was going. I wanted to talk to her to see if she's all right."

Lester stood and put his hands on his hips. "Now you got me to wondering if I shouldn't be worried myself."

That was the last thing I wanted him to do. I gave a little chuckle. "Hey, no need for that. How about we make a pact? If I hear from her, I'll let you know. And if you hear from her, you let me know. Deal?" I offered my hand.

He took my hand in his, and we shook on it. "Deal."

"Good. If you have a piece of paper, I'll write my numbers down for you."

Lester nodded. "And I'll do the same for you."

I drove away from Lester's wondering why Emmy's lamp had been on the past night. And why she hadn't told the man who seemed to be her best friend that she was leaving. And where in the world she was going. My parents always told a neighbor when they'd be gone, even if it was just overnight, so they could keep an eye on their place.

Emmy Anders kept secrets, including two very big ones: her real name was Emaline Andersohn, and she was the prime suspect in her husband's suspicious death. Jeepers creepers, creepers jeepers. Would we ever see Emmy again? Maybe she had driven across the Canadian border by now. She'd taken on another identity at least once, so what would stop her from doing it again?

I pulled into the lot behind the shops and parked, wishing I didn't have to go to work. Emmy's past and her strange behavior after the police questioned her about Molly's death troubled me no end. How could I even start looking for her when she'd kept the details of her life under lock and key?

Pinky was adding coffee grounds to one of her machines when I walked through the door. "What's wrong?" she said.

I slipped off my coat and laid it on a counter stool. I'd never had a good poker face with my friends. "It's Emmy. I'd like to find out where she is. I just talked to one of her neighbors—you know Lester who used to own the gas station?"

"Sure, I know Lester. Cami, it's up to the police to find her."

"There's nothing wrong with helping them."

"They're the police. They have their own special ways of finding people."

It was better to drop the whole subject. "That's true. Have you been busy?" I walked to the other side of the counter and stood beside her.

"No more than usual. Enough so I didn't think about Molly every single, solitary minute."

"I dreamed about her last night. Molly, I mean. Actually, it was Molly's spirit, and she was telling me her killers were in the shop."

Pinky let out a little scream and covered her ears. "That is too scary. See, that proves you have extraterrestrial powers." She dropped her hands to her sides.

"You mean . . . Never mind." She had trouble with the word extrasensory. "Getting back to the dream; the shop was full of people, but all their faces were fuzzy, so I couldn't make out who they were. And when Molly talked, she didn't have a voice, so I had to read her lips."

Pinky covered her ears again. "Molly's ghost was in your shop? What if it comes here for real?" She moved her hands to her shoulders, crossing her chest.

I went on, "Then after I woke up, I wondered if she had really said, 'My killer is in the shop,' instead of 'My killers are in the shop.'"

She shook her hands out to release some nervous energy. "I can't stand it. If I have a dream like that I'll probably die of fright right then and there in my sleep. So if that happens, you'll know why I kicked the bucket."

I reached over and put my hands on hers to stop the shaking. "People don't die from dreams." They didn't, did they? "Pinky, if you ever have a nightmare like that, call me right away and we'll talk through it."

"Okay." She didn't sound convinced. And I'd be surprised if she'd ever had a nightmare in her entire lifetime. Once Pinky was asleep, she slept like a rock. When we were young and had slumber parties, Erin and I could laugh and talk and even tickle her, but she'd be dead to the world until morning.

The shop door bell dinged, and Clint came in looking as forbidding as all get out. "We got the autopsy report this morning."

Pinky grabbed my hand and squeezed. "Tell us, Clint. I can't stand it anymore," she said.

Putting aside the tragic fate Molly had suffered, I knew the autopsy results could greatly impact our businesses and maybe even bring them to a sudden end.

Clint was carrying a thin briefcase and pulled out a small stack of papers. He held it up, and we read the two highlighted phrases on the cover sheet: "Cause of Death: Cyanide Poisoning" and "Manner of Death: Homicide."

The panicky feeling that had become all too familiar the

past two days spread through me and started my heart pounding. "I was hoping you were wrong about the poisoning, Clint." But I'd known all along he'd been right. Even my dreams of Molly's talkative spirit supported his theory.

He gave a single nod. "So was I. When you detected that odor of almonds in her coffee cup, that all but convinced me cyanide was the murder weapon."

Murder weapon, yikes. "So the police and the medical examiner are positive Molly didn't take the poison herself?" I said.

"Proof positive. We thoroughly searched Molly's discarded clothes and other possessions, including her vehicle, and found no signs of cyanide. And there were no containers with traces of the poison anywhere that we could locate on these premises—in Brew Ha-Ha or Curio Finds."

Clint sounded like a robot, as though he had been fed the information and was spitting it out to an audience at a conference with other robots. Maybe that was the way he coped when he was dealing with an investigation of a tragic death. And a homicide besides.

"Molly's ghost came to Cami last night and told her that her killers were in the shop." The words spilled out of Pinky's mouth before I had time to put my hand over it.

Clint's eyes narrowed on me, and I felt my face warm up. "Say what?"

I gave Pinky a light kick in the calf. "It was only a dream." Only. Right.

"A dream. Well, go ahead and humor me. I like a good story," he said.

"I think it all started when I read *Macbeth* before falling asleep. You know, Macbeth kills King Duncan and hires murderers to kill his friend Banquo. And then Banquo's ghost comes to him, and it drives Macbeth insane—"

"Why in the devil were you reading *Macbeth*?"

"Well, I started thinking about . . . Okay, it was a dumb idea, and it didn't help me fall asleep, after all."

Clint nodded like he understood. "You think it started with the ghost in *Macbeth*; let's just leave it at that. I would like to hear more about your dream, however."

I'm not sure why I told him, but I did. He kept his eyes on me and didn't even blink through the short narration. "Are you some kind of psychic?"

"No."

Pinky gave her thigh a slap. "That's the word I was looking for: 'psychic.' Cami, you do have some sort of psychic thing going on."

"Finding pennies from heaven is not being psychic."

"Pennies from heaven?"

"Clint, it is nothing, really. And Pinky, can we please just drop the subject?"

"For the record, I don't believe in ghosts, but if you have some sort of connection with them, and they tell you anything that will help solve this case, I'd consider listening to it," Clint said.

Was he kidding? Sorry to disappoint everyone, but I was not psychic. "Okay, then."

"And neither one of you has heard from Emmy?"

"No, but Cami talked to her neighbor." Pinky was on a roll, giving Clint all kinds of information.

"You don't say."

"You know Lester who owned the gas station all those years?"

"Of course."

"It turns out that he's a friend of Emmy. But he doesn't know where she went, either."

"Hmmph." Clint turned to me. "And you were planning to share that with our office, Camryn?"

I hadn't thought that far ahead, but yes, I would have. "Of course."

"Just let the boys and girls in blue do their job, and you stay out of the investigation."

"Unless a ghost gives me a good lead, that is."

The sour look on his face told me he didn't appreciate my sarcasm.

Pinky pointed at her coffee dispenser. "Clint, can I get you something to drink?"

He put the autopsy report back in his case then glanced up at the whiteboard where Pinky wrote her special of the day. "I guess I could use a coffee to go. A medium blend with cream sounds good to me today."

Pinky served him up, and I cringed when he took a loud slurp. I wondered if they heard him all the way next door. As much as I wanted him to take his coffee and leave, I needed an answer to a question. "You told Molly's husband about the report?"

"Of course, I contacted him first thing, before I came here."

I weighed my words. "How did he take it? I mean, did he say anything that seemed like he was blaming Pinky or me in any way?"

Clint's eyebrows lifted. "What are you talking about?"

"Well, um, I was just wondering."

"I think she's wondering if Will Dalton is going to sue us," Pinky said. So Pinky had been worrying about the same thing.

Clint slurped another sip of coffee before he answered. "Sue you? I wouldn't know about that. I stopped by his house, but no one answered the door. Frankly, I thought he'd be home, and maybe he was. I was able to reach him on his cell phone; not the best way to deliver this kind of news. Mr. Dalton didn't have much to say at all. I got the impression he hasn't started processing what happened to his wife. I wouldn't be surprised if he gets back to me when he's past the initial shock."

If something like that had happened to one of my loved ones, I was sure I'd be stuck in that initial state of shock forever.

Clint started for the door. "I'm going to Molly's mother's house next. She's pretty distraught."

"I've wanted to talk to her but haven't gotten there yet," I said.

"You're welcome to come with me now."

"Really?" I looked at Pinky, and she nodded. Since Clint was actually being decent for a change, I'd put up with a short car ride and try to block out the unpleasant sounds his noisy coffee drinking habit produced. I grabbed my coat from the stool, slipped it on, and followed him to his police car.

Clint unlocked it and we got in. He set his cup in a holder and handed his briefcase to me. "I usually throw it on that seat." I laid it on my lap and buckled up. I'd been in his police car a couple of times before, and each time I noticed something new. It was filled with gadgets and buttons and switches. We drove the mile or so to Mrs. Ryland's, the house I'd been by the night Molly had died.

"Is she expecting you?" I asked when he parked at the curb.

"Yup, I talked to her earlier."

When we got out of the car, I gave Clint back his briefcase, relieved I wasn't the one who had to tell Mrs. Ryland the cause of her daughter's death. Clint rang the bell and waited. He was about to ring it again when Mrs. Ryland opened the door. She was stooped over with what looked like osteoporosis, and grief was written all over her face. She was around sixty years old, a tiny, lovely-looking woman.

"Please come in, Officer." She glanced at me. "Oh, you're Cami Brooks. Molly talked about you, and she was very excited you gave her a job."

I nodded. "I don't know what to say except how sorry I am, especially for you, Mrs. Ryland."

"Thank you. Let's sit in the kitchen and talk."

The house was very well kept on the inside. Mrs. Ryland had quality furniture pieces that shone from polishing. She sat down on a chair that had a soft, thick pillow on the seat and said, "Please, sit down."

Clint settled on a chair, laid the briefcase on the table, then opened it and pulled out the document with the ominous words. He didn't say anything when he handed it to Mrs. Ryland. She gasped and shook her head as her eyes traveled down the sheet. When she'd read the first page, she turned to the next. She was privy to all the personal, detailed information Pinky and I hadn't been allowed to see. Not that I'd want to.

"There must be some mistake. There is not a person on earth I can think of who would poison my daughter. At least I don't think Troy would."

What was the poor woman talking about?

Clint seemed to sprout antennae as he leaned forward and pulled a notepad and pen from his pocket in one fluid movement. "Maybe you could tell us about this Troy person."

Mrs. Ryland had been dry-eyed until that moment, when

the floodgates opened. "I didn't know. I swear I didn't know. Looking back on it, I should have, but I was blinded by love." It was one of those moments when part of me wanted to hear the rest of the story, but the other part knew it was not going to be good. "Then after it was too late, the only thing I could think of was to cover it up and go on with life as best as we could." Definitely not good.

Clint lifted his hand up in a halt sign. "Mrs. Ryland, I want you to stop right there. Before you go on, you may want to talk to an attorney first."

"No, it's been long enough, nearly twenty years. I would have gone to my grave without confessing, but now that Molly's gone, there's no point."

Clint's face turned a shade darker. "All right. Mrs. Ryland, you are not under arrest, but if you are about to confess to a crime, I'm going to read you your rights."

Mrs. Ryland nodded and dabbed at her tears with a napkin she'd snatched from its holder. Clint pulled out a little card with the words "MIRANDA WARNING" printed on top. He read each of the five rights to Mrs. Ryland while I sat right there, hoping I wouldn't keel over from all the suspense. I think Clint had forgotten I was there, because he didn't tell me to wait in the other room while he conducted his official business. Or maybe he wanted a witness.

Mrs. Ryland said she understood each one of her rights and then blurted out, "Molly killed her stepfather, and I protected her all these years."

I think the main reason I didn't collapse was because my body had stiffened from the shock. Clint, with the best poker face I'd ever seen, looked her in the eyes and said, "Why don't you start from the beginning, Mrs. Ryland."

8

If I lived to be one hundred, I doubted I would ever forget a single word that came out of Mrs. Ryland's mouth that morning. I felt like pulling a Pinky and covering my ears, but I didn't want to cause a distraction.

"I got remarried when Molly was twelve. She had been such a happy and outgoing little girl until then. She got quieter and insisted on dressing in baggy clothes. At first I thought it was because she hated growing up. I had a friend who told me her daughter had been sullen all through puberty. I though Molly would grow out of it. It wasn't until after my husband died that Molly told me what he'd been doing to her for over four years. I have never felt sicker in all my life."

"You said Molly killed him. Can you tell me more about that? How she did it?" Clint said.

"When she'd had enough of the abuse, she substituted my

husband's heart medication with an antibiotic she'd gotten. I guess he didn't notice the difference. He died in bed, in his sleep. The coroner ruled it was natural, due to a bad heart. He had a bad heart, all right. An evil one, as it were. The day after he was buried, Molly told me what she'd done. I didn't believe it at first, but it eventually sunk in.

"It was such a terrible thing, but I didn't blame her. I only wished she had told me about the abuse before it came to that. Here she was, barely seventeen, with her whole life ahead of her. I know we should have gone to the police, but the man was dead and buried. And Molly spending years in jail wouldn't have brought him back."

Mrs. Ryland sniffled and wiped her nose. "But then of all things, she went and told her stepbrother, my husband's son, what she'd done."

Clint kept his voice steady, like he was having a casual conversation. "Why did she do that?"

"Troy was singing his father's praises, talking about what a wonderful man he was and how the good die young. Molly was disgusted and told him what his father was really like, and how she stopped him for good."

"You don't say. And did Troy believe her?"

"Yes, he did, and he said he was going to go to the police. I was scared for Molly, and I did something I should never have done."

How could it get any worse?

"What was that?" Clint said, with more of an edge to his voice.

"I offered him my portion of my husband's life insurance policy—twenty thousand dollars—if he'd move away and leave Molly alone."

Mrs. Ryland had gotten herself in deeper and deeper as she went along.

I think Clint was counting to ten, because it took him that long to answer. "What did he do then?"

"Troy took the money and did stay away for a few years. But then when he found out Molly had married the very wealthy Will Dalton, he started blackmailing her." Mrs. Ryland and Molly had been secretly living a real-life soap opera. "About two months ago, Molly told him, 'No more.' She told him to go to the police with his story. It was his word against hers, and he had no proof she'd done anything to his father."

"I take it Troy didn't like that."

"No, he did not, but he stopped pestering her. We weren't sure what he was thinking, or what he'd do about it. Molly figured he knew better than to push the issue, since he might be in about as much trouble as she'd be."

Obviously, Molly should never have killed her stepfather, but she did have a reason a jury of her peers might understand and sympathize with. Troy had actually profited financially by threatening to expose Molly and the crime she had committed against his father.

"Did Will Dalton know about this blackmail scheme?" Clint asked.

Mrs. Ryland shook her head. "No, he gave Molly a generous allowance and thought she was spending the money on clothes and her hair and massages and lunches. He didn't seem to notice or didn't care. If she wanted a new living room set, that was fine with him. As long as she was busy so he could work, he didn't care what she spent." That would be fun for about a month.

"How much did Troy extort from Molly?"

"Five thousand dollars a month."

"Five *thousand*?" Clint said, and I silently repeated, "Five thousand," about eight times, trying to comprehend that Will would think nothing of Molly spending that kind of money on nonessentials, month after month.

Mrs. Ryland nodded and got teary eyed again. "Now that I'm really thinking about it, Troy may have decided he'd get back at Molly once and for all: first for killing his father, and then for cutting down his money tree. Who else could it be?"

Besides Emmy, or Ramona and Peter Zimmer?

Clint blew out a puff of air. "That's what we intend to find out, Mrs. Ryland. Can you tell me where Troy lives?"

"Molly sent his cashier's check to a post-office box in St. Paul. We didn't know where he lived."

"Do you have the number of the box?"

"It's in a file box with my addresses. I'll get it for you." She grimaced when she pushed herself up. She was obviously in pain.

Clint pulled on his earlobe while he read over his notes. Mrs. Ryland got the box out of a kitchen cupboard and returned with it to the table. She pulled out a card and handed it to Clint who wrote the information in his notebook. "I'll need Troy's full name and date of birth."

Mrs. Ryland told Clint what she knew about Troy. He was six years older than Molly and out of the house when his father married her mother.

"Do you have a picture of Troy?" Clint asked.

"Not anymore. Molly threw them all away."

"How about a description?"

"He was the same height as his father, six-one. He has more of a round face. Dark brown hair, and a medium-sized nose, thinner lips." She pointed to her own features as she described him.

Clint jotted it all down, and when he finished writing, he put his notebook and pen in his pocket and stood up. "Irene Ryland, I regret having to do this under the circumstances, but I'm placing you under arrest for accessory after the fact in the murder of your husband. The statute of limitations has run out for the crime of bribery, but there is no limitation on murder."

Mrs. Ryland didn't look surprised, but I was. My mouth dropped open, and I gasped on top of it all. "Clint—" I started to protest, but the way he looked at me stopped me in my tracks. There was fire in his eyes, making it crystal clear he did not want me to interfere when he was doing his job.

"Do you need to turn anything off in the house, or attend to a pet?" Clint said.

"No. But I'll need a coat."

"Yes, of course. And how about medications? Are you taking any?"

Mrs. Ryland nodded. "They're in that cupboard." She pointed, and Clint found a quart-sized plastic bag with several bottles in it. He held it up. "This it?"

"Yes," she said.

"And you should grab that pillow, if you need it to be more comfortable. I'm not going to place you in handcuffs, but I have to ask if you have anything on your person that might be used as a weapon?"

"No." Poor Mrs. Ryland. People had been shocked enough by Molly's death, and they'd be blown away when everything her mother had confessed was brought to light.

Clint handed me the briefcase and the bag of meds. We went to the front closet together. Mrs. Ryland pulled a coat off a hanger, and Clint helped her put it on. "My keys and wallet are in the pockets," she said.

Clint reached in to double-check. "Okay. Let's go. Camryn, make sure the door is secure behind us."

He put Mrs. Ryland in the backseat of his police car like she was a criminal. In reality she was but didn't seem like one. I got into the passenger seat, wishing I could trade places with Mrs. Ryland for her ride to the county jail.

When Clint got in and started the car, I noticed it was after 10:30. I had lost all track of time. He drove to Brew Ha-Ha's door and stopped at the curb. "Time you got back to work, right, Camryn?"

"Um, yes it is." I turned around and glanced at the forlorn-looking little lady on the other side of the cage. "I'm so sorry for all of this, Mrs. Ryland. I'll come and visit you, if that'd be all right."

"That would be very nice. Thank you, Cami."

I nodded, took a quick look at Clint, and opened the car door. I set the meds and briefcase on the seat then closed the door and hurried into Pinky's shop. She would never believe what Mrs. Ryland had told us about Molly, the cover-up, and the bribery scheme.

"It was that bad, huh?" Pinky said when she saw me. "I didn't dare call to ask why you were taking so long. Clint thinks I'm snoopy enough."

"It was worse than bad." I looked around. "Nobody else here, in either shop?"

"No, the ten o'clock crowd has come and gone."

I lowered my voice anyway. "Molly's mother is on her way to jail. Molly's *mother*."

"Holy moly. What did she do, freak out and attack Clint or what?"

"Pinky, you're going to have to sit down when I tell you this story, seriously." I led the way to the back, then we sat down across the table from each other and I gave her every detail I remembered. She was in a state of stunned silence. I finished by saying, "So now we know what happened the summer between junior and senior year when Molly came back like a totally different person."

"Oh. My. God. That is crazier than crazy. And Molly, she lived with her stepfather doing those things for years. I don't blame her one little bit for what she did, but why didn't she tell her mother what had been going on before then?"

"You would never have been able to keep something like that secret."

"No, and I can't understand how anyone else can, either."

"It's something we can't ask her now. Maybe it was fear, threats against her or her mother. Maybe she was worried no one would believe her," Pinky said.

"It's starting to make sense why Molly dressed the way she did during those years, it was to play down her beauty. I know someone else that happened to, someone I worked with. She told me she had wanted to be as unattractive as possible, thinking her abuser would leave her alone. Unfortunately, it didn't work. But she got out safely, eventually," I said.

Pinky put her elbows on the table and dropped her chin into her hands. "We were really lucky growing up, having pretty normal families."

"We were."

"What about Molly's mother? What's going to happen? She's not young and is kind of disabled besides."

"I don't know, but when I asked if it'd be okay to visit her, I think she was happy I offered."

"Good. I'll go with you after we close the shops tonight."

Mark stopped by in the early afternoon with the news that Clint was trying to pull some strings to try to get Mrs. Ryland into court before the end of the day. "In any case, Clint did have a talk with the prosecutor and asked him, when she does make her first appearance, if he'd consider asking the judge to release Mrs. Ryland on her own recognizance."

"Recognizance?" Pinky said.

"Instead of bail. It means that she promises to return for her next court date." Mark shook his head. "Man, I hear stories every day, but what a shocker about Molly's stepfather. I think the guy had it coming myself, but we're not living in the Wild West. We have to play by the rules, with guys like me to enforce the law."

"I know, but did Clint really have to arrest Mrs. Ryland, for pity's sake?" Pinky said.

Mark nodded. "As much as he hated to, yes. He is bound to his duty."

"What about Molly's stepbrother, the one who was blackmailing her? Her mother thinks he might have been the killer," I said.

"That's what I hear, and we'll track him down." He lowered his voice. "And here's something to keep under your hats for now—Clint is working on writing up a warrant to search Emmy's house, and then he'll have to get a judge to sign it."

"Why would you search Emmy's house?" I said.

"For answers, like where she might have gone and . . . other things."

"It doesn't seem right that you guys can go in there when Emmy isn't home," Pinky said.

Mark lifted his hands, palms turned toward the ceiling. "Hey, she's the one who left in a big hurry right in the middle of a murder investigation. She could have stayed and defended herself."

Mark got a radio call from the county dispatcher to check on a suspicious vehicle that was cruising around a neighborhood. He said, "Copy that," and ran out the door.

"Is it just me, or does it seem like people are calling the police for things like that more and more?" Pinky said.

"It does. Remember how we used to drive around for hours after we got our driver's licenses?"

Pinky smiled. "We must have looked pretty suspicious ourselves, like we were casing houses or something."

"Except everyone in town knew who owned each and every vehicle back then."

"That is so true, and we couldn't have gotten away with a single bad thing even if we'd wanted to."

I chuckled. "You are so right about that."

"Not that we were Goody Two-Shoes all the time."

Fond old memories came to mind. "That's true. We did have a few prankster moments. But all for fun." I heard someone in my shop, gave Pinky a wave, and left to help my customer.

....

Shortly before six o'clock, I was preparing to lock up for the night when I got a call on the shop phone from a frantic-sounding Emmy Anders. "Camryn, there are two police cars at my house and the lights are on inside. What am I going to do?"

"Where are you, Emmy?"

"Sitting in my car outside your shop. I didn't know where else to go."

Jiminy Cricket! And she was calling from the cell phone she said she didn't have. "Come in, Emmy. My door is open." I rushed over to it and looked out, concerned Emmy might panic and drive away. She was parked on the other side of the street and got out of her car and walked faster than normal to my door. I pushed it open and held it as she hurried in, bringing a large dose of cold night air with her.

Her face had the most forlorn expression I'd ever seen and prompted me to give her a bear hug that rivaled my dad's. "I'll lock the shop doors. Go sit down at one of Pinky's tables; I won't be a minute." She nodded and headed into Brew Ha-Ha. I closed up my side, turned off the lights, then went to lock Pinky's door. Pinky herself was standing on the other side of it with her hand on the knob. It gave me a start, and I jumped a few inches. Not that I was feeling guilty about harboring a fugitive or anything. Pinky pulled the door open and stepped inside.

"Man alive, Pinky."

Pinky screwed up her face. "Are you that nervous about visiting Molly's mom?"

"No." I leaned closer and whispered. *"Emmy's* here."

"Here, here?" she whispered back.

I pointed behind me. "Back there, here."

"Holy moly, Cami. Why?"

"The police are at her house, and she got scared and came here."

"She can't hide out here."

"I know that. Let's go talk to her."

"Crapola, Cami. I don't like this one little bit."

"You don't have to stay."

"Of course I do." A good story drew Pinky in like a magnet.

Emmy's eyebrows shot up when I rounded the corner in the back area with Pinky in tow. She had a napkin in her hands and was twisting it around and around. "I'm scared," she said.

Pinky and I joined her at the table, and when Emmy looked from me to Pinky, I wondered if she thought we were closing in on her. That's what her expression seemed to be saying as she drew her hands to her chest in a protective gesture.

"I would be, too," Pinky said, and Emmy made an inhaling noise that sounded like she was trying to catch her breath.

"What Pinky means is that it is perfectly natural to be scared given everything that's been going on," I said, hoping to ease Emmy's anxiety a little. "Right, Pinky?" I nudged her foot under the table.

"Oh, right. What Cami said."

"Where have you been the last two days?" I said.

"At a friend's house in Minneapolis. Do you have any idea why the police are in my house?"

I didn't think they'd want me to say much about it. "Um, maybe they wanted to talk to you some more about Molly, and then you left without telling anybody where you were going. Maybe they were worried about you."

"Or something," Pinky said. I gave her ankle another nudge.

"Police cannot go into someone's house without the owner's permission, unless they have a search warrant," Emmy said with a good deal of conviction.

I'm sure the expression on Pinky's face and my own told her obtaining a search warrant was what the police had done, all right.

Emmy shook her head. "What on earth would they be looking for?"

"Um, well, they asked me where you were—" I started.

"So Cami asked your neighbor Lester where you were—" Pinky interrupted.

Emmy raised her eyebrows. "Lester?"

I leaned in closer to Emmy. "Anyway, none of us knew where you'd gone, and since we didn't hear from you—until now, that is—I'd say they are probably trying to find out the name of the friend you left here to go help."

Emmy's eyes narrowed, and she focused them on me. "You know more than you are letting on."

My guilty heart pounded, and I threw the ball back in her court to change the subject. "You told me you didn't have a cell phone, and I found out you do, after all."

Emmy looked down at her hands and nodded.

I pushed on. "Why didn't you want me to have that number? When you keep secrets, it makes it seem like you have something to hide."

"Like what your name really is," Pinky blurted out. I was too astounded to even give her a nudge that time.

Emmy's frown disappeared, and her eyes opened wide. "My real name? You must mean my full name, Emaline Grace Andersohn." She looked down again and spoke so quietly I could barely hear her. "So you've heard the story of my past. And that's the reason the police are at my house. They are looking for something to try to tie me to Molly's death."

I would not lie to her, so I kept silent. And thankfully, Pinky did, too. She'd blabbed enough, thank you very much. And if Emmy made a run for it, we'd all be in trouble. At least she was probably one of the few people on earth I could actually catch up to in a race. But how could I tackle her without breaking any bones or hurting her somehow? It was probably why Clint hadn't handcuffed Molly's mother. He didn't want to cause her any more pain than she was already in.

Molly's mother. That's why Pinky had come back to the shop; we were planning to visit her in jail. Instead, we were sitting with another older woman who'd also been there and done that. And she might be in trouble again.

"I want you both to know that I didn't do what I was accused of back then. I was heartbroken when my husband died." Her lips turned down and quivered.

"Emmy, you're saying you did not poison your husband?" I said.

"No, I did not." She looked me directly in the eyes.

Either she was telling the truth or she was a very convincing liar. "Why did the police think you did?"

"I worked for a hardware store, and we sold poisons. According to my boss, a bottle of cyanide was missing from the inventory. I had access to it, of course. And I was with

Howard when he died. They thought I'd given it to him and gotten rid of the evidence before I called for help."

It did sound a little suspicious, and it made some sense that the authorities thought she was guilty of the crime. Something deep inside me believed Emmy was sincere and truthful, but still, there was something about her story that caused me to doubt her.

Pinky's cell phone rang from wherever she had it tucked away on her person, about the same instant mine did. Pinky flapped her hands and jumped up like she was on the dance floor. She headed to her back room, and I went the other direction to answer my phone. It was difficult for me to block out Pinky's loud telephone voice when I was concentrating on something else. She always talked about a hundred decibels above normal on the phone, no matter how much I'd nagged her to keep it down. We'd made a pact long ago that if I was on the phone or talking to someone and she got a call, she'd take her amplified voice to an opposite corner.

I glanced at the display and winced when I saw it was Clint. I had no choice but to answer it. The woman he was looking for was sitting in the coffee shop, and I was probably in enough trouble for not calling him the minute Emmy called me to tell me she was outside. I went into Curio Finds so Emmy wouldn't overhear the conversation. "Hello?"

"Camryn, it's Clint." Even without caller ID, I'd be able to pick out his distinctive baritone voice anywhere.

"Clint, Emmy's here," I said as the first line of defense. "Where?"

He'd called my cell phone, so he wouldn't know where I was. "Brew Ha-Ha."

"Why in tarnation didn't you call me?"

"She just got here a few minutes ago, and Pinky and I were trying to calm her down."

"Calm her down from what?"

"She was on her way home when she spotted your police cars and saw the lights on in her house. She didn't know what else to do."

"I'm on my way, and whatever you need to do, do not allow her to leave."

I went back to Pinky's sitting area, relieved that Emmy had not escaped when we weren't keeping close watch. Pinky joined us from the back room. "The police are on their way?" Emmy said.

I would have sworn I had talked more quietly than that. "How did you know?"

Emmy pointed at Pinky. "She was talking to Officer Mark."

Pinky's shoulders and hands lifted a tad. "Sorry, Emmy, but they said they needed to talk to you."

"Like last time," she said, looking as sad dog as it got.

A loud knocking on Brew Ha-Ha's door reminded us it was locked. Pinky ran to open it, and I stayed with Emmy. She slowly stood, and I moved to her side as a way of offering my support while Clint and Mark talked to her. But there was to be no talking. Clint arrived first, looked at me, and said, "Camryn, step aside." He meant business, and I did as he said, then he moved in close to Emmy and pulled a set of handcuffs from his belt. "Emaline Andersohn, I'm placing you under arrest for the murder of Molly Dalton. Hold out your hands."

Emmy lifted one hand but put the other on the table and leaned on it for support.

"Clint—" I started, but he cut me off.

"Mark, I need your help."

Mark understood what Clint meant and moved behind Emmy in case she fell. I was worried about that myself.

Emmy's voice was shaky. "Why in the world would you arrest me for that?"

Clint closed a cuff on her free hand. "Because we found the bottle of cyanide in your garage."

If someone had touched me with a feather, I would have fallen over. Apparently Pinky felt the same way, because she collapsed onto a chair.

Emmy had the opposite reaction. She raised her hand from the table and stood up straighter. "That's impossible. Where was it?"

"We'll talk about that later." Clint put a cuff on her other hand. "Let's go."

I moved behind Pinky's chair, and we watched helplessly as Clint and Mark led Emmy away. When they rounded the corner on their way out, Pinky stood up and the two of us walked to where we could see them go out the door.

"Do you believe what just happened?" Pinky said.

"No. And it's the second time today I've witnessed a little old lady getting arrested. I'm beginning to feel like a bad-luck charm."

"Cami, I actually thought Emmy was telling the truth when she said she hadn't killed her husband."

"I know, me too. She seemed as sincere as could be."

Pinky turned to face me. "So what do we do now?"

I thought awhile. "Remember what we were planning to do?"

"What?"

"Visit Molly's mother in the county jail."

Pinky bopped her forehead with the heel of her hand. "That's what I came back for. And to let you know I talked to Erin about it, too. She had to go to a meeting but wants to hear how it goes."

"Of course. Oh, and I called the jail and found out visiting hours are from six to eight tonight. So we better get a move on."

Pinky and I walked to Buffalo County Courthouse, which also housed the jail, since it was only three blocks away. Prior to our friend Archie Newberry's arrest the month before, neither of us had ever visited anyone in our county jail, thankfully. The only county business I'd ever had was when I needed a copy of my birth certificate and to get my driver's license and vehicle plates.

Pinky glanced up at the camera above where the female lobby officer was sitting in a glass-enclosed area. "I don't know why I didn't notice all these cameras when Archie was here, but that's the third one I've seen so far tonight," she whispered.

"Just don't panic and do something goofy, and you won't have to worry about it," I said quietly out of the side of my mouth.

"This is way too nerve-racking, but I'll try to think about why we're here instead of the fact we're being watched."

There was a line of open booths where a number of people were seated on stools and talking via phones to inmates on the other side of glass partitions. The inmates had doors on their side. We approached the officer to tell her why we were there.

"Good evening, can I help you?" She was no-nonsense but polite.

"Yes, we'd like to see Irene Ryland. Please."

The officer looked at her computer screen, pushed a few buttons, then nodded slightly. "Do you have your driver's licenses with you?"

My wallet was in my coat pocket, and I found what she needed and handed it over.

"I locked my purse in my car. I'm sorry. I forgot I needed it," Pinky said.

The officer looked at Pinky. "I recognize you from the coffee shop. What's your full name and date of birth?"

She wrote down the information Pinky gave her, handed back my driver's license, and pushed a button on her radio. "Lobby to Central Control, send Ryland from zero-four-two to visiting." Then she said to us, "Take visiting booth E."

We walked down the line to the fifth booth. "You sit on the stool, since you're the one she'll be expecting," Pinky said.

I discreetly moved my eyes to the right and then the left without moving my head to see if I recognized any of the inmates in the visiting booths next to me. One looked familiar, but I didn't know why.

A few minutes later, Mrs. Ryland and a jailer walked up to the door on the other side of the booth. There was a loud click, and the jailer pulled the door open for Mrs. Ryland then shut it when she was safely inside. The orange jumpsuit looked like it was at least three sizes too big. She had her sitting pillow with her. The corners of her lips moved into a little smile as she set the pillow down and lowered her body onto the stool. She lifted the phone to her ear. Everything she did took some effort, and I hoped she wasn't hurting too badly, physically speaking. I knew that time and maybe therapy would help with the emotional pain.

"Thank you for coming to see me." She pointed behind me. "And I see you brought Alice with you. Molly thought so highly of both of you."

I held the phone away from my ear enough so Pinky could hear, too. "Thank you for saying that. We can't tell you how bad we feel about what happened to her. We'd like to offer you whatever support we can." A lot of good people did bad things for what they thought was a good reason at the time.

"That is very kind of the both of you."

"Did you get into court today?" I said.

"No, the officers told me they were too busy up there. It'll be tomorrow, then. But, no matter, I think I'll be in here for a long time, maybe for the rest of my life."

What a thing to face. "Is there anything we can do?" I said.

"No, but it's good of you to ask. And don't worry about me. I'll be fine. The food is pretty good, and they gave me an extra mattress so I'll be more comfortable." It seemed the Buffalo County jailers had heart. "There are only a few other women here, so it's quiet in our section, our cellblock. But there was something strange when we walked past the booking area just now. I saw that one of the women from my church was getting fingerprinted. I can't imagine what that kind soul is here for."

An alarm went off in my brain, and Pinky stuck her knee in my back. What should I tell Mrs. Ryland? "Pinky and I happen to know about that. But, um, I guess we can't say anything yet."

She nodded. "I understand. Oh my, I hope I wasn't speaking out of turn by telling you that."

"Um, no, of course not." Mark had told us many times that the names of people who got arrested and those who were in jail was public record. "Well, I guess we have to go for now, but we'll check back. And if you need anything, be sure to call me. I'll accept the charges." We'd learned when Archie was in jail that inmates either had to buy a calling card or make collect calls.

"Thank you again," Mrs. Ryland said and pushed herself up.

The jailer standing by waited for the click that popped the door lock then pulled it open enough to let Mrs. Ryland out. She turned and waved as she was escorted away.

I got up, and Pinky and I headed out of the jail lobby. The north wind hit us as we stepped away from the protection of the building. "Brrr. I'm going to call Clint and check to be sure they don't put Emmy in the same cellblock as Mrs. Ryland." I pulled out my phone.

"Holy moly, I didn't even think of that."

Clint answered right away and assured me that the jail staff knew who was who and what their charges were. They would keep the two women in separate blocks. "You don't have to tell me how to do my job, Camryn."

My blood pressure rose after he barked out his last sentence. I was only trying to help. "I wouldn't presume to be that smart, Assistant Chief Lonsbury." I hung up before he said another word.

"What was that all about?" Pinky said.

"Just Clint being his normal irritating, exasperating self, telling me to mind my own business. He had made sure the jailers knew that Irene was Molly's mother, so Emmy and Irene would be separated."

"What a mess, huh? And speaking of Molly's mother, I hadn't seen her in, like, forever and didn't realize she'd gone that far downhill, healthwise. She wouldn't be able to hurt a fly even if she wanted to. But I suppose she could create a scene with Emmy," Pinky said.

"You are right on. You know, I've been thinking about this since this morning when Mrs. Ryland told us what she'd done. As much as I love you and all my friends and my family, I wouldn't do what she did to protect Molly. I think I've always known that I'd be in way more trouble trying to cover something up than confessing right off the bat."

"Not to mention the fact that it's against the law. My parents drilled the same thing into me."

Pinky elbowed my arm. "You know, Cami, when all that stuff happened with Archie last month, and now with Emmy and Molly and her mother, it all makes me realize that I could never do Mark's and Clint's job. Can you imagine how hard it would be to arrest people you know, especially if that person happened to be your friend? Whenever I think of our dear Archie being hauled off to jail, it makes me want to cry. And sometimes I do."

"I do, too. But the one good thing that came out of that is Archie is in a place where he's getting the treatment he needed all these years."

"That's the other thing, the real sad part; he suffered in silence forever. I wish he had told us, or someone, what was going on. I mean, he'd been having nightmares since Vietnam, for crying out loud."

"Pinky, even if he had, would we have known Archie had PTSD and was on the brink of going into combat mode if he felt threatened? But you're right; if he had gotten help years ago, Jerrell Powers would probably still be alive."

Pinky shrugged then nodded. "I've heard some of my customers talk about Veterans' Services and how they've helped with all kinds of things. I'm sure Archie was around when some of those guys talked about it, too. If he had gone to see those Veterans' Services people, they would have asked the right questions and figured out that's what Archie had."

"Yeah, you're right. The sad thing is that Archie was too proud to ask for help. Or maybe to figure out he needed help. Anyway, we've got to take another trip to St. Peter soon and visit him."

"Yes, we do. And in the meantime, he loves getting our letters. He went on and on about that the last time I talked to him on the phone."

"Our sweet, old-fashioned, quirky friend."

Pinky, Erin, and I had known Archie since childhood, and he was unlike anyone else we knew. He was at home communicating with the trees in his parks, and he had a way of making kids feel important.

We crossed the street to the front of our shops where Pinky's car was parked. "I don't think we should tell Archie about Molly and everything else just yet. You know how he obsesses about things, and it might interrupt the progress he's making with his treatment," I said.

"I agree, but I just don't know how to keep it secret from

him." Archie had always been in on everything that was happening in our lives.

"Maybe we better hold off on the visits for a while and send lots of letters instead," I suggested.

She nodded. "He'll understand, knowing how busy the shops get at this time of year, and how tough it is for us to get away. We'll get down there Thanksgiving week, and Christmas, for sure." Archie had been sent to a treatment center that was nearly two hours away by car.

"Yes we will, for sure. The more he feels our love and faith in him, the better for his healing. It'd be great if he gets released to outpatient therapy in a few months."

Pinky nodded. " I miss seeing him almost every day, like before."

"Me too. And thanks for going to the jail to visit Mrs. Ryland with me, Pink."

"Sure. At least it sounds like they're trying to make her as comfortable as possible there."

"Yes, that is a relief. So, any idea what time Erin's meeting will be over?"

"No, probably not late."

"I'll call her tonight and give her the latest unbelievable news."

"Okay, and I better get some baking done." She pointed at my shop window. "You left your bathroom light on."

I turned around to look for myself. There was a sliver of light spilling into the shop. "That's odd. I didn't use that bathroom; I used yours. I sure don't remember turning the light on."

"Maybe some nosy customer did. You know, someone who wanted to see the place where Molly died."

"I would have seen it was on when I turned off the overhead lights."

"Erin said Molly might be haunting the place. Plus, you told me you saw her ghost."

"Erin didn't say that exactly, and I did not see her ghost. It was a dream."

"Are you going to go turn it off?"

"I suppose with the old electrical system in the shop I'd better."

"You don't sound like you want to."

"Well, it's not that I'm scared, but all that ghost talk is kind of unnerving."

"Do you want me to go with you?"

"Sure, if you want to."

"Want to? That's sort of an exaggeration. But you'd do the same for me, right?"

"Right." I fished in my pocket and pulled out my keys. Pinky stayed close beside me when I opened the front door and threw on the light switch. As light replaced the darkness, it felt ten times safer going into the shop. I still walked slowly to the bathroom with my ears tuned for any unusual sound.

"Hello?" I called out for no good reason.

"Do you think a ghost is going to answer you?" Pinky whispered.

I gave her a small shove. "No more ghost talk." We got to the bathroom, and I pulled the door open enough to see inside. Its creak gave me a start, and I made a mental note to grease the hinges in the morning. "See, no one here." Yes, I breathed a sigh of relief.

We checked the storeroom and small office next.

"Do you think we should take a look around my shop?" Pinky said.

"If you want to." I took one last glance in the bathroom then turned off the light and shut the door.

"I suppose we should."

I picked up one of the heavier snow globes from a shelf to use as a weapon if the need arose. When we got to the archway, Pinky reached around the corner and turned on her shop lights. We walked through to the back, checking her back room and bathroom. No one hiding anywhere. Not that I'd thought there would be.

The light being on in Curio Finds was odd, but there could have been a short in the old electrical system. Except the switch had been flipped on. It wouldn't hurt to talk to my parents about having the system checked, anyway. We definitely did not want a fire.

"A last peek behind my counter and we're outta here," Pinky whispered.

I followed her for the final search then replaced the snow globe we hadn't needed for defense purposes after all.

"I think we've had enough excitement for one day," Pinky said.

"One very, very, very long day," I said, thinking back to all that had happened since morning. It seemed like a week ago. "Yes, we have." We closed up for the second time that evening. "Pinky, if I ask you something, will you promise not to laugh?"

She was on the driver's side of her car. "I promise to try not to."

Typical Pinky. "This is going to sound silly, but do you mind giving me a ride to my car?"

She didn't laugh. "Of course I don't mind." She hit the button on her door and unlocked the passenger side. "I don't blame you for not wanting to walk down the alley after dark. You never know who you might run into, now, do you?"

"You are right about that." I'd had that very experience with a man the past month, and with all the scary things going on, I was definitely on edge. Pinky drove around the block to access the back lot and pulled up so close to my car, I could barely squeeze out without scratching her door.

"I'll make sure your car starts before I take off," she said.

"Thanks, Pink." My car roared to life at the turn of the key. I sat there for a minute, staring at the back of our shop, half expecting to see a light come on inside. I drove to my parents' house and let myself in. They were happy to see me, but not so with the news I shared: first what Molly's stepfather had done to her, and how she had stopped him. And then all the bad things that had triggered.

My parents were flabbergasted. "To think all that was going on right under our noses," Mom said.

"Secrets, secrets, secrets. And not a one of them was the kind that should have been kept," Dad added.

"But those are the secrets that people keep all the time. And that makes them all the worse as the years pass by," I said.

Dad reached over and patted my hand. "You always were a bright little girl. And you grew into an even brighter young woman."

"Thanks, Dad."

Mom smiled. "I'd like to think you got it all from your mother's and my side, but you had a very smart father, too." As my biological mother's sister, Mom talked often of her, and of my father to a lesser extent. I was only five years old when they died, and I was welcomed into the Vanelli family, my aunt and uncle's household. Mom did her best to keep memories of Berta and Connor Brooks alive for all of us.

I was not done talking about the day's dramatic events. "And you're not going to believe this, but Clint arrested Emmy Anders for Molly's murder."

"Mercy me, why?" Mom said.

"It started with her background. She was the number one suspect in her husband's death. He just happened to die from cyanide poisoning, too. Her real name is Emaline Andersohn."

My dad scratched his head. "Now that name has a familiar ring to it. Emaline is not a name you hear every day."

"I guess it was in the papers and on the news sometime in the last couple of years."

"Sure, now I remember," Dad said.

"Emmy is *that* woman?" Mom didn't sound convinced.

I nodded. "She admitted that's who she is, all right. And this is the part you can't repeat; the police found cyanide in her garage."

"She is a churchgoing woman. I just don't know what to believe about all this," Mom said.

"I haven't really processed it, that is for sure."

"Land sakes," Mom said. "I ordered flowers for Irene Ryland this afternoon, so I better call the florist first thing tomorrow to tell them to hold off on the delivery. We can't very well say to send them to the jail instead."

"They don't let the inmates get flowers in there, anyway. Clint thinks they'll probably release Mrs. Ryland after she goes to court and the judge sees she's not much of a threat to society. But she'll have to go to trial eventually."

"Cami, I don't know what to think about any of this," Mom said.

"Me, either. Sorry to deliver all this bad news and run, but I should get going."

Dad leaned close to my face and put his hand on mine. "Cami, if it turns out Emmy is some sort of serial killer, we're very grateful that she was stopped in her tracks and you weren't harmed in any way."

A chill passed through me, raising goose bumps on my whole body. Was it possible Emmy Anders was not the kind little old lady she seemed to be and was actually a demented killer? If that was the case, she may have other victims the police had not yet linked her to.

Jiminy Cricket, I needed to rein in my overactive imagination, because my rational brain did not believe any of it. Emmy had been found not guilty of poisoning her husband, although it didn't look good for her when the police found cyanide in her garage. But there were many uses for the poison, right?

I nodded at Dad and swallowed, trying to move the lump out of my throat. I gave each of my parents a reassuring hug. If Emmy really was Molly's killer, we'd all be thankful she had been caught.

9

When I got home, I parked in the front of the house so I didn't have to cross the backyard in the dark. Clint had told me to install better lighting, and his warnings about taking personal safety precautions were starting to get to me. The windy night was playing tricks with the leafless branches of the trees, making them look like long arms reaching out for victims. My imagination was not my best friend at the moment.

I climbed out of my car as fast as I could, locked it, and looked around for anyone who may be lurking in the neighborhood. "Hello," a voice called from behind me, and I stopped breathing for a few seconds. I held on tight to my keys, prepared to use them as a weapon if I had to. The voice belonged to my next-door neighbor who appeared from beside the giant oak on the boulevard. My fear of what trees could do was not so outlandish after all. They provided great hiding places.

"Oh, hi, have a nice evening," I said and made a mad dash for my front door. When I glanced back, my neighbor was standing there, holding on to a dog's leash. I hadn't even noticed the dog a moment ago, proof that people had tunnel vision when they're afraid. The poor guy probably wondered what my problem was, and I had to wonder the same thing. I let myself in and took another look at the moving branches before I closed the door on them. "You need to get a grip," I told myself.

Logically, I knew it was silly to be so scared, but since I could not seem to steer my brain toward logic at that particular moment, I had to distract myself in another way. I turned on the light in the front entry then opened the closet door and hung up my coat. I wandered into the living room, turned on the lamps, and stood for a moment, appreciating the few treasures that were still in the house from Sandra, the former owner. Sandra was a special woman in my life mainly because she'd been my birth mother's best lifetime friend. Sadly, my mother's life was only twenty-seven years long.

Sandra was gracious, kind, and giving to a fault. And it seemed to me when I moved into her house that it still retained the same positive energy it had when she was alive. The little bird in her cuckoo clock startled me when it popped out. I took a look at it: 7:30 p.m. Too much had happened in the last ninety minutes, and it would take time for it all to sink in. My stomach rumbled a bit, reminding me I hadn't had dinner. I'd bought the ingredients to make a chicken stir fry the night before Molly's death, and I figured if I didn't use them soon, they'd spoil.

I gathered the frying pan, sesame seed oil, teriyaki sauce, and a pound of sliced chicken breasts. Then I grabbed two cloves of garlic, fresh ginger root, a can of sliced water chestnuts, an onion, and a pint of baby bella mushrooms. A bag of baby carrots, a head of broccoli, and a small bag of fresh green beans joined the rest of the ingredients, and I was ready to get cooking. I added a couple of teaspoons of oil to the pan, peeled and pressed the garlic, and added it in, too. Next, I grated some ginger then peeled and sliced the onion and slid it in the pan, then turned on the burner. When the onions had softened a bit, I stirred in the chicken and took an appreciative sniff of the yummy smells.

When the chicken had browned, I added the mushrooms, water chestnuts, and vegetables and cooked them until they were soft but not mushy. Then I sprinkled some teriyaki sauce over the dish and declared it ready to eat. As I pulled a plate out of the cupboard, I thought of the family dinners I'd had growing up and how different they were from the more recent years when I'd lived alone. It was more fun to cook for family or friends, but I liked good food, and there was nothing like a home-cooked meal, in my opinion.

The sound of my ringing doorbell caused me to lose the grip on the plate. Fortunately, it was about a half inch from the countertop and didn't have far to fall. I had been way too jumpy since I'd found poor Molly dead in the bathroom, and I hoped I'd get over it before too long. If the police would just get to the bottom of her murder, that would be a great help to my emotional state.

I rushed to the living room window and pulled back the curtain to see who was at my door. Of all the bad luck; it was Clinton Lonsbury. Probably there to chew me out for something I may or may not have done.

He knocked on the door, obviously impatient that it took me more than thirty seconds to let him in. "Camryn, it's Clint."

I unlocked the door and pulled it open. "Yes?"

"Do you mind if I come in?" When I didn't object right off the bat, he stepped in and turned his head toward the kitchen. "What is that?"

I whipped around to see what he was referring to. "What?"

"Food. It smells good enough to eat."

"Oh, well, I hope so."

"Am I interrupting your supper?"

"Not yet. I was just about to sit down."

He nodded. "I'll take off, then. I just stopped by to apologize for being short with you." Which time was he talking about? He was "short" with me all the time. "You were trying to be helpful when you said Mrs. Ryland and Mrs. Andersohn should be separated, and I took it the wrong way."

"Oh, okay." Somehow his apology broke down my defenses, or maybe it was that I didn't want to be alone what with the wind howling outside. Or maybe it was because I hadn't cooked for anyone else for a while. Whatever the reason, I said, "Have you had supper?"

His eyebrows rose. "Why, no, I haven't had a chance."

"If you like chicken and vegetable stir fry, you're welcome to join me. When I cook, it always ends up being enough to feed at least six people."

He actually smiled then slipped out of his jacket and laid it on the couch on his way to the kitchen. It was there he discovered something about me he may not have believed, had he not seen it with his own eyes. I was a very messy cook. Very, very messy. But as Mom had told me many times over the years, "Cami, now I'm not saying this to hurt your feelings, but when you cook or bake, no one makes that much of a mess." Then she'd smile and finish, "Or can clean up better than you can." My claim to fame. Little-known fame. In all the years I'd been on my own, very few people had seen my kitchen in its meltdown state.

Clint set one foot in the kitchen and stopped cold. "You must have one good therapy session planned."

The man was insufferable. I'd let it slip that I found cleaning therapeutic, and he had found several occasions to rub it my face after that. "Yes, that's the sole reason I cook."

He looked at me long enough to make me blush then turned his attention to the pan on the stove. Clint walked over and inhaled like he was taking his last breath on earth. When he turned and gave me a big, genuine smile of appreciation, my color deepened, and something inside of me melted a bit. For that one moment in time, I let myself admire what a hunk he was when he allowed a happy expression to crack through his normal granite exterior.

"Can I do anything to help?" Clint asked. He was sincere, and I immediately forgave him for the therapy crack.

Of course his question meant that I should answer him. It should have been simple enough, but the state of my kitchen distracted me. I had never had a guest for dinner with utensils and food scraps scattered around, filling the counter spaces. I wouldn't be able to relax surrounded by the mess while we ate. "Um, do you ever drink beer?"

He smiled again. "I have been known to do that on occasion."

I felt more melting deep inside of me. "How about, like, now?"

His eyebrows went up and down once. "That sounds good."

I opened the refrigerator door. I had bought a Minnesota brewers' sampler pack with three different beers. Actually, two kinds of beer and a pale ale. I pulled out the pack and set it on the counter. "Any preference?"

Clint stepped closer and lifted one of the pale ales from the case. "One of my favorites."

I found a bottle opener in a drawer and handed it to him. "If you could take your drink into the living room, maybe catch the news on TV for a few minutes, I'll finish up in here."

The way he frowned at me seemed to say, *Are you serious?*

"Please," I said.

He cracked the top off his bottle, nodded, then went into the next room. I heard voices on the television a minute later. I drove into a frenzied cleanup, discarding onion and garlic peels and all the other waste I had created. Then I loaded the dishwasher with all the food preparation supplies and wiped down the stove and counter. The small dining room was off the kitchen. I had never had a meal there but kept a tablecloth on the table, just in case. I added a plate to the one I had taken out before Clint arrived, grabbed utensils and napkins, and set the table. Then I scooped the stir fry into a large bowl, added a serving spoon, and put it and the bottle of teriyaki sauce on the table.

I went to the doorway of the kitchen to call Clint to the

table. He was sitting on the edge of the couch watching a nature show. "All set," I said, and he clicked off the television with the remote he was holding. He stood up, grabbed his drink from the coffee table, and came into the kitchen.

"How did you do that so fast? I don't think I took three sips of beer."

I shrugged. "I learned early on that the faster I got done with my chores, the sooner I got to play."

"Just what kind of play are you proposing here?" He raised his eyebrows.

In retrospect, I realized I had set myself up for that one, but it was too late to take back my words. "Or go shopping, or meet my friends, or eat. Like now. And we should, before the food gets cold."

"We should. Where would you like me to sit?"

I pointed at the table. "Either place. Would you like another drink?"

Clint shook his head. "I'm still nursing this one."

I got a pale ale for myself then sat across from Clint. I'd set the food on the table in between the place settings and now pushed the bowl closer to him. "Help yourself. I would have made rice to go with it if I'd known you were coming."

"Thanks, this looks hearty enough without rice. I don't do much cooking myself." He dished a generous portion onto his plate.

"We had a home-cooked meal every night growing up. I notice the difference in how I feel eating good food versus junk food."

Clint stabbed a piece of chicken and popped it in his mouth. He raised his eyebrows and smiled. "That's what I'm talking about."

The corners of my lips lifted as I dished stir fry onto my own plate. We held off on talking while we ate, and thankfully, it was more difficult to argue about things when our mouths were full.

After Clint had polished off a second helping, he leaned back in his chair and rubbed his stomach. "That was the best meal I've had in a long time."

Really? "Thank you. I have ice cream, if you're still hungry."

"I'm stuffed, but thanks, anyway."

"I'm glad you stopped by and stayed for dinner. I was feeling kind of jumpy when I got home."

He studied my face. "Jumpy?"

"With everything that has happened the last couple of days, it's almost too much to process. And after I told my parents about Emmy, my dad said what if Emmy turns out to be a serial killer with other victims nobody knows about."

Clint frowned. "In any case, it's something we can look into; track where she's lived and if there have been any suspicious deaths in the area."

That made me feel even worse for Emmy, whether she deserved it or not. If she had hurt others, she needed to pay for her crimes. Maybe I was naïve. And I had been fooled by people before, but I wasn't convinced Emmy had killed either her husband or Molly Dalton.

"Have you told Irene Ryland why Emmy is in jail?" I asked.

Clint shook his head. "Mark and I talked about it and felt it was best to wait until after they make their court appearances, see what happens there. We felt she has enough to deal with for now. We did inform Will Dalton, however."

"And what did he say?"

"Not much, just, 'Good, I had my suspicions about her.'"

"I'm surprised Will Dalton even knows Emmy."

"It's a small town."

"But what about Emmy would make him suspicious in the first place?"

"I asked him what he'd meant, what gave him 'suspicions,' and he said it was more of a gut feeling, no real reason. So when I told him what her real name was, it convinced him he was probably right about his gut feelings."

"Or he's just trying to act like a know-it-all."

"That's a possibility, too." Clint got out of his chair and picked up his plate. "I'll get these washed up," he said.

"Don't worry about it. I have a dishwasher."

Clint carried his plate to the kitchen, and I followed with my own. He glanced down at his watch. "If you're sure, then, I'll get out of your hair."

It was close to nine o'clock, much later than my usual dinner hour. Clint went into the living room, picked up his coat from the couch, slipped it on, and then turned to me. I was surprised when he stuck his right hand out, like he wanted to shake mine. "Thanks again."

Not knowing what else to do, I shook his hand. His grip was firm, and his hand was warm and comforting. That surprised me a little. Not the firm and warm part; it was the comforting part that threw me off. "You're welcome."

"And there's something I wanted to give you, if it's all right." He dropped his hand, and I wondered what in the world he might have stuffed in his pocket for me that I may or may not want to accept. But he didn't reach into his pocket; his hands came toward me instead. One slipped around my waist and settled in the middle of my back. The other lifted my chin, and his mouth closed over mine for a brief kiss. The whole thing lasted a nanosecond, but my heart rate seemed to soar into triple digits, like I had just run a fast sprint.

Clint's lips were still near mine when he whispered, "Good night, Camryn." Then he slipped out the door. I was momentarily tempted to go after him to beg him to come back for one more kiss. And then I remembered who he was and who I was, and that rushing after him would be a bad idea indeed.

I considered calling Pinky and Erin to tell them about the crazy evening: how Clint had stopped over, how we'd had dinner together, and then how he'd kissed me out of the blue—the very last thing in the world I'd expected. I had to admit we'd shared a fairly pleasant meal together, but that was mostly because we hadn't talked much.

Clint took his eating very seriously, and it seemed it was the only thing he could concentrate on at the time. That had cut down substantially on our propensity to disagree. Then he *kissed* me. He must have been overcome with gratitude for the home-cooked meal to do that. But what if he tried to do it again sometime? How in the world would I handle that? Golly.

I went into the dining room and started cleaning up the rest of our meal. As distracting as Clint's visit had turned out to be, there were critical things going on in our small community. All the things Molly's mother had been part of umpteen years ago had come to light and landed her in jail. Then Emmy Anders—or Andersohn—was arrested for Molly's murder because the police found cyanide in her garage. Mind-boggling events. Would either of the women sleep a wink tonight?

The only thing our friend Archie Newberry had complained about when he was in jail, before he went to the treatment center, was the hard, thin mattress on the metal bed. "These old shoulders of mine kinda like a softer place to rest on."

Archie. Pinky and I had agreed to keep him in the dark about the latest happenings for as long as possible. He didn't watch television, so we felt fairly sure he wouldn't hear about it. When he was further along in his psychological healing and could handle the news better, we'd decide on the best way to tell him.

I put the leftover stir fry in a plastic container and snapped on the lid. After I'd put it in the refrigerator, I heard a light scraping, like a tapping noise, near the dining room window. My first thought was that it was a woodpecker. But it was late, and the ones that wintered over, that didn't migrate south for the winter, would be in their shelters for the night. I turned off the dining area light, went over to the window, and opened the blind. There was enough light from the streetlamp to make out the offender—a large branch had broken off, and the wind was pushing it against the house and window. If the wind pushed much harder, the branch might break the window.

I did not want to go out in the frosty, windy night, but I had no choice. I slipped into a quilted jacket and boots then went out the front door to the south side of the house. I ignored the moving, reaching branches that had given me a fright earlier and resolutely marched to the broken one. It was six or seven feet long, and the base of it had a diameter that would be the right size for firewood. I got ahold of the heavy end and tugged until it moved then kept going until it was far enough away from the house.

I started back inside but almost fainted on the spot when a white ghostlike object floated by. I was frozen in my tracks and thanking God out loud that it hadn't come toward me. When my irrational terror settled down, and I could see better, I recognized it was a tall kitchen garbage bag that had taken on a ghostly appearance in the buffeting wind. I stood there for another second, chiding myself for being such a big baby. Ghosts didn't look like the cartoony white-sheet version, anyway. They looked like the people they had been, but different. Like Molly had been in my dream. That thought sent me rushing into the house.

Maybe I was officially cracking up. Perhaps the stress of getting ousted from my position in Washington had finally caught up with me. That got me thinking about Senator Ramona Zimmer, who was about to be ousted herself. She had actually accused me of costing her the election. She was really grasping at straws, but it was possible that wild notion had warped her brain. Enough to have me killed? If that was the case, her plans had gone awry when either she or Peter or the mystery man who was looking for me poisoned the wrong girl. Oh my.

I started shaking my hands the way Pinky did when she felt nervous. The results on the letter Ramona had delivered were not back from the crime lab, and I was getting impatient. If the letter contained poison, that should prove to the police that the Zimmers were the ones who had killed Molly. Unless . . . Emmy had killed Molly after all. And her death gave the Zimmers the idea to poison another girl—namely me—in Curio Finds to make it look like a serial killer was on the loose.

I had caught Ramona completely off guard when I came in and found her at my counter. She may have thought I'd trustingly open the envelope, inhale the contents, and die before I could tell anyone what had happened.

Then one more thought hit me. What if that man who was in the store asking about the woman who fit my description was not working for the Zimmers after all? What if he was asking for Molly because of some other connection they had? And who was that strange guy Ramona brought to her house when Peter wasn't home? The man had looked like he would be staying awhile.

My head hurt from all the bad thoughts circling around in my brain. I needed to do something calming, but what? It was too dark to go for a walk, even if I bundled up against the cold and armed myself with a canister of Mace. Plus, if the Zimmers had it in for me, the Mace might not be enough to ward them off. I grudgingly admitted Clint was right. I needed to take a self-defense class. After all, the same kinds of things, good and bad, happened in small towns, rural areas, and big cities.

Clint. It was the strangest thing, but thinking about him and the way his lips caressed mine for that brief moment gave me a sense of reassurance. Yes, we butted heads on a regular basis, and we had virtually nothing in common. Not to mention that the way he slurped his coffee drove me bananas. But there was a part of me, way deep down inside, that liked and respected him.

When my phone rang and I saw it was the man of the hour

calling, I debated whether I should answer it or not. But it might be important. "Hello, Clint."

"Camryn, I wanted to thank you again for the delicious meal. And to make sure you locked your door after I left. I forgot to remind you, and I know you don't always remember to do that."

That's what Clint did, and it drove me up a tree. He'd draw me in and then insult me. But I was not about to get all hyped up again, so before I said a word, I took a breath and bit my tongue. "You're welcome, and I did remember to lock the door." *I'm not quite as feebleminded as you think I am.* "I've gotta go, but thanks for calling. 'Night." I hung up. It didn't matter whether he was done talking or not—I was. Clint had effectively reminded me how we clashed way too much and way too often.

10

She came to me for the second time in the middle of the night. A pale Molly in all her otherworldly glory was back in Curio Finds, and I was the only one who seemed to notice. I was standing behind my checkout counter, and she moved in a smooth and graceful way. "Did you see them?" she asked.

"Who?" I said.

"The ones who put that there." She glanced down at the counter. When my own eyes followed her gaze, I saw the coffee cup and knew it was *the* one with the poison because a strong odor of almonds was emanating from it.

"No, I'm sorry, I didn't."

"I think there were two of them, but maybe it was only one. The one who brought it to me."

"Molly, what did they look like? Was it a man, a woman?"

"Look around," she said and faded to nothing.

I did what she'd said, but everyone's faces were fuzzy, and then they all disappeared, too. I was alone in the shop when all the lights went out and total blackness engulfed me.

When I awoke, I was sitting upright in my bed with my hands clamped tight over my eyes. I was panting. When everything went dark in my dream, I had screamed bloody murder, but not a sound had escaped from my mouth. I was completely mute. My throat hurt, like I had strained it. And whether I had screamed out loud or silently didn't matter, because there was no one else in the house to come to my rescue.

I gripped the blankets and pulled them around my chest as I tried to calm down and convince myself that a dream was only a dream and nothing to be afraid of. I was grateful the orange red glow from the dial on my alarm clock gave off some light. When I looked at it and saw it was only 3:01 a.m., I felt even more distressed. Who would I dare wake up in the middle of the night to talk about my bad dream, terrifying or not?

I turned on the reading lamp on the nightstand then got out of bed and pulled on a flannel robe and the furry pink bunny slippers Pinky had given me. I went to the kitchen for a cup of tea, turning on lights along the way. I fished through the assortment in my cupboard and settled on a bedtime tea with chamomile and spearmint. I heated a mug of water in the microwave then dropped the tea bag in and put a saucer over it to let it steep.

My heart was quieting down, and I breathed in slowly though my nose and out through my mouth a few times, the way Mom had taught me to do when I was upset. My breathing was back to normal in about a minute. Why were things so much scarier in the middle of the night? At least the howling wind had died down.

"Okay, Molly, your ghost has to just quit it." I gave my forehead a light bop. "You are losing it, Cami. It was *your* dream, after all."

The tea was ready, and I carried it into the living room, turned on a reading lamp, and settled on the couch. I felt I owed it to Molly to help find out who had poisoned her, especially if the final hit was meant for me. Wasn't there some unwritten rule about that, like I would need to take care of her family until death do us part? I had money put away and could bail Molly's mother out of jail if it came to that. Did Molly's husband Will even care that his mother-in-law was locked up?

And then there was Molly's stepbrother. He sounded like a real piece of work. He'd actually taken money to keep quiet about his father's murder instead of going to the police with the information. Then on top of it all, he had extorted thousands of dollars a month from Molly until she finally put a stop to it. In my opinion, he was lower than low and seemed a likely suspect in her murder. He certainly had more of a motive than Emmy did. And he could have been the one in the shop who'd asked for the blonde that worked there.

I set my tea on the coffee table and went to my desk for a pad and pen then carried them back to the couch. I set the pad on the coffee table and leaned over it, pen in hand, ready for action. I thought back over the last month when we'd had a murder in town and remembered how I had worried that my friends, Erin, Pinky, and Mark, were involved in some way. I felt awful about having even a smidgen of doubt about them, but I'd tried to be as objective as possible. And they all had reasons to want Jerrell Powers out of the picture. Instead it was Archie, whom I had not initially suspected, that sadly turned out to be the guilty one.

I thought back to the afternoon Molly died. I poked my pen into the pad a few times, debating whose name to write down first as a suspect. Emmy was with Molly right before she died and was the Brooks Landing Police Department's prime suspect. I hoped to have a real heart-to-heart with her soon. I printed her name then jotted down all the things that had come to light about her past and the evidence the police had found in her garage.

Molly's stepbrother was a prime suspect as far as I was concerned. The problem was finding out where he was. Troy Ryland fit the general description of the mystery man that had talked to Pinky. If Molly had seen Troy, even if she didn't want to tell us about him, it seemed she would have given something away by her reaction. At the time, none of the rest of us knew about Troy, or how he had blackmailed Molly. I didn't blame her for wanting to keep that under wraps forever.

But say he came in, greeted her, said something nice, asked her to forgive him, then handed her a cup of laced coffee, disguised as a peace offering. Poor Molly would have been none the wiser. "Okay, Troy Ryland, you get an asterisk by your name. Make that three." And then I underlined his name, twice.

That left Peter and Ramona Zimmer, and I wrote a page of reasons why I thought it might be them, with a possible accomplice. Molly had said "they" when she talked about her killers. *Cami, you keep forgetting, she told you that in your dreams.* It was becoming more and more clear to me what people meant when they said they felt like they were in the Twilight Zone.

I laid the pen down, took a final sip of tea, and stood up. I left the lamp on in the living room, just because, and headed back to bed. The Shakespeare volume of works that included *Macbeth* was lying on my nightstand. I turned it over so the title was covered. No matter what my imagination came up with when it ran wild, it did not hold a candle to Shakespeare's, thank goodness.

My alarm woke me up at 8:00 a.m. I smiled when I opened my eyes and saw it was light out. Remarkably, I had slept the rest of the night without any more unwelcomed dream visits from you know who. The first person that came to mind was Emmy. I needed to talk to her. And the second person I thought of was Molly's mother. Clint said she would go before the judge today, and I hoped Emmy would, too. Whether either one of them would be released was the big unknown. I'd made a vow the night before that I would help Mrs. Ryland, and I hoped if they did set bail it would be an amount I could manage. As far as Emmy was concerned, her bail might be steep and way beyond my means. And I wasn't completely convinced she was innocent. Evidence was evidence.

I called Mark Weston's cell phone. "Good morning, Cami, what's up?"

"Morning. Hey, Mark, I was wondering how I'd find out about court today? Like if Emmy or Mrs. Ryland will be going before the judge?"

"Well, court admin makes up a calendar, and their names should be on it. How about I check it out for you?"

"I'd appreciate it."

"So, Cami, did you hear that they're not having a funeral for Molly?"

"What do you mean?" Everyone who lived and died in Brooks Landing had a funeral.

"I talked to Ike over at the funeral home and he told me. He said her husband wants to keep it limited to an intimate few."

"Like her mother, his parents?"

"I have no idea, probably something like that. According to Ike, Mr. Dalton does not want it to turn into a circus."

"I don't think it's possible for a funeral to turn into a circus. People are more considerate than that."

"I agree with you on that one."

"You'd think he'd appreciate people coming to pay their respects."

"I sure would. He must be having a lot of trouble dealing with it all and just can't face what happened to his wife."

"You have a point there."

"And when it comes right down to it, it's none of our beeswax."

"I know, but still."

I heard Mark's badge number being called over his police radio. "Gotta go. I'll get back to you about the court calendar," he said.

"Thanks."

Mark was right—it was not our business whether Will Dalton had a service for Molly or not, but it seemed that a man in his position would want one. His parents were upper middle class, known for their social gatherings. Will was a partner in a large law firm with a ton of colleagues. Although

Molly didn't say much about their social life or friends, she'd mention events here and there. They may have felt more like obligations than fun, but I remembered feeling a little jealous when she told us about a fund-raiser gala they were going to earlier in the fall. There wasn't much occasion for my friends and me to get dressed to the nines.

Whether it was my business or not, I found the local phone directory and looked up the number for Walters Funeral Services. Ike Walters answered, and his voice was soft and soothing. "Walters Chapel. How can I be of service to you?"

"Hi, Mr. Walters, it's Cami Brooks."

"Oh, Cami, always a pleasure. How are your folks? Well, I hope?"

"Pretty good. Mom's doing much better, thanks."

"Good to hear."

"Mr. Walters, I was wondering about Molly Dalton's service."

"Well, Cami, it's at three o'clock this afternoon, at Will Dalton's home. But I expect it will be small, family, maybe a few friends. It's private, closed to the public, invitation only."

I had never heard of an "invitation only" funeral or memorial service. "I'm sorry to hear that. I know a number of our classmates would like to be there."

"Well, yes, that is unfortunate, and it's been my experience that when people share stories and kind words about the deceased, it helps their loved ones move through the grieving process a little better. But it's not right for me to question decisions the bereaved make. I follow their wishes and do the best job I can for them."

Mr. Walters was very good at it, too. "Okay, and of course

you are right. I appreciate the info, Mr. Walters, and we'll see you in Brew Ha-Ha one of these days."

"You can count on it. Good-bye, Cami."

"'Bye."

I knew where I'd be at about 2:30 that afternoon if I was able to arrange it—watching to see who made the cut and got invited to Molly's memorial service. Her mother had made no mention of it when we'd talked to her in the jail, so I had to wonder if she even knew about it. Mark called me back a while later to say both women were scheduled that morning and should make it to court sometime between 11:00 and noon. If Pinky was comfortable with handling the business in both shops, I'd head over to the Buffalo County Courthouse and sit in on the proceedings.

I got to Brew Ha-Ha before nine. Pinky raised her eyebrows when she saw me. "Holy moly, you're early."

"I'm hoping for a couple of breaks later so I thought I'd help out now."

"Okay." She drew out the word. "Where are you planning to break to?" I told her about the private service for Molly. "Her mother is in jail, for crying out loud. That would be just plain wrong if Will Dalton went ahead and had it without her," she said.

"I know, and I plan to ask Mrs. Ryland what she knows about it, if I get the chance. Which brings me to the other reason for a break. Mark found out both Emmy and Mrs. Ryland are scheduled for their court appearances sometime between eleven and noon."

Her eyebrows went together. "Not at the same time, I hope?"

I shrugged. "According to what Clint said, the jailers are keeping them separated. I'd think everyone at the courthouse knows about that by now."

"Let's hope so."

"Anyway, I want to be there—for both of them. And don't go all freaky on me, but if Mrs. Ryland's bail isn't outrageous, I'm going to spring for it."

"Cami, are you kidding?"

"No, I feel I owe it to Molly."

"How did you figure that one?"

"In case the poison was meant for me."

"I wish you wouldn't keep saying that."

"I don't keep saying it; this is only the second time. And here's another thing not to freak out about, but Molly's ghost was back in my dreams again last night, saying the same thing she said last time, that her killers were in the shop. And then she said she thought there were two, but maybe there really was only one killer after all."

Pinky put her hand on my shoulder. "Cami, this is just not like you. I mean, actually listening to a ghost tell you crazy stuff in your dreams."

"I agree, and it doesn't make sense to me, either. I know it's got to be my own subconscious coming up with those things, but Molly seems completely real and certain about what she's saying."

"That's because the killer was in the shop and gave her a cup of coffee. It could have been Emmy for all we know. Molly didn't give you any names, did she?"

"Well, no."

"And even if she did, you could not very well go to the

police and tell them a ghost in your dream told you who poisoned her."

"Yes, I know, it is crazy, crazier, craziest." I made a secret vow that from then on, I'd be careful what I said to Pinky about Molly's murder. "And of course I know Molly's ghost is just a figment of my imagination." At least my rational self knew that. My middle-of-the-night irrational self was confused and had sent the jury out with hopes that a verdict was forthcoming. The decision on whether I was of sound mind could not come soon enough, that was for darn sure.

"All this ghost talk is starting to rub off on me, and I've been praying it stays in your dreams. Early in the morning I've seen shadows in your shop that seem to be moving, and they've given me enough of a start. If Molly's ghost shows up for real, I don't know what I'll do—after I come to from a dead faint, that is."

"Pinky, there is no need to worry about that. We've got enough to deal with."

B rew Ha-Ha was not overly busy at 10:50 a.m., so I headed to the courthouse with Pinky's mixed blessings. I stopped at the court administration office to check in and then headed as directed to Courtroom 2. The heavy wooden door creaked when I opened it, and a few people in the back rows turned and gave me a quick once-over. The judge was sitting at his bench, and the nameplate in front of him read "Judge Roger Terney." Judge Terney had the same color hair as Santa Claus and had a similar older yet ageless look. The public seating was on church pew–like benches, and I sat in an empty row, four rows from the back.

Judge Terney was studying the paper he held. He set it down, and his eyes moved to the well-dressed young man standing with his attorney in front of the bench. "Given the recommendation by the prosecuting attorney and your admission of guilt, I am sentencing you to thirty days in the Buffalo County Jail. Since you are gainfully employed, you will be eligible for work release." He tapped his gavel. The young man said something quietly, maybe "thank you" to the judge, then left with his attorney.

A door on the other side of the jury box opened, and Emmy came through it wearing an orange jumpsuit and handcuffs. *Handcuffs? Really?* I supposed it was required, but still. A uniformed jailer was close behind her. He pointed at the jury box, and Emmy climbed the step then sat down in a leather chair. I hoped she would notice me, but she was focused on the judge. The jailer stood near her, outside the box. My heart went out to her; I couldn't help it.

The judge called her to go before him and asked her to state her full name. "Emaline Grace Andersohn," she said. *Grace.* If anyone needed grace right then, it was Emmy.

"Mrs. Andersohn, the purpose of the first appearance is for the court to inform you of the charges against you and let you know your rights, including the right to a public defender if you are unable to hire an attorney. You will also have the opportunity to enter a plea." He then read Emmy her rights and asked if she understood. Emmy said she did.

The judge looked at the bailiff. "Deputy Garrison, give the defendant a copy of the complaint." The court clerk handed it to the deputy, who gave it to Emmy. She glanced at it then lifted her head to look at the judge. He read the list of what she was charged with, but the only thing I clearly heard was the first charge, "Murder in the first degree." A pulse started pounding in my ears as my mind locked on those five awful words.

Emmy was standing there looking old and fragile, and I was surprised she didn't topple over. When the judge finished the list, he asked Emmy if she understood the charges against her, and she said she did. Then he asked if she was ready to enter a plea.

"Yes, Your Honor. I plead not guilty."

There was whispering in the rows behind me. I had no clue who the people were, or if they knew Emmy or Molly or how Molly had died in Curio Finds.

"A plea of not guilty is hereby entered." Judge Terney wrote something down then looked up at Emmy. "Bail is set at five hundred thousand dollars. You are dismissed." Then he rapped the gavel.

Emmy's head hung low as she walked back to the jailer, and then the two of them left the courtroom. Five hundred thousand dollars was a lot of money. Three more people, all men, were brought to court before Mrs. Ryland was. I didn't know there was so much going on in the county. It seemed like Emmy had gotten the book thrown at her, and I could only imagine what Judge Terney would do to Mrs. Ryland.

The judge went through the same spiel with her as he had with the others. She, too, understood her rights. Her charges sounded almost as ominous as Emmy's had: accessory after the fact for murder in the first degree, bribery, aiding an offender, and obstructing justice, all felony-level crimes. She agreed that she understood the charges and was ready to enter a plea. "I'm guilty, Judge Terney."

The judge nodded and studied her for a long moment. "I have read the complaint from the Brooks Landing Police, and the circumstances. Therefore, I am releasing you on your own recognizance with the expectation that you will return for your next appearance, which will be?" He stopped and looked at the clerk, who looked at the calendar and said, "November twenty-third at nine a.m."

Mrs. Ryland nodded and said, "I will be here." Then she left with the jailer.

I slipped out of the courtroom and headed down to the jail lobby. The officer looked up from her computer. "Can I help you?"

"Yes, Judge Terney just told Irene Ryland she was free to go, and I'd like to give her a ride home, if she needs one."

"And what is your name?"

"Camryn Brooks."

She raised her eyebrows, making it clear to me that she was well aware of the recent crimes I'd been involved with. Not that I was directly involved, but close enough. Or maybe my name brought to mind the D.C. scandal. "Are you a relative or a friend?"

"A sort of friend. Actually, I'm more her daughter's friend. But if you tell her I'm here and can give her a ride, it will save her from having to call someone else. I just need to go get my car, which is a few blocks away."

The way the officer stared at me made me nervous, and I rambled on. "I will call booking and let them know," she finally said.

"Thank you. I'll be back soon."

"It'll be at least fifteen minutes until Ms. Ryland is out, depending on what else they have going on back there."

I nodded, thinking I'd said enough already, and braced myself for the breezy walk back to the shops.

When I went into Brew Ha-Ha, Pinky stopped in her tracks. She had an expectant look on her face. "Tell me what happened."

"I didn't have to bail Molly's mom out after all because the judge released her. Emmy did not fare as well, I'm afraid. Her bail was set at half a million dollars."

"Holy moly, that's way out of our league."

"That means the bond is fifty thousand. If it was for you or Erin, I'd borrow from my inheritance and retirement fund to put up the bond, but for Emmy?"

"You got that right. Oh, and speaking of Erin, she called and said she's coming in after school to help out. She wants to get more familiar with all the stuff on your shelves."

"Good, because I have something I'd like to do and I don't know how long it's going to take."

"Such as?"

"I'll tell you later. I offered to give Mrs. Ryland a ride home from jail, so I've got to run. Thanks for helping me out here."

"Cami, you're not thinking of going to Will Dalton's house—"

I pretended not to hear her and waved on the way out the door.

Mrs. Ryland tried to smile when she spotted me in the jail lobby, but her lips were trembling. I went to her, took her small bag, then offered my arm to lean on. "This is very kind of you, Cami. I didn't know how I was going to tell Will about all of this, so this buys me a little time. He was the last one I wanted to have to call for a ride."

"No problem at all. My car isn't far." In fact it was the closest one in the lot to the door, after the handicapped spots. Even with her crippling disease, Mrs. Ryland walked smoothly and fairly quickly. And she was as silent as a kitten or cat burglar. When we were in the car and driving away, I said as gingerly as possible, "Mrs. Ryland, you haven't said anything about a service for Molly."

"No, it hasn't been set. I expected to meet with Will, but he hasn't called to do that yet."

"Actually, I found out this morning that he's planning to have one at his house today."

She turned her head to look at me. "What?"

"It sounds like it's going to be small."

"I don't understand." Mrs. Ryland looked down and paused a moment. "But then again, I haven't been home the last two days if he's been trying to call me."

"I'm sure that's it."

When I stopped in front of her house, Mrs. Ryland said, "Do you mind seeing me in the door? I'm feeling a little shaky."

"I'd be happy to, and I'll wait while you check your messages, if you'd like."

"That'd be nice." She reached over and patted my hand. "Molly always helped me with whatever I needed. I don't know what I'm going to do without her."

"You call me anytime, for any reason. And I know Pinky feels the same way. We're happy to do whatever we can."

Tears formed in Mrs. Ryland's eyes, and a small smile played at her lips. I went around and helped her out of the car and up the one step to a side entry door. Her bent, arthritic fingers fought to get the proper grip on her house key. I was ready to join the fight when she finally won the battle and got her door open. We went into the kitchen, and I saw the light on her answering machine was blinking—a good sign. Interestingly enough, there was no message from Will Dalton, however.

Mrs. Ryland picked up the phone and dialed a number. "Will, it's Irene. I was gone overnight and may have missed your call. I'm home now, so please call me." She hung up and leaned on the counter for support. "It's probably not the kind of thing he wanted to leave on my machine."

"That's true. When I heard there might be a service today, I called Ike Walters, and he confirmed it was at three o'clock. So if you'd like a ride to Will's house, I'm free to do that."

"Oh, well, I can drive myself."

"I thought maybe you'd like the company."

She reached over and touched my hand. "That would be nice if you're sure it's not too much trouble?"

"No trouble at all." Besides helping out Mrs. Ryland, it also gave me the opportunity to see who was in with the in crowd. "I'll be back to get you at two thirty."

She nodded.

.

Pinky had a few people drinking beverages at her counter, and she was helping a customer in Curio Finds. I took over in my shop, but the woman was just browsing. At the first opportunity, I pulled Pinky aside in her back area and summed up the latest on Mrs. Ryland.

"Cami, it's nice that you're helping Molly's mother out and all, but you can't just crash the memorial service. Even I know what 'private' means."

That brought a smile to my face. "Pinky, you *know* what private means, but—"

She waved her hand between our faces. "Pshaw, whatever. Okay, well, you go do your thing and bring back a full report." Pinky's long arm reached around my back and gave it a pat, then she headed back to her service counter.

I went back and forth about calling the jail and leaving a message for Emmy, asking her to call me. In the end, I decided it would be better to talk to her in person instead. During a lull between customers, I sat down at my checkout counter with a pen and paper. Emmy was weighing heavily on my mind. The police had evidence against her, and maybe she was guilty, but a number of other suspects took turns bubbling to the surface. Peter and Ramona Zimmer. Molly's stepbrother. The unknown man who was in the shop looking for the blonde. And then there was the man with his suitcase that Ramona Zimmer let into her house. Five possibilities in addition to Emmy.

My shop door opened, and when I saw a tall man with a round face staring and walking toward me, my heart stopped beating for a few seconds. I glanced at his hands to see if he was carrying any kind of weapon or an envelope that may be filled with suspicious powder. Nothing I could see, anyway. I heard Pinky moving around next door, and it calmed me to know that help was just one loud, bloody-murder scream away. "C-c-can I help you?"

He shook his head and pursed his lips like he was holding back words that were trying to escape. There was something familiar about him. "Do we know each other from somewhere?" I asked, unable to stop myself. He shook his head again, and it felt like hundreds of pins and needles pricked at my shoulders and the back of my neck. The man broke eye contact and walked around the shop, looking at the shelves. He stopped near the back of the store and glanced first at the bathroom door, and then toward the storeroom area. He gave me one final stare, nodded, then headed into Brew Ha-Ha.

I got off my seat and followed him, stopping by the archway opening to spy from the short distance. The coffee shop area was deserted, so Pinky was either in the bathroom or her back room. The man walked up to the counter and read the menu above it until he caught my reflection, as I was hovering and peeking around the edge of the archway. I would have moved, ducked behind it, except my feet were frozen in place. He turned, and I wondered if he was going to ask me for a cup of coffee. Instead, he turned again and walked out Pinky's door. He was one strange dude, and I wondered if his elevator went to the top floor. Maybe he was casing the joint or had some other mysterious motivation.

Pinky apparently heard the bell on her door ding, because she appeared from the back room. "Did someone come in?" she asked.

"No, someone just left."

"Why are you standing there looking so weird, Cami?"

"There was a man in here, first in my shop and then in yours. And I'm trying to figure out what he was up to." I explained the encounter and then said, "You know that mystery man who was in here asking for the blonde the day Molly died?"

"Of course."

"From the way you described the guy, it might have been him, back for a return visit."

Pinky came up beside me and leaned in close. "Why would he come back here and then just look around without saying a word?"

"You know how they say criminals like to return to the scene of the crime?"

Pinky grabbed my shoulders. "Cami, you have a way of scaring the bejeebers out of me."

I gave her hand a pat. "I wish you could have seen him. You're the only one who would know if this man and that man are one and the same."

Pinky raised her eyebrows and shrugged one shoulder. "Maybe. Like I said, I would have paid better attention to him if I'd known what was about to go down."

"He also looks a lot like that guy who was with Ramona Zimmer the other night. But I didn't get a close enough look at him and don't think I could pick him out of a lineup."

"What I think is that you should call the police."

"And tell them what? A man was in our shops, looked around, then left without saying a word?"

"I guess you're right." She looked up at her clock. "Betty Boop says it's about time for you to get a move on."

I looked at the clock, too. "I guess, and I have no idea if this will be a quick trip or what, so wish me luck, Pink."

"All right, luck. But I think you're going to need more than that going into the lion's den. And Erin should be here by three thirty, so don't worry if you're there for a while. Just bring back all the juicy news you can gather from the rich and famous."

I rolled my eyes then gathered my coat, hat, and gloves, and left. Mrs. Ryland was waiting by the door when I pulled up. I got out of the car to assist her. I worried that if she fell, she'd break in a bunch of places. Her black cashmere wool coat, no doubt a gift from Molly, was buttoned up to her neck. It had a hood, which I pulled up over her head. "All set?"

Her shoulders lifted slightly. "Nothing in life really prepares you for this. You know, Will never called back, so I hope he got my message."

I nodded and offered her my arm.

11

There was only a handful of vehicles parked in front of
Will Dalton's home. Very, very expensive ones: a black
Lexus SUV, a Bentley, a Porsche, an Aston Martin. I read
the logo on one model and saw it was a Lamborghini. I
considered parking my Subaru down the street a ways but
chided myself for being silly. I owned it free and clear and
knew that not everyone who drove top-of-the-line vehicles
could afford them any more than I could.

"I haven't been here for quite some time," Mrs. Ryland
said.

I didn't ask her the reason why. Instead, I said, "I'm going
to pull right into the driveway so we won't have far to walk."

The more time I spent with Mrs. Ryland, the more questions I thought of to ask her. And the fact that Will did not
consult his wife's mother about her final arrangements was

unheard of. The least he should have done was make sure she knew about the service, and then sent a car to pick her up. The Bentley would have been a nice, smooth ride for Mrs. Ryland.

Mrs. Ryland sucked in a breath that sounded to me like she was calling for the courage to go in, or maybe even to go on at all. Her hesitation gave me cold feet, and I considered telling her to go in without me. But that wouldn't have been fair, so I jumped out of the car before I changed my mind. She was partway out of her seat when I got to her side. Instead of taking my arm, she reached for my hand and held on tight all the way to the front door. I rang the bell, and a melodious series of perfectly pitched chimes sounded inside.

A few seconds later the door opened, and who but Will's young red-haired assistant stood there looking at us like we were yesterday's trash. Her eyebrows were nearly touching her hairline, and her pouty mouth was half open. "Yes?"

Something about her being there, coupled with her superior attitude, got my dander up. It's entirely possible I pressed back against the door just enough to throw her slightly off balance. Not on purpose, of course, but before she could regain her composure I said, "Surely, you know Molly's mother." Yes, I sounded snotty and snooty, but Ms. Assistant needed to know Mrs. Ryland deserved respect, and she had to give it to her.

"Oh." Her eyebrows shot up impossibly higher as I pushed past her, dragging Mrs. Ryland with me. I was feeling rather righteous until I came face-to-face with Will Dalton. His cold gaze released some butterflies in my stomach and at once reminded me he was not a person to taunt or toy with. I was a memorial service crasher, and the way he was staring me down made it seem like the worst possible thing to be at that moment in time.

Then, as if a fairy godmother waved a magic wand, his icy, cold expression changed to a seemingly sincere, warm one. Will took his mother-in-law's hand and led her into an adjoining room. There was an urn on a pedestal table and some chairs in a circle around it. I counted eight others in the room besides the three of us. Ms. Assistant must have stayed back for door duty.

Will helped Mrs. Ryland out of her coat and onto a chair in the circle. He hadn't asked me to leave, so I stayed close then sat down next to Mrs. Ryland. Will walked over to a man in a high-priced suit and said something too quietly for me to hear. It couldn't have been the minister, because he wouldn't have that kind of money for clothes. The man glanced over at Mrs. Ryland and me and then said something back to Will. I thought for a moment that we'd met somewhere, but I dismissed that notion in a split second. We certainly did not run in the same circles.

None of the people there sought out Mrs. Ryland to express their sympathies, and I found that strange. Molly was her daughter, after all. Will was not the only one here who had suffered a loss. I leaned over to Mrs. Ryland's ear and whispered, "Do you know all of these people?"

"No, not a one. Except Will, of course."

If no one from Will's family was there—and Mrs. Ryland would know them—who were these people?

"All right, I think everyone is here, so let's begin," Will said.

The few invited mourners took their seats, except for the man Will had talked to. He had moved someplace behind

Mrs. Ryland and me, and I didn't want to turn around to see where. There were four men and three women. Thankfully, Ms. Assistant did not come in and join the group.

Will sat down across from us and directed his attention to Mrs. Ryland. "Irene, would you like to say a few words?"

She drew in a quick breath and thought for a minute. "I didn't prepare anything, so I'll just say Molly was a special person and the most caring and loving daughter a mother could hope for . . . And she didn't deserve to die like that." Mrs. Ryland broke down, and the tears flowed freely. When I put an arm around her, she leaned into me.

Will looked down at his folded hands and nodded. His reaction struck me as off, and I wasn't sure why. After a while, he lifted his head and zeroed in on me. "Ms. Brooks?"

I was beyond surprised. What in the world could I come up with to say about Molly on the spot? I had worked on overcoming my fear of public speaking for many years, but this strange gathering did nothing to ease my anxiety. Plus, I figured it was best to keep my mouth shut, that way there was nothing that could be used against me in a court of law. I was more and more convinced that was where Will Dalton would drag us someday. I shrugged my shoulders slightly and shook my head.

"Anyone else?" Will asked of the small group. Several made nice comments, but nothing seemed heartfelt. Finally, it was Will's turn. He studied the urn holding Molly's ashes and opened his mouth, but instead of talking, he let out a wail that honestly scared me half out of my wits. Mrs. Ryland jumped right out of my half hug and sucked in a little gasp of air. Will pulled a hankie out of his front pocket and buried his face in it for a long time, crying silently.

When he finished, he wiped his nose then stuck the hankie in his pants pocket.

He stood up, and the rest of us followed suit. Will cleared his throat. "Thank you all for coming. There are refreshments in the dining room, but I'm going to have to excuse myself." He left the room without another word. It was one of life's awkward moments when I, for one, had not a clue what to do next. I had already pushed the envelope being there without an invitation and felt it was up to Molly's mother to make the call.

"Should we go get something to eat?" I asked Mrs. Ryland, looking around to see if anyone else was heading in that direction.

She shook her head. "I'd like to go home." I picked her coat up from the back of the chair Will had hung it on. I hadn't taken my own off, so that saved a step. No one paid much attention to us as we made our way out of the library and then through the front door. Ms. Assistant had left her post. Maybe her next duty was to serve whatever lunch Will had for his guests in the dining room.

When we were back in my car, I wanted to tell Mrs. Ryland that Molly's service was, hands down, the most bizarre gathering I had ever attended. But I didn't want to openly speak ill of her son-in-law, and it was not because I feared a lawsuit. A list of unkind words describing how I felt about Will Dalton's behavior came to mind, and at the top of the list was "insulting." Molly's service was anything but respectful, not only to her memory, but also in the way her mother was treated.

After witnessing Will Dalton in action, it was easier for me to understand why Molly was lonely in her marriage.

Did he really care about anyone besides himself and his own interests?

Mrs. Ryland and I were both quiet all the way to her house. When we got there, I asked if it'd be all right if I came in for a bit. "Please do, Cami." After we had settled down at the kitchen table, Mrs. Ryland looked me in the eyes. "I'm not sure Molly even still loved Will."

That was unexpected. "Really? What makes you think that?"

"He's turned into . . . well, you saw how he acted. He's gotten himself too wrapped up in his legal practice and other business to have much of a family life. He didn't even plan a real funeral for his wife. What kind of a husband does that?" She lowered her voice to a whisper. "Molly's minister wasn't even there, like she would have wanted."

"It was very unusual, that is for sure. And frankly, I would have expected that you'd be in on the planning. You know Molly better than anyone, even Will."

Her eyes filled with tears. "I know. She should have had a proper service, one that anyone could come to. Anyone that wanted to be there."

I reached over and gently closed my hand over hers. "You can still have one, you know. And I think you should."

She nodded. "I'll talk to the minister."

"Mrs. Ryland, this is sort of a prying question, but did Molly ever talk about leaving Will, getting a divorce?"

"She didn't, but I suggested it when I saw how unhappy she was."

"And what did she say about that?"

"She didn't want to even think about that. She thought maybe if they had children that would make them close again.

Molly wouldn't go into details, but I think she was either seeing a fertility doctor or looking into adoption. I wanted to tell her that children do not make a bad marriage better, but I kept that to myself because a baby would have brought her such joy."

Her lips quivered, and I gave her a minute before I switched gears. "Okay, this is a change of subject, but there's something you need to know. I'm just going to come right out and say it. Emmy Anders was arrested for Molly's murder yesterday. That's why she's in jail."

Mrs. Ryland stared at me for a while before she responded. "Emmy Anders? How could that be? I've talked to her at church a few times, and she seemed kind, hardly a violent type."

I nodded. "I guess we don't always know."

"But why on earth would the police think she killed Molly?" She was so matter-of-fact it was obvious the news hadn't sunk in.

"You'll have to talk to them, but let's just say the reason they're convinced is because of something she was charged with in the past, and because of some evidence they found at her house. Assistant Chief Lonsbury was planning to talk to you, but I wanted you to know before you heard it from someone else."

Except Will Dalton, maybe. It would have been the natural thing for him to do before or after the service—take his mother-in-law aside to talk about Emmy's arrest. They were the two most invested in seeing that justice was served.

Mrs. Ryland nodded. "What an awful thing."

"The police may be right, but I'm not convinced. And I

feel I owe it to Molly to find out the truth so she can rest in peace."

Mrs. Ryland grabbed my hand in both of her bony ones and squeezed. I was surprised she had so much strength. "I want to help, so tell me what I can do."

Oh boy. "Um, I don't know if that's such a good idea. I mean, the police would not be happy if they knew what I was up to in the first place, and if they found out I'd dragged you into it all, they would be doubly unhappy. I don't want to get you in any more trouble than you're already in." I hadn't meant to bring up the crime she was charged with committing. "Sorry."

Mrs. Ryland lifted a hand like it was all right. "Cami, Molly is my daughter. I let her down when I married her stepfather and didn't see what was going on. I have never been able to forgive myself for that. *I'm* the one who owes it to her to find out the truth. Then when I die we can both rest in peace. Together."

Molly's mother's face held the most earnest, determined look, and I couldn't disappoint her. Mark would kill me and Clint would want to do something even worse if they knew what I was about to agree to. "All right, Mrs. Ryland, you're in."

"Good." She tapped her hands on the table.

"And there is something important you can do, when you're up to it, of course."

"What's that?"

"Help me find your stepson. We need to locate Troy."

She gave a single nod. "So you *do* think Troy . . . was involved in . . ."

"I honestly have no idea. But we know he blackmailed Molly, until she cut him off, that is."

She let out a noisy breath of air. "I'll see what I can do, but I'm not even sure where to start."

"His photo would be a good place to begin."

She rubbed one hand with the other. "Molly may have missed one somehow. I'll see what I can find."

"Thanks. Pinky mentioned someone who was in her shop shortly before Molly died. It was a man asking for a blonde who worked there. If Pinky saw a picture of Troy, she could tell us if it was him or not."

"But Molly knows Troy, and if she had seen him, the least she would have done was to call me right away and tell me."

That was a good point. "I have my doubts it was Troy, because like you said, Molly knew him. Whoever that man is, he probably had nothing to do with what happened. But it's good to eliminate all the people I have questions about."

"That is a wise way to go about it."

"We don't have the authority to go to the county and ask them to do one of those composite drawings, but . . ." I thought a moment. "I know of someone, an artist who's one of Pinky's regular customers. She might be talented at drawing faces or at least know someone who is. We'd need your help to do that, of course."

Mrs. Ryland nodded. "Cami, you should go into police work."

The suggestion made me smile. "No thanks, I'm way happier staying in the background."

"I'll let you know if I happen to locate a picture of Troy. Or even his father, since Troy looked just like him."

"If you find one, great. If not, we look for an artist." I held out my hand for her. "We have a sort-of plan, Mrs. Ryland." When she took my hand in hers, we shook on it.

"It's a place to start. And please, call me Irene."

When I got back to the shops, the looks on their faces told me Pinky and Erin were ready to hear the details about Molly's private service. There were no customers around, and they dragged me to a back table. "Spit it out, every single word," Pinky said.

"Okay, this is going to sound nasty, but I don't think Will Dalton has a caring bone in his body."

"What makes you say that?" Erin said.

"Not only did he not tell Molly's mother about the service in the first place, he didn't even introduce her to the other people who were there."

"*No,*" Erin and Pinky said together.

"And when Will saw me, he gave me the coldest stare ever. But then he seemed to catch himself and put on this show, acting like he was glad Mrs. Ryland was there after all. At least he didn't kick me out. And none of his family was there. It was like he invited eight strangers who didn't even really know Molly to show up, say a few words about her, and then have lunch."

Pinky leaned forward, crossed her arms, and plopped her hands on her shoulders. "In my whole life, I've never heard anything even close to that."

"I know. Get this, when it was Will's turn to speak, he broke down and cried instead of saying a word about Molly.

At least he acted like he was crying. I'm not so sure. And then he excused himself and disappeared."

"Okay, that is strange," Erin said.

I nodded. "We didn't even stay for lunch. Mrs. Ryland had no idea who the people were, and it was obvious she'd had enough."

"I wouldn't mind eating with a bunch of strangers, so I'd have stayed. I bet it was good, too. And Cami, you might have found out why Will thought those people were special enough to make the cut," Pinky said.

"I didn't have the stomach for it—either the people or the food, no matter how good or fancy it might have been."

"So you think Will was putting on an act?" Erin asked.

"It seemed that way to me. When Molly's mom said a few words about her, Will's reaction struck me as wrong, and I figured out why that was on the way over here."

"What was it?" Pinky said.

"So if I said, 'Molly didn't deserve to die like that,' show me what you'd do." Both Pinky and Erin shook their heads. "I thought so. That's what I would have done. You shook your heads because you are agreeing that, 'No, she did not deserve that.' You know what Will did? He nodded."

"I don't know; some people might nod," Pinky said.

"That's true. They would if they thought she deserved what she got," I said.

"Pinky, think about it. Cami is right." Erin reached over and gave my wrist a squeeze. "Great observation, Cami. I seriously doubt I would have caught that."

"If you were watching Will Dalton like I was, you would have."

....

Pinky left for home after we'd finished talking. I hadn't revealed that Mrs. Ryland—Irene—was my new partner in crime solving. There was no sense dragging them into it. After all, Irene was a felon. Knowing Erin, she would make me swear to cease and desist, and Pinky would inadvertently tell Mark what I was up to. It was all going to come out eventually, anyway.

Erin spent time studying the various snow globes and where they had come from, how old they were, and so on. My parents had written up cards for the ones we had a history on. Erin was one sharp cookie and memorized information on a number of the snow globes in short order. "Gee whiz, Cami, I don't know why I never really paid much attention before. You have some very cool and unique snow globes."

"We do. You know, when I was young I thought all snow globes were special. Now I know some are more so than others. So are you feeling more comfortable, like you can run the place alone, if you have to?"

She set a snow globe down and looked at me. "Why, you're not planning on leaving, are you?"

I chuckled. "No, but there might be a time when Pinky or I need to run somewhere for a few minutes. We really appreciate you filling in, Erin. It's been slow lately, but it'll start to pick up, and by Black Friday, look out."

She nodded. "And since I'm off from school Thanksgiving weekend, I can be here just about whenever you need me."

"Good to know. I haven't been through a Black Friday yet, working on the retail side of it. And I am not looking forward to it, at all." I checked the time. "Erin, feel free to take off anytime."

"All right, I'll get going then and will catch you later."

It seemed like three days had passed instead of just one when closing time finally rolled around. Between the court proceedings, the odd man's visit to our shops, Molly's memorial service, making a pact with Irene Ryland, and working in between it all, it was an emotional and stressful day.

But there was something else I needed to do.

I locked up the shops and drove my car over to the courthouse. Although it was only a few blocks, it was cold out, and I didn't want to walk back for my car. I braced myself against the brisk wind and wondered what kind of a winter was ahead of us. If the near-freezing mid-November temperatures were any indication, it could be a doozy. I'd grown accustomed to the milder weather in Washington, D.C., these last years, and it'd be my first full Minnesota winter in a long time.

When I walked into the jail lobby, I got quite the surprise. Irene Ryland was leaving one side of a visiting booth, and Emmy Anders was leaving the other. Was visiting the person accused of killing your daughter even allowed? Why would Irene want to do that? Not to mention how awkward it would be for Emmy.

"What are you doing here?" I said when Irene came toward me.

She waved me over toward some chairs on the other side of the lobby, and we sat down. "I had to ask her. I needed to know what she'd say about Molly," Irene explained.

"To tell you the truth, I'm surprised she agreed to see you."

"Emmy knew me from church, and she knew Molly from your shops, of course. But she didn't know she was my daughter."

"I guess that explains it. So what did you all say?"

"I asked her if she knew what happened to Molly, and she said she didn't. She assured me she had nothing to do with her death."

"Anything else?"

"She apologized to me. Emmy said she and Molly had not gotten along very well, and she was sorry she'd been crabby to her. She was having a bad day." It had been a bad day for all of us, Molly in particular. "Emmy said she did not poison Molly and thinks she was framed."

"Framed?"

"That's what she said. She told me what happened with her husband, and that she was accused of killing him, too. She thinks someone planted evidence at her house that would make her look like the guilty one."

"Really? That's what she said?"

Irene nodded. "Emmy looked me straight in the eyes when she said she didn't do it, and then she said, 'Cross my heart and hope to die.' I believed her."

Cross my heart and hope to die? "Okay, well I'm holding on to the hope that we get to the bottom of what happened very soon."

"Cami, are you here to talk to Emmy, too?"

"Yes. I haven't known her that long, but I'm not convinced she's guilty. And if she isn't, I want to do what I can for her and get to the bottom of Molly's death like we discussed."

Irene nodded then stood up. "The last two days have taken a toll, and I need to get home."

I gave her a gentle hug. "Get a good night's sleep." I watched her walk out and get into a waiting cab, then I went to the booth where the officer sat. I handed him my driver's license and asked if I could please see Emaline Andersohn. He checked my identification then told me to take a seat in visiting booth B. I put my license back and waited for Emmy. It took a number of minutes until she got there.

Emmy picked up the phone with one hand and touched her heart with the other. "Thanks for coming to see me, Camryn."

"You're welcome. I wanted to let you know I was in court earlier today, when you went before the judge."

"I didn't see you there." She frowned slightly. "So you know about my bail."

"Yes."

"I'm getting the money together to get out."

Irene hadn't mentioned that. "You are? Five hundred thousand is a big chunk of change."

She lifted her shoulders in a small shrug. "I know it could have been worse. I need to put up ten percent of the bail to bond out. Since I don't have any family around, my best friend from childhood is helping me. Her name is on my bank accounts. I made sure of it after my husband died, in case something happens to me. My attorney advised me to do that, otherwise things get tied up for a long time. And I'm glad I did it now that I can't get to the bank myself."

"It's good to have a trusted friend. Emmy, I talked to Molly's mother, and she told me about the visit you two had."

Emmy shook her head. "When she said that Molly was her daughter, I didn't know what to say. All I could do was tell her how sorry I was for her loss, but that I was innocent of what I was charged with. I did not poison Molly." She pointed her finger into the little ledge in front of her to emphasize each of the last five words.

She almost had me convinced. "The question is, who did? Irene said you think someone planted the evidence in your garage?"

"I can't think of how else it got there."

"But how would anyone do that?"

"I'm going to check my garage doors and windows when they release me."

"The other question is why."

"If someone knew of my past, they'd think I'd be a good person to pin it on."

That was a stretch, but I didn't want to argue the point. "Emmy, you've had a couple of days to think about it. Was there anyone in the shops—a man, in particular—that acted suspicious to you?"

"There were a lot of people there that day, and then we had all that commotion with the broken snow globe. The woman who broke it acted suspicious, but there was no one else who stands out in my mind. The people all kind of blurred together." Blurred, like the faces in my dreams. A small shiver crawled up my spine.

"When do you think you'll get out?"

"I'm not sure of the time, but it should be in the morning. My friend is meeting with the bondsman first thing."

"Good." At least I hoped it was. "Call me if you need a ride, all right?"

Her wrinkles deepened when she smiled. "Thank you, Camryn, for coming to see me and for believing me."

I hadn't specifically said that I did but, "You're welcome," came out of my mouth, anyway.

It was a relief to get in my car knowing I was headed for home and a meal of leftovers. My relief was short-lived, however, when I drove by Curio Finds and saw a sliver of light inside the shop. "You have got to be kidding me," I said out loud. There was no vehicle coming from either direction, so I did a U-turn in the middle of the road and parked in front of the shop.

It was the bathroom light again, and I know I'd turned it off. I was positive. There was no way I was going in there alone, and Erin lived the closest. I pulled out my phone and dialed her number, grateful when she answered right away. "Hi, Erin, are you busy?"

"Just finished some takeout and was about to correct some papers. What's up?"

"I'm sitting in my car in front of the shop. There's a light on inside, and I'm afraid to go in alone."

"Cami, are you serious?"

"Yes, the light was not on when I left, but it is now."

"You need to call the police. If someone's in there, you and I can't go traipsing in there unarmed."

"I don't think anyone—a person, at least—is in there, because it's happened before. Last time Pinky and I checked and no one was hiding anywhere."

"Cami, I will go down there on one condition: call Mark and have him meet us."

"Okay." The problem was that when I called Mark, he happened to be with Clint, and Clint decided he should come on down, too. One little unexplained light was turning into a dog and pony show.

Erin got there first, followed by Mark and Clint in their separate police cars a minute later. It was the first time I'd seen Clint since we'd kissed, and having a crowd around eased what might have been an awkward moment. I had my key ready to open the door as soon as we were all assembled.

Mark pointed at the shop window. "Cami, so you turned off all the lights except the security one, and then when you drove by twenty minutes later the bathroom light was on?"

"Yes."

"Go ahead and unlock the door, and Mark and I will check it out," Clint said.

I did just that, but as soon as they stepped into the shop, the light went out. Erin grabbed my gloved hand in hers, and when I looked at her, all I saw was her dark eyes open wide. I pulled her with me into the shop, and we nearly bumped into Mark's back.

"What the hey?" Mark said. Both he and Clint drew their guns then crept toward the bathroom.

Erin and I huddled near the front window, trying to prepare ourselves for whatever lay ahead, but it was over almost before it began. Clint took out his flashlight, flipped the switch with his free hand, and pushed the door wide open with his foot as Mark trained his gun on whomever might be inside.

"Nobody there," Clint mouthed then tilted his head toward the storeroom. He and Mark checked that, the small office, and all of Brew Ha-Ha.

When they came back into Curio Finds, their guns were back in their holsters. "If I hadn't seen it with my own eyes, I wouldn't have believed it," Mark said.

"The last time this happened, the light stayed on until I turned the switch off."

"This happened before?" Clint said.

I didn't want to explain and nodded instead. "I'm going to get an electrician in to check the wiring."

"Smart idea to help prevent a fire call here," Clint said. So much for a worry-free evening. I'd be imagining an electrical fire smoldering in the building all night long.

Mark stuck his nose up in the air. "I don't detect any hot wires or burning smells in here."

Clint took a few sniffs himself. "You're right, and it could be a fluke. Maybe the switch wasn't completely off and the vibrations we produced coming into the shop made it go down all the way."

"Or the place is haunted," Mark said.

I reached over and gave him a little shove. "None of that kind of talk, please."

Mark shrugged. "So what are you girls doing the rest of the night?"

"Correcting papers," Erin said.

"On a Friday night?" I said.

She smiled. "Then I'll be free for the rest of the weekend."

As I thought of a clever response, Mark honed in on me. "Cami, I know what I was going to ask you about. When I stopped in for coffee this afternoon, Pinky said you were at Will Dalton's house with Mrs. Ryland. I was wondering how that went."

Erin crossed her arms on her chest. "Just wait until you hear about that."

It didn't take long to fill them in on every detail, including what I thought about Will Dalton's behavior and how he had excluded Molly's mother.

Clint dropped his head back. "Ahhh, that's what I meant to do when I got word Irene Ryland had been released from jail. I meant to advise her that Emaline Andersohn, aka Emmy Anders, is in custody on suspicion of her daughter's murder. I got tied up on another case and forgot to take care of it."

"I told her about it after we got back from the memorial service. And you should know that Irene went to see Emmy in jail a little while ago."

"What?" Clint said, and Erin and Mark seemed equally surprised.

"I sure didn't expect her to do that, especially not today. But I think she needed to look Emmy in the eyes and ask her if she did it," I said.

"And Mrs. Andersohn said she was innocent, of course."

I shrugged. Clint could talk to Irene if he wanted a recap of their visit. "And something else you'll be notified of soon: Emmy is bailing out of jail."

"*What?*" all three of them said in perfect unison.

When I was in my car again, driving away from the shop, I shoved the mystery of the bathroom light to the back of my mind. I started mulling over all the things that had happened in the past days and wondered for the thousandth time who had killed Molly and why. And then Will Dalton worked his way back into my thoughts and made me more and more irritated. I know people do strange things under duress, but was that any kind of excuse for excluding Irene Ryland from her daughter's memorial service?

Maybe Molly had told Will her mother thought she should divorce him. That would make a guy angry, especially one who was used to getting whatever he wanted. Had he ever even lost a case in court? From what I'd heard about his reputation as a trial lawyer, I doubted it.

I wanted to keep my distance from Will but felt compelled to drive by his house. It was a little after seven, about four hours since Molly's service. I wondered how long people had stayed around after their host's sudden departure. I turned onto his street and saw his outside lights were on and lit up both the front of the house and the side by the attached garage. There was one car in the driveway—the Porsche I had parked next to earlier.

A man came out the front door and headed that direction. He looked like the man who'd spoken privately to Will at the service but had not said anything in Molly's honor. I drove past, then when I was out of sight from any prying eyes in the Dalton home, I turned around and pulled ahead enough to have a decent view of the man. He got into his car, started it, then let it idle for some minutes before he took off.

I had the irrational desire to follow him but was worried he might notice me. When he took a left at the end of the block and was out of sight, I sped up and decided to give it a shot. I checked my gas gauge. No problem there. I forgot about how weary I had been just minutes before. I was on my third or fourth wind of the day, so what the heck.

The Porsche headed west on Highway 44 out of Brooks Landing. I wondered if the man was headed home, or where else he might be going. He seemed to be the last to leave the

Daltons' home, so he had to have a close connection to Will. A friend or colleague or both. Will's law firm was in Minneapolis, about forty miles from Brooks Landing. The man might live a good long distance away, maybe on the other side of Minneapolis. People commuted many miles to jobs in the metropolitan area.

When we drove past the road that led to the Zimmers' home, I thought about how their lives would spiral even further downward if they had, in fact, tried to poison me. Emmy said she believed someone planted the cyanide to make her look guilty. Either she was trying to shift the blame away from herself or it was the truth. But I didn't see how the Zimmers could have had anything to do with that. They had no connection to Emmy unless they'd had some past dealings with her, before she moved to Brooks Landing. And what were the chances of that? But I still could not rule out the Zimmers' possible involvement in Molly's death.

And Emmy. Maybe she hadn't killed Molly, but that didn't mean she hadn't killed her husband. She said she didn't know where her husband had gotten the cyanide, but that could just be a convenient ploy to hide the truth that she had killed before and would kill again. It would have been quite the surprise to her when the Brooks Landing police force had found the hidden stash of poison.

There were many unknowns about Emmy. When she was out of jail and on the loose, I'd try to keep a watch on her, see what she was up to. And if she did something criminal, the police were just a phone call away.

I followed the Porsche and managed to keep at least one car between us all the way to Plymouth, a suburb of Minneapolis that was twenty-five miles from Brooks Landing.

He moved into a left turn lane at a stoplight, and I wasn't sure what to do. The traffic was light, so I waited until the turn arrow was green. After he turned, I did a quick maneuver into the lane and followed. That may have earned me a stop by the police if there had been any around.

The Porsche turned into an affluent neighborhood, but not as fancy as the one Dalton lived in. He pulled into a driveway, the garage door opened, and he drove in. When he got out of his car, I got a close enough look to confirm it was the guy who had exchanged private words with Will Dalton. Then he pushed a button, the door closed, and it was the end of my spying. As I drove by, something in his yard sparked my interest: a "House for Sale" sign. A classier, upscale house would better match his new-looking Porsche.

I memorized the Realtor's name and phone number. When I was farther down the block, I pulled over, found an old receipt and pen in my purse, and wrote down the information. When my adoptive sister Susan was looking to buy a home, she had gotten information on it from the county's website, including the owner, home value, and yearly taxes. I was drawn to learning more about this mysterious man. There was something about him and the way he acted around Will Dalton that concerned me. Perhaps he was his personal bodyguard or something. I circled back for his house number. If I found out his name, Mark might be willing to run a check on him to see if he had a criminal record. The man gave off those kind of vibes, in my opinion.

As I drove back to Brooks Landing I thought of all the questions I wanted to ask Molly: Were you seeing a fertility doctor? Were you thinking of adopting? Were you thinking of leaving Will Dalton? And who were the people at your memorial service, people your mother didn't even know? Did you know them, and what did you think of the big guy with the full face who seemed to be in cahoots with your husband?

When I got close to Orten I made a spur-of-the-moment decision. I turned off the highway and drove to the Zimmers' house. The senator may have gone back to Washington, weekend or not. I wondered if she'd keep her connections there; maybe try out her skills as a lobbyist. Then again, if she was guilty of murder, or attempted murder, her career would no longer matter.

There were lights on in the house, and I crept by as slowly as I dared. The curtains were open, and I barely processed what I observed. Ramona and the man I'd seen in her garage were in each other's arms. They were hugging, in plain sight. What was going on? Had she dumped Peter and taken up with a new man in a matter of a few days? I pulled over to the curb and turned off my car, confident no one would see who I was in the dark.

The man put on an overcoat and turned so I got a good view of his face. He looked familiar, but I couldn't place him. He was several inches taller than Ramona, had short dark brown hair, had a round face, not unlike the shape of Ramona's, and wore glasses. I studied him for the few seconds, then it hit me. He looked a lot like the strange man who had been in the shops that morning, the man who'd left so abruptly, but I couldn't tell for sure.

A taxi drove up and stopped in front of the Zimmers' house. I slumped down in the seat as far as I could. The man walked out the front door with a suitcase and got in the cab. Ramona waved at him from inside then closed the door when the taxi left.

I sat for a moment wondering what to do with this latest information then started my car and drove away. My phone rang, and I saw it was Pinky calling. "Hi, what's up?" I said, after switching to hands-free mode.

"Are you home?" she asked.

"Uh, no, I'm just out for a drive."

"Cami, what in the world has gotten into you going for drives like this at night? Are you near downtown?"

I wasn't far from downtown Orten. "No, I'm a ways out. Why do you ask?"

"Well, I had to run to the store—I didn't have enough blueberries for my next batch of muffins. Anyway, I just drove by our shops and noticed the bathroom light is on in Curio Finds. I even stopped to make sure it wasn't a reflection, and the light is definitely on."

Again? "That is too odd. The same thing happened earlier tonight, so I called Erin. And she made me call Mark, who was with Clint. All three of them showed up to help me check it out. But the light went off as soon as we stepped inside the store."

Pinky's voice rose in volume. "Get out of here. That's like the third time it's happened. Do you think Molly's ghost is haunting the shop?"

"No, I do not. I mean, this light thing could have been going on for weeks and we just didn't know about it. We need to get the wiring checked, so do you know a good electrician?"

"Yeah, but you should find out who your parents usually use."

"All right, I'll give my dad a call. Thanks for letting me know about the light, Pink."

"Sure thing. See you in the morning."

I hung up then glanced at the time on the clock. It was 8:27, still early enough to call Dad. I pulled over to dial my parents' number then got back on the road when the phone started ringing. Mom answered. "Hi, it's me. I have a question for Dad if he's there."

She chuckled. "Since I'm here, you can bet he is, too. Here you go."

Her laugh lightened my heart. My parents had spent a lot of quality time together since Mom was diagnosed with cancer.

Dad cleared his throat. "Cami, all things considered, how are you holding up? Mom and I have been wondering if there have been any new developments in Molly's case."

"Some pretty big things happened today, actually. I'll tell you all about them tomorrow when we have more time, if that's okay. The reason I'm calling is to get the name of your favorite electrician. I think there's something wrong with the wiring at the shop, because the bathroom light keeps coming on by itself."

"Say what?"

I told him again then added, "Yes, it's happened at least three times now. And it's kind of freaky. Pinky just called me to say it was on, and that's the second time tonight."

"I better run down there."

"You don't have to do that. I'm out . . . running an errand, so I'll pop by in about ten minutes."

"You call me right away if you smell smoke. Otherwise, I'll get ahold of the electrician first thing in the morning.

That'll be one less thing for you to worry about. How does that sound?"

It sounded wonderful. "Thanks, Dad."

I drove into Brooks Landing, parked in front of Curio Finds, and wondered if the wires had started smoldering in the past couple of hours. The light was on in the bathroom when Pinky had been by a short time ago, but it wasn't on now. There had to be a logical explanation. So far we'd ruled out anyone hiding in the shops.

My dad had asked me to check for signs of burning wires, and the only thing that got me out of the car was my devotion to my parents. I sent up a prayer that all would be well, turned the key in the shop lock, and opened the door. I had a keen sense of smell—in fact, I'd learned I could even detect cyanide—so I reasoned there was no cause to step all the way into the shop.

Instead, I stuck my head in and sniffed the air, right, left, and in between. Roasted coffee beans was the predominant aroma. Nothing burning, no hot smells. That was a good enough test to assure me all was well in Curio Finds. And the wiring would get a thorough check in the morning.

I turned around and headed home for the second time that night. This time it was for real. When I let myself in the back door, I saw that the light on my answering machine was blinking. I slipped out of my coat and dropped it on a chair then leaned against the counter while I pushed play on the machine.

The first message was from Irene Ryland thanking me again for helping her and for taking her to Molly's service.

The second was a disturbing one from Will Dalton. "Ms.

Brooks, to let you know, I think it was inappropriate and unfortunate that you forced your way into my home today, particularly given the circumstances of my wife's death." *Inappropriate, unfortunate, forced, wife's death.* Oh my.

His voice held a tone of controlled anger, like he was talking with his jaw clamped shut. I had unthinkingly made things worse for Pinky and my parents and me. And now the question was, what was Will planning to do about it?

I wanted to call Pinky and warn her, but then she'd forget what she was doing and burn the blueberry muffins she was baking. And I couldn't deliver upsetting news like that to my parents so late in the evening. Erin was the best choice at the moment.

I called her on my cell phone so I could play the message left on my home machine. "Hi, Erin, still correcting papers?"

"Oh no, it was only a few assignments."

"Well, do you have time to listen to something? It's a message I got from Molly's husband."

"I can hear in your voice that it's not good."

"No, it is not. Here you go." I turned the volume up and held my cell phone close to the machine.

"*Cami!*" she yelled when it stopped. "Play it again." I did so two more times. When I put the phone back to my ear, Erin said, "You are in such deep doo-doo, and I'm wondering what we need to do about it."

My stomach tightened when she voiced what I already knew—I had made an awful situation even worse. But there were two bright spots to focus on. Neither Pinky nor I had committed a crime, despite what Will may try to pin on us. And we had a strong team of supporters who would help us through the worst of the worst.

"Will Dalton has all the money in the world and can make things pretty miserable for Pinky and my family if he wants to. Knowing you're there for us means a lot, Erin," I said.

"We've all had our turns needing help over the years."

"It's hard to believe, but this makes the whole scandal with the Zimmers seem pretty minor."

"I guess, and the bright spot in all of that is that it brought you back to Brooks Landing."

"Very true." I paused for a second. "I should tell you what I did tonight."

"What?"

I filled Erin in on my trip to Will Dalton's house, following his friend home to Plymouth, and then swinging by the Zimmers' house and watching Ramona and her house guest bidding each other a warm good-bye.

"Cami Brooks, are you turning into a spy or what?"

"Well, maybe I am. There are strange things going on with all these people, and I want to find out what they're up to."

"I'll give you that much. Molly's husband sounds like he's fallen off the deep end. And that Ramona has some nerve casting stones at you when it sounds like she's involved in some hanky-panky of her own. Which reminds me, when are you supposed to get the results back on that poison pen letter she dropped off for you?"

"I'm hoping early next week. Clint didn't know for sure. If it turns out there is poison in the letter, I think it's the link to Molly's death. What a thing to have to tell her mother; Molly was not the intended victim after all. I was."

"That'd be a tough one for sure."

"And then we have the case of the bathroom light in the shop."

"It's turned into a case?"

"Practically. Pinky drove by a while ago, and the light was on again. By the time I got there to check it out, it was off."

"You are getting it checked before the place burns down, I hope."

"Dad is on it. Erin, remember how we used to look forward to Friday nights so we could go out and have fun?"

"Yeah, now it's all about schoolwork and spying."

I laughed. "Thanks for listening. I feel a hundred percent better than I did a few minutes ago."

"Anytime, my friend. And feel free to call if you need help in the shops tomorrow. I have nothing planned."

"Will do. 'Bye for now."

Talking to Erin perked me up and also relaxed me at the same time. My stomach gave another growl, reminding me it had been over twelve hours since breakfast, my only meal of the day. I opened the refrigerator, pulled out the stir fry leftovers, and was about to dish some up when my cell phone rang.

"Camryn, it's Clint."

"Hi."

"I thought you'd want to know the light is on in your shop bathroom again, if you want to run down here."

"Pinky noticed the same thing about an hour ago. And when I went to check, it was off and I didn't smell any wires burning. What's causing it is beyond me, but we're getting the wiring checked, and I'm holding on to the hope that everything will be fine until morning."

"If you say so. I'll have the night patrol pay extra attention, watch for any smoke, and so on."

He deserved credit for that. "Thanks, Clint. Have a good night."

"And the same to you, Camryn."

As I spooned stir fry onto a plate, I thought about the bizarre bathroom light situation and wondered how it had started all of a sudden. "Molly, I know I'm really just talking to myself and that you can't hear me. But hypothetically speaking, if you have anything to do with that light going on and off, will you just quit it? Please."

I heated my meal in the microwave and poured myself a glass of milk. I was tired, weary right down to my bones, and hoped the milk would help settle my nerves enough for a restful night's sleep. I sat down with my dinner at the kitchen table and thought back on a day packed full of unimaginable events. Hopefully it'd be easier to digest my food than it was to digest everything that had happened since morning.

Molly's mother had been released from jail, and Emmy would bail out tomorrow. After demonstrating poor judgment, strange behavior, and leaving me that message, it was anyone's guess what Will Dalton would do next. And Ramona Zimmer may have lost her mind, was all I could figure. I knew people killed others for reasons that made no sense to anyone else. But risking spending the rest of her days in prison because she lost an election and thought I should pay with my life was not anywhere close to rational, if that was, indeed, the case.

To top things off, if she'd taken up with a man and convinced him to do the dirty deed, that was exponentially worse. There had been no sign of her husband, Peter, the last two times I'd scoped out their house. It was possible he had either moved on to his next gift horse or Ramona had finally given him his marching orders.

My mind switched to Emmy Anders and how she had gone from sweet little old lady to crabby employee to murder suspect in a few short days. It seemed the police had no inclination to look beyond her as the guilty party. If she proved to be the one responsible, so be it. If not, we owed it to Molly and Irene Ryland and . . . Will Dalton to find out who was. I gave myself a pinch in the arm because I'd grudgingly forced myself to include him.

Molly's stepbrother definitely needed to be tracked down. At least he was on the police's radar. They knew he had blackmailed Molly for thousands and thousands of dollars. If he was capable of doing that, it wasn't too much of a stretch to think he'd seek revenge when the money stream came to an abrupt halt.

I finished the last bite of food, put my dishes in the sink, then went into my bedroom and put on my pajamas. I didn't care that I wasn't out with friends doing something exciting. All I wanted was a boring, uneventful end to the day and a dreamless sleep. I got half my wish.

Molly's ghost came to me right before it was time to get up the next morning. Irene Ryland and I were in Molly's den with a number of people who all had their backs to us. Molly came up to her mother and me and smiled. She reached out toward us but didn't touch us. "I'm glad you found each other," she said. My alarm rang before either her mother or I could answer.

"Another minute and I would have missed your visit, Molly." I turned off the alarm and smiled. My heart wasn't pounding, and I wasn't scared out of my wits. Was I getting used to Molly's ghost visiting me in my dreams? Maybe I was less afraid because it was morning, or maybe it was because Irene was there, too. I did not know. "Molly, we will find out the truth so you can rest in peace." And I can quit obsessing about what really happened in Curio Finds on that fateful day.

12

I was barely out of bed when Irene Ryland phoned. "Cami, I hope I'm not calling too early."

"No, not at all."

"I wanted you to know that I was going through some boxes this morning and found a picture of Troy."

"That is great news! Would it be okay if I stopped by your house this morning before I go to work?"

"Of course."

"Wonderful." I did a quick calculation of when I needed to be at the shops. I tried to get there a little earlier on Saturdays. "All right then, I'll be over in about thirty minutes if that works."

"That's fine, and I'll have coffee ready."

Coffee sounded good. "Thanks."

I wanted the Brooks Landing Police to know about the

photo, and to see if there were any updates on Troy Ryland, but I didn't feel like talking to Clint, so I called Mark on his work cell phone. It was official business, after all.

"Hi, Mark, are you working today?"

"Oh yeah, out on patrol cruising around the neighborhoods so the folks know we're looking out for them."

"I've heard people appreciate that. Do you have a minute?"

"Sure, what's up?"

"I just got off the phone with Molly's mother. She found a photo of Troy Ryland, and I'm going over there to check it out."

"Clint will be glad to hear it. We've been running up against brick walls trying to find the guy. He doesn't have a Minnesota driver's license or even an ID. He's never been arrested. No mug shots, fingerprints. And the post-office box in St. Paul belongs to a guy with a different name. And it has for years."

No driver's license or identification in Minnesota? And the P.O. box number that Irene gave Clint is not in Troy's name? "That's odd. So it's possible he moved away to parts unknown."

"Seems like it's more than just possible." Mark got a call via the police radio, answered the dispatcher, then said, "I was going to offer to meet you over at Mrs. Ryland's place, but I gotta take this gas drive-off call."

"No biggie, I'll see what she has and let you know."

"Roger that."

M y dad phoned as I was putting on my makeup. "Good morning, sweetie. Allen, the electrician we like, will be down to the shop about nine thirty. He thought that should give him enough time to size things up before you open. And if he needs to replace any wiring, we'll figure out the best time to get that done."

"I'm glad. It'll be a relief to get it checked out."

"Yes, indeed. Mom and I don't have much planned for the day, so give a shout if you need me."

"Thanks, Dad, will do."

I sped through the rest of my morning routine and arrived at Irene's house a few minutes ahead of schedule. When she opened the door, my heart went out to her. I saw the drawn look of exhaustion on her face and tried to imagine what it was like to be in her shoes. Her life had gone from normal, as she knew it, to anything but. I gave her a hug, careful not to squeeze as tightly as I wanted to.

She patted my arms when we'd finished. "Thank you, Cami, I needed that. Come right in. The coffee is ready, and Troy's picture is on the kitchen table."

I followed Irene, once again surprised that despite her medical condition, she had a fairly sprightly gait. If push came to shove, she would probably beat me in a footrace. She walked to the table, picked up the photo, then handed it to me. It was an older snapshot of a young man some distance from the camera. He was standing by a tree and had one hand raised like he was waving. I was hoping for a close-up shot, but this would have to do.

As I studied the photo, Irene set a cup of coffee on the table in front of me. "When was this photo taken?" I asked.

"It must have been around the time I married his father, or within a few years, anyway. Troy would have been eighteen when we got married. His face hasn't changed much over the years; at least, it hadn't. Unless he gained or lost a lot of weight since the last time I saw him, or grew a beard, something like that."

"You know what? It's something to go on. And how old is Troy now?"

She thought for a few seconds. "He'd be forty-three, a little more than six years older than Molly."

I held up the picture. "Is it all right if I take this to the police? They haven't been able to locate a photo of Troy. I guess he doesn't have a driver's license."

"He used to, I think, unless he was driving out here without a license back then."

"I don't know the answer to that. I'm sitting here thinking that maybe the police can do one of those face-aging things to get a better idea of what Troy looks like now."

"That is a very good idea." Irene sighed. "It's about impossible for us older ones to keep up with all the latest technology."

I smiled and didn't correct her by saying face-aging computer programs had been around as long as I could remember. And she wasn't that old. "Irene, you gave the assistant police chief Troy's P.O. box number the other day."

"Yes, I did."

"Any idea how long he'd had the box?"

"Not really. Years, I guess."

Years, that's what I was hoping. He must have rented it under a different name. "Hmm, maybe we can save the police some time and legwork by checking to see if he still has the box. It might be worthwhile to pay a visit to the St. Paul Post Office."

"I'm not sure I understand. I don't think the postal workers are allowed to tell people who rents the boxes."

"I'm sure you're right about that. What I was thinking is . . . well, I used to have a post-office box myself, and I didn't get my mail every day. If I wasn't expecting anything special, sometimes it'd be a few days before I checked. Anyway, when I had mail or maybe when my box was getting too full, I'd get a text message from the post office telling me that. I say we send Troy a letter of some sort to that box, something marked "Important" that entices him to go there to pick it up. I'll arrange to have the next day off, and I just bet he'll show up to get his mail."

Irene tapped the table. "I'll go with you."

I shook my head. "Thanks, but I don't think that'd work, because Troy knows you, and if sees you, who knows what might happen. He doesn't know me. If it works out, I'll try to take a photo of him that I can hand over to the police. Maybe between the St. Paul and Brooks Landing police departments, they can set up some sort of sting to catch him and put him behind bars for a long, long time."

She smiled. "That would be a very good thing." Then her face sobered and she grabbed ahold of my hand. "Especially if it turns out Troy took my Molly's life."

Her words took my breath away, and I nodded. "Especially then."

I walked into Brew Ha-Ha and did my best to look pleasant when I greeted Pinky and her Saturday morning customers. The weekend crowd was different from weekday regulars. People were more relaxed and gave the impression they had no better place to be. I caught Pinky's attention and tipped my head toward my shop. "Got a second?"

She nodded, threw the towel she was holding on the back counter, and followed me.

"Okay, you're busy, so I'll just tell you two quick things. An electrician will be here at nine thirty to check out that goofy bathroom light." I pulled the picture of Troy out of my purse. "And Irene Ryland found this. I know it's old and it's a small image, but does he look familiar to you? As in, could he have been the one in the shops the day Molly died?"

Pinky took the photo, moved her head right then left, and shrugged. "Holy moly, Cami, I don't know. It's possible, but I wouldn't swear to it. If I saw him in person I think I'd recognize him, but I sure can't tell from this little photo. How long ago was this taken, anyway?"

"Probably twenty years."

She shook her head. "Nope, sorry, I can't tell much from this."

"I'm going to see if we can get a face-aging thing done. That should help."

"Maybe." The bell on her door dinged. "Duty calls."

"Do you need my help?"

She shook her head on the way out. "I'm good for now, anyway."

I turned the lights on in Curio Finds but kept the sign turned to "Closed" for the time being. Allen the electrician came in with his small bag of equipment a few minutes later. He was around fifty, and his lips were turned up in a perpetual smile.

"Hi, Cami, it's been some years since I've seen you. You're looking good as ever."

"Thanks, Allen, and you, too. I appreciate your quick response, and on a Saturday, besides."

"No problem. Saturday, Monday, makes no difference to

me." He pointed to the back storeroom. "The electrical box is back there, if memory serves."

"Yes, it is."

"And your dad said it's the bathroom light that's been acting up, huh?"

Acting up was a good way to describe it. I nodded.

"I'll take a look at that first. The problem might be with the switch." He went in and flipped the switch up and down a few times then removed the plate and had a look. "Seems to be fine. Wires aren't loose and don't have any little breaks or anything." I followed Allen into the storeroom. He slipped off his canvas jacket and dropped it on the floor. He opened the small metal door of the electrical box. It had a single row of fuses in it. He pointed. "It's nice they're marked." He tapped one of the fuses. "This here is the one to the bathroom, the office, and the storeroom. I'll see if there's a loose wire."

"*Cami*," Pinky called from the archway.

"Carry on, Allen. It sounds like Pinky needs help in the coffee shop, so I'll be next door if you need me."

"Okie doke."

After I helped serve about a dozen daily specials, I returned to see if Allen had figured out the problem. He closed the fuse box and turned when he heard me behind him. "Well, there is no problem with any of the wires that I can find. They are all intact and working just fine." He tapped the wire tester he was holding against his shoulder.

"What's causing the light to act up?"

"You got me. I can put a new switch in the bathroom for the heck of it."

"Sure, go ahead, just in case it turns out to be that after all." I was in the "better safe than sorry" camp when it came to anything electrical.

Allen had completed his job by the time Curio Finds was open for business. I phoned my parents, and Mom answered. "Cami, I was just about to call you to let you know the florist is delivering the flowers to Irene Ryland today. It's a lovely basket, and I included all of our names, if you'll pass that on to Pinky."

"Sure thing. And can you pass something on to Dad?"

"What is it?" I gave her the lowdown on Allen's inspection then ended the call when a customer came in. I had a small rush of people in the next half hour, did some great business, then nothing. I sat down on the stool behind my counter and was thinking about the electrician's inconclusive findings when Emmy Anders walked through the door. Her sudden arrival gave me a bit of a start.

Pinky picked that second to pop her head into the archway, and when she saw Emmy, her mouth dropped open like she expected the worst was about to happen. Emmy had her back to Pinky and missed her reaction. Besides, in my opinion, the worst had already happened. Molly Dalton had died in our shop.

At the moment, all I longed for was world peace.

"Emmy, hi." My cheeriness sounded less than genuine. I struggled to find something more to say, but my mind had drawn a blank.

Emmy's eyes darted toward the bathroom then back to me. The look on her face was difficult to read: maybe it was a mixed bag of regret and a sense of caution. "Hi, Cami. I feel a little funny asking you this, but I was wondering if you might be able to break away sometime this morning to give me a ride home."

Pinky's eyebrows shot up, and she could hold her tongue no longer. "Hi, Emmy. Cami can break away right now. Everything is under control in the shops, right Cami?" I could read between the lines and figured out that Pinky did not want Emmy hanging around in case a customer came in and recognized her.

And I had offered to give her a ride. "Um, right. Now is a fine time to run you home."

Emmy smiled and nodded. "Thank you, dearie."

"Let me grab my coat and purse." I hurried to the back room and got what I needed. I fished the keys out of my pocket and ushered Emmy out the door. The cold air made both of us pull our collars up around our necks on the walk to my car.

When we were inside and after I'd started the engine, Emmy turned and answered the question before I asked it. "After I bonded out they turned me loose and I was too embarrassed to call my neighbor, Lester, to come and pick me up. I hope you don't mind me showing up unannounced like that."

"Of course not. I'm glad you did."

"I know I have some work ahead of me to prove to everyone that I am innocent."

I looked Emmy squarely in the eyes and believed in my heart of hearts she was telling the truth. But I needed a final assurance. I lifted my right arm. "Emmy, raise your right hand." She looked puzzled but did as I asked. "Do you swear once and for all that you had nothing whatsoever to do with Molly's death?"

Her lips curled up then her face turned solemn. "I do so swear, before God and before you, Camryn Brooks."

That sealed the deal for me. I reached over, took her hand in mine, and we shook hands.

"Tell me what I can do to help you," I said as I moved my left hand to the steering wheel and my right to the gear shift.

"I am grateful for your offer, but I just don't know yet. You have no idea how much your friendship and support means to me. I can't adequately tell you."

I nodded and shifted into drive. "The way you said it was ten times more than adequate. I do have one question, though."

"What's that?"

"Why did you leave the night Molly was killed? It wasn't because your friend needed help, was it?"

Emmy shook her head. "No. Well she is sick, but her daughter is staying with her. I didn't know what to think when the police came over and told me about Molly. They questioned me about what I knew, and I didn't know anything. It brought back all those terrible memories of when Howard died. I had to leave town for a day or two."

"I've been wondering about it, so thanks for leveling with me."

Clint was my second unexpected visitor at the shop that day. He was wearing street clothes and his normal stern look. He walked toward me with purpose, and I felt myself tensing up. "Officer Mark tells me Irene Ryland found a photo of her miscreant stepson and you were picking it up so we could have a look."

"Yes and yes. I meant to get back to Mark about it. He usually stops in earlier than this."

"Calls for service have kept him pretty busy today. Do you have the photo here?"

I nodded. "I'll get it." I retrieved it for him then handed it over.

Clint stared at it for a while. "How old was he in the photo?"

"Somewhere between eighteen and early twenties, Irene thinks. He'd be forty-three now."

"So we'd be safe to age him twenty-two to twenty-four years."

"We?"

He nodded. "As in me. We have a software program at the PD that does computer-generated age progression."

"Our PD? Brooks Landing?"

A hint of a smile crossed Clint's face. "Yes, we can do that even out here in Hicksville. Wonders never cease."

I guess not. I had planned on asking Mark about getting an aged image of Troy, but it seemed Clint was a step ahead. "When do you think you might work on that?"

He opened his jacket and slid the photo in his shirt pocket. "As soon as I get back to the PD."

I was curious about the process. "Would be all right if I came along and watched?"

He frowned while he thought about it. "Well, I suppose that would be okay."

"Let me talk to Pinky, see if it's all right to leave." *Again.* Erin had volunteered to come in, so that was an option.

I felt Clint following behind me. Pinky's eyes rose up over my head, and she smiled at him. "What are you two cooking up?" she said.

Clint patted his pocket. "Something that requires detective skills more than culinary skills: bringing this bad boy's appearance into the right decade."

Pinky was puzzled. I laughed when I guessed what she was thinking. "Clint's not talking about himself. He's got the old picture of Troy in his pocket."

"Oh, okay."

She still didn't understand, so I added, "They have a computer program at the police station that ages faces. He's going to use it on Troy's picture and said I could watch."

Pinky smiled. "Aha."

I glanced around and saw people at the back tables. "Erin offered to come in today if we need her."

Pinky threw her towel on the counter. "You can thank your lucky stars, because she called a minute ago and is on her way in."

"Good."

"So grab yourselves a cup of something and get going. And I want to see what that computer program comes up with, okay?"

Clint nodded. "I'll make some copies to distribute."

"While you're at it, Clint, maybe you can make some target-sized copies so we can throw darts at it."

I wasn't sure if Pinky said that to show off in front of Clint or if she was that angry at Troy for what he had done to Molly. Either way, it brought a smile to Clint's face. And if the opportunity presented itself, I'd be up for throwing darts at the guy's picture myself. "Right," he said then turned to me. "Do you want a coffee or something?"

"No, I'm good. I'll go get my coat."

When I was ready, I spotted Clint putting a cover on a

to-go cup behind Pinky's serving counter. Great, I'd have a noisy, slurping detective on my hands. But he was willing to let me watch the process, so I would be polite, and if I felt too annoyed by the sounds, I'd excuse myself, go into the bathroom at the station, and scream silently.

We headed out to his truck. I had ridden in it once before when he picked me up from a costume party. I was dressed as Marilyn Monroe—long story. As I climbed in this time, I noticed it was much easier to gain access to the high seat without a dress and spike heels on.

"Buckle up," he said, as if I wasn't going to. *Just go with the flow, Cami.* And then he took a noisy, slurpy sip of his coffee, and I pushed the seat belt together with an extra loud snap.

It was a short ride to the city hall where the police station was housed. Since it was Saturday, the doors to the city offices and police department were locked, but there was a woman sitting at the front desk going through papers. "We staff the office during the day on Saturdays and Sundays, mostly for phone calls. And then if a citizen stops by, someone is here and can step up to the front window," he explained.

I nodded and smiled at Margaret, the same woman who had been at the front desk on my previous visit there. She frowned and nodded once in my direction.

Clint led the way to his office, set his coffee on his desk, dropped into his chair, then turned on his computer. He shrugged off his wool jacket then pulled it out from behind his back and tossed it on a side chair. He pulled the photo from his pocket and laid it on his desk. "Pull that chair around so you'll have a better view."

I slipped off my coat and hung it on the back of the chair. It was on wheels and moved easily. I pushed it closer to Clint but tried to keep as much distance between us as possible. Clint picked up the photo, put it in a scanner, then sent the image to his computer. He logged in then worked on cropping the photo. After he got rid of the background, Troy's face was front and center. He enlarged the image and made it sharper. Next he opened the software program and uploaded Troy's edited photo. After he'd punched in some data, two versions of an older Troy appeared on the screen within a minute. One image depicted a man who had lived a harder life than his counterpart.

"Amazing," I said.

"It wasn't that long ago we had to have it done manually by a specialist. Now it's a slam dunk. I'd show you what I'll supposedly look like in twenty years, but I wouldn't want to scare you."

Since Clint's looks had improved as he'd aged so far, I doubted he'd be anywhere close to scary looking as he closed in on sixty. "I'll use the chair arms for support and brace myself," I quipped.

His lips parted slightly when he grinned. "Maybe some other time. We'll do your photo at the same time."

Was he kidding? Because that would never happen. There were other, much less painful ways to embarrass myself. "We'll see."

"I'll get this updated image out to the departments around the state in an attempt to locate him. We didn't find Troy Ryland in Minnesota records, so if he's still around, he's got to be hiding under another identity." Clint raised his eyebrows. "Not that it worked out so well for Emaline Andersohn, who I understand bailed out of jail this a.m."

"She came over to the shop, and I gave her a ride home."

Clint swung his chair around so we were face-to-face,

and it felt surprisingly natural. "You don't say. Are you two bosom buddies now or what?"

"Or what. She needed a lift and I gave it to her. It's that simple." It wasn't that simple, but it was not the time to talk about the oath I had asked Emmy to take and the promise I made to help her. "Clint, the evidence you found at Emmy's house, the cyanide? How did you find it?"

"We geared up for a thorough search, but as it turned out it was a fairly easy discovery. It was in a box with some glass ornaments, not very well hidden at all. Who knows, maybe Emaline thought it was. Or maybe she figured we'd never look her way in the first place. Or that we wouldn't figure out who she was."

"If it was me, I'd make sure to get rid of the evidence."

"You'd think, Camryn. But it's downright surprising how many people don't. And we have to consider the possibility that she planned to use it again on someone else." My dad had wondered the same thing. Was there any possibility Emmy was a serial killer who'd been stopped in her tracks?

"I don't believe that, and if I was a member of a jury it'd be a hard sell to prove it."

"Suit yourself, but I'd be willing to wager a bet that if Judge Terney believed Ms. Andersohn had the means to make a five hundred thousand dollar bail, he would have set it a lot higher. Usually you see a million or two on a murder suspect."

Clint's cell phone rang. "No," he said when he looked at the display. "It's our local reporter." I thought he'd let the call go to voicemail, but he braved it out instead. "Hello, Sandy . . . Yes, I can confirm that . . . What? . . . No, I can't go into details, but we'll be checking in with her. . . . She can't leave the state. . . . That's correct. . . . Sorry, but I have no further comments. Have a good one." He pushed end on his phone and shook his head. "The media will be all over this one for a day or so until they move on to the next big story. The *Star Tribune* should be calling anytime."

Clint turned back to his computer and sent an e-mail containing pertinent information on Troy, including his younger and older images, to his selected contacts. Then he printed a number of copies of the images. "An eleven-by-sixteen is the largest sheet I can print from here. Not quite the target size that Pinky asked for."

Was he serious? "You're really giving one to Pinky to throw darts at?"

"No, I was making an observation. That'd be a good example of what could get a police officer in trouble. I keep my nose clean."

That was true from all I knew about him. "That's smart. Mind if I take a closer look at the pictures?"

He handed me a copy, and I got goose bumps when it hit me that Troy's older image reminded me a little of three men I'd seen recently: the odd-acting man in the store, the man who stayed with Ramona Zimmer at her house, and the man who acted like Will Dalton's best friend. The one I'd followed home, all the way to Plymouth.

If the men were all standing side by side, their differences would probably be obvious. But their overall looks were similar. Faces on the full side, high foreheads, rounder noses, and thin lips. A general description that would fit a number of guys I knew. The man in the store and Ramona's friend looked more like the clean-living version of Troy, and Will's friend like the hard-living one. I reminded myself that they weren't real photos of Troy; they were images the computer program had conjured up as possibilities.

"I'll stop by Irene Ryland's and give her back the photo. And I'd like her opinion of how close Troy matches up to one of these images."

I was planning to visit or at least touch base with Irene myself and was tempted to ask if I could tag along. But on second thought, I decided it was better to let Clint do his thing, then I'd do mine later in the day. "As tough as this is, I know Irene would appreciate that. And if I can get a copy to show Pinky . . . Okay, I know Emmy is your suspect, but there was that someone in the shop not long before Molly died, someone who fits Troy's—and some others'—descriptions. Anyway, he asked for 'the blonde'; that could have been either Molly or me. The trouble is, Pinky's the only one we know of who saw him."

"You're back to him, are you?"

"I'm curious."

Clint's eyebrows and shoulders both lifted a tad as he handed me the photo. "If Pinky does anything more than look at these images, I don't want to know about it. Understood?"

"Yes. Sir." Then I braced myself as he lifted his coffee cup to his mouth and sucked in the noisiest gulp ever. He did it to irritate me; there was no question about it.

Clint dropped me off at my shop. Erin was behind the counter in Brew Ha-Ha. Her straight black hair was pulled into a ponytail and showed off her beautiful Vietnamese-American face. Pinky was waiting on a customer in Curio Finds. Her headband had worked its way down her forehead, and her curls were bouncing as she flapped around pointing to snow globes the older gentleman might like. I offered to take over, but the two of them had formed an immediate bond and didn't need me.

I hung up my coat and purse then carried the images of Troy into Brew Ha-Ha to show Erin. She was talking to a customer, so I went behind the counter, laid the photos aside, and helped myself to a decaf. When her last customer was served, I pulled Erin out of earshot and handed her the paper. "Have you ever seen this character around town?"

She looked it over. "Troy Ryland, huh? Around age twenty then fast forwarded to forty-three. The stepbrother Molly never mentioned, to me anyhow."

I shook my head. "No, and if she hadn't kept secret about him, she just might be alive now."

"What? *Cami*." She lowered her voice to a whisper. "Now you're thinking Troy killed Molly?"

"I don't know what to think except he needs to be behind bars." I pointed at the pictures. "And now the police have something to help them identify him."

Irene Ryland phoned me in the early afternoon to extend her thanks for the beautiful floral arrangement. "And Assistant Chief Lonsbury stopped by earlier," she added.

"Did that go okay?" It had to have been better than the last time he'd been to her house and ended up arresting her.

"Yes, he tried to return the old photo of Troy, but I told him to keep it. Then he showed me what the computer came up with, aging Troy to look more like he'd look now."

"And what'd you think, between the two images?"

"Judging from the last time I saw him, he looks a lot like the cleaner-living version, believe it or not."

"That's good information for the police. Irene, I have a favor to ask you."

"What is it?"

"I was wondering if you'd send Troy that letter we talked about, maybe write 'Urgent' or 'Important' on the envelope. If we can get it in the mail today, it'll be in St. Paul on Monday for sure. I know the P.O. number isn't in his name, but the same person has had the box for years, so it must be Troy, don't you think?"

"I would think so."

"We have no way of knowing how often he picks up his mail, but if he's on text alert, he'll hopefully pick it up on Tuesday. Maybe Wednesday. It might be a long day waiting for him to show up, but I think it's worth a try."

Irene made a lip-smacking sound. "Shouldn't the police be doing that?"

"Like I said before, this will save their resources. According to our police, they checked and there is no Troy Ryland who rents a mailbox at the downtown St. Paul Post Office. If we find out that he does, we will pass it along to them."

"I'll do it on one condition; that you take me with you. Yes, Troy knows me, but I can make myself look different. Molly bought me a wig a few years ago. She asked me to wear it when I went with her to a fancy party."

"Irene, it could get to be a very long day."

"I think we can narrow it down some."

"How?"

"Troy's father always said Troy would have to work an

afternoon shift because he was such a night owl. I think we'd be safe if we got there by noon."

A couple came in the front door. "I have to go, but we'll talk later."

"Okay, good-bye, Cami."

The afternoon was surprisingly busy at both shops, but I found my mind often wandering back to thoughts of Molly. I hadn't used the shop bathroom since she'd died there, and had not yet given it a good cleaning. When I was finally alone in the shop, I walked over to the bathroom door, opened it, stood on the threshold, and stared inside without reaching in to turn on the light. It was a normal little room where something very abnormal had occurred. The light flickered on and off, making my heart thump in my chest. "That did not happen," I said and shut the door.

I went in the storeroom and leaned against the wall until my heart rate slowed down to normal. It was possible all the stress was getting to me and I was hallucinating.

"Cami, where are you?" Pinky called out.

I stepped out of the room. "Here."

"Erin gave me the sheet on Troy Ryland a couple of hours ago, and I was wondering if that's my copy."

I smiled at the thought of what she wanted it for. "Not specifically. I may need it."

"Whatever for?"

"Um, well, to compare it to someone else. So what do you think? Do either of the older versions look familiar to you, like the man that asked for the blonde that day?"

She shrugged. "I've looked at it like a hundred times, and all I can say is maybe. I'd need to see him in person."

That could be happening sooner rather than later. "I know what you mean. He has pretty ordinary-looking features." That reminded me of something else I planned to take care of. "I need to call my sister, unless you wanted something."

"Not really. Erin and I are going to sit down for a while before I take off and hoped you would join us."

"Sure, as soon as I make this short call."

Pinky left when I picked up the shop phone and dialed my sister Susan's number. She sounded out of breath when she answered, "H'lo?"

"Susan, are you running?"

"Just up the steps from the basement to get the phone. So how is everything going? Mom and Dad have been worried about you. We all have."

"Thanks. It's been an awful week, and we couldn't feel worse about Molly, but we're hanging in there as best we can."

"You're strong, Cami. A lot stronger than I'd be if that happened to me."

"Don't be too sure about that. Susan, I have a question that might seem strange. I'm wondering how you looked up the information on your house before you bought it. You know, like who owned it."

"You're thinking of buying a house?"

"Well, sometime maybe. Someone wanted to know." Yes, that someone was me.

"Oh, well, it's easy. Go to the county website and click

the tab marked property search, type in the address, and it should give you the information you need."

That was easy enough. I jotted the instructions on a piece of paper. "Thanks, Susan."

"We're looking forward to Thanksgiving dinner at Mom and Dad's. See you then."

My parents liked having all of us under their roof at least once a month, and for every holiday possible. "Yes, see you then."

If I didn't have a chance to look up Will's friend at work, I'd do it when I got home. Pinky and Erin were sitting at a table in the back area of the coffee shop, and I joined them. There was so much to tell them, I didn't know where to start. So I blurted out the juiciest bit first. "Clint kissed me."

"*Cami*," Erin squealed.

"*Cami*," Pinky screeched even louder. Then they both grabbed my hands and squeezed until they turned blue.

"Ouch!" I said in protest, and they eased their grips.

"Tell us every single detail and leave nothing out," Pinky said.

"There's not all that much to tell. He stopped over when I was making dinner. He hadn't eaten, so I invited him to join me, we ate, then he gave me a quick kiss good night, and left."

"Pinky said not to leave anything out, and you are. Like did you kiss him back and how was it?" Erin gave my hand a tap.

"I had no clue he was going to do that, and I'm not sure if I kissed him back or not. It happened so fast. And I don't think it should happen again."

"What are you talking about?" Pinky said.

"Because what kind of life would we have together? We'd be fighting all the time."

Erin held up a hand. "Whoa, Nellie. You are jumping from point A to point Z here. There are lots of things that happen between those two points."

"Whatever."

And that was as much as I could say on the subject, because the subject himself walked into Brew Ha-Ha, and he wouldn't have been much of a detective if he couldn't figure out what we were talking about. It was obvious from the way Pinky and Erin kept looking from Clint to me and back again that I had told them about our evening. He smiled and shrugged his shoulders. "Camryn, do you have a minute?"

Great, those were eavesdropping words to Pinky. I nodded, stood up, and followed him into Curio Finds. "Something happen?"

"Why no, I stopped by to see if I could buy you dinner. I owe you one." He had such a way with words.

"I don't look at it that way."

"Well, you have to eat."

"Clint—"

He lifted his hands like he was requesting a truce. "Let me start over, Camryn, it's been a tough week, and I think it's been especially hard on you. I thought going out for dinner might offer you a little distraction, help you relax."

I didn't know whether to be grateful or suspicious. "Oh, well, thank you." Any kind of distraction sounded nice. "Where were you thinking of going?"

"Maybe the golf course restaurant, the Golfers Glen. Have you been there since they've remodeled?"

I shook my head. "Do I need to change clothes?"

He looked me over from my teal pullover sweater to my black pants. "No, you're fine. You'll be done with work at six?"

"Yes."

"How about I pick you up at your house at six thirty?"

"Okay." That'd give me a little time to freshen up.

"Okay," he said with a nod then headed out the door.

Erin and Pinky stepped in from the other side of the archway. They had been listening, all right. "Cami's got a date, Cami's got a date," Pinky said in a singsongy voice, sounding more like a six-year-old than a thirty-six-year-old.

"You two! I feel like we're back in high school half the time. The only reason I said yes is because I was too tired to say no."

"Uh-huh, and you have to eat," Erin said.

I patted my hips and smiled. "Yes, I'd hate to waste away."

Before I closed up for the day, I stuck my head in the shop bathroom and wiggled the light switch. "Okay now, no more monkey business. You're off, and you need to stay that way."

I hurried home, not planning to do more than freshen up, but I decided to jump in the shower instead. I let the hot water pound on my back for a minute as I soaped up then rinsed, wishing the cares of the week could wash away, too. Like that was remotely possible.

When I climbed out of the shower, there wasn't much time to spare, so I dressed first, in case Clint was early. I put on a calf-length dark gray skirt and a light gray crewneck of the softest wool. It felt comforting when I stretched my arms into it then pulled it around my middle. I added a sterling three-chain necklace to dress it up a tad.

I brushed my shoulder-length hair, put on a little makeup, then went to the front closet for my boots and coat. I was ready and waiting when Clint pulled up and stopped in front of my house. I flipped on the outside light, turned the lock on the door, and was on the front stoop by the time he got out of his truck.

He walked to the passenger side and opened the door. A gust of wind hit me. "Brrr," I said. Clint helped me in then got in himself and drove the couple of miles to the golf course west of town. The upper level lot, next to the main restaurant entrance, was full. "They're busier than I would have expected this early. I'll park in the back, and we'll use that door." As he drove to the lower lot, I realized that in his line of work, Clint would know all about back entrances.

As it turned out, it was the entrance the golfers used when they got off the course. We blew in the door with the wind and walked up the steps to the restaurant. The hostess recognized Clint. "Long time no see. Would you like to hang up your coats?" Clint helped me out of mine and disappeared into the coatroom with it for a minute.

When he returned, the hostess smiled and asked where we wanted to sit. "We've got a big anniversary party going on in the main dining room, so it's a little noisy in there. But there are seats in either the sports bar or the smaller dining room."

Clint looked at me. "The smaller dining room okay with you?"

"Sure."

"Right this way." The hostess led us to a room with

double-wide glass doors that could be pulled shut for private gatherings. There were a few tables available, and she seated us near the back, on the other side of the area where the waitstaff had a counter for their supplies. She laid menus on the table. "Your server will be with you momentarily."

I looked around at the woodsy décor. "It's nice in here."

"Even better, the food is great." He picked up the menus and handed one to me. After I'd had a minute to study it, he said, "What looks good to you?"

Beef tenderloin, grilled jumbo shrimp, baby back ribs, pasta dishes. There was nothing on the menu that didn't look good. My eating habits had been more miss than hit the past few days. "What are you going to have?"

"Prime rib."

I took another look at the menu and debated for a minute. "I'll go with the seafood platter."

We talked about life in general as the server brought us wine, took our orders, and delivered our meal in courses. Clint was genial and did not make one aggravating comment throughout the entire evening. When we'd finished, the server scooped up our plates. "Can I offer you dessert, coffee?" she said.

Please say no to the coffee, Clint. "I don't even have room for a sip of water. Thanks, though." And Clint shook his head.

The server left, and I closed my eyes for a second, savoring my satisfaction with the delicious meal.

"Let's get you home. We don't want you falling asleep here, especially if you snore." He sounded serious.

My eyes popped open and found Clint's. I hoped to find a smile on his face, but it wasn't there. The man was hands down the most exasperating person I'd ever spent both professional and personal time with. "You need to work on your bedside manner, Doc."

His eyebrows rose, and he picked up the check the server had left on the table.

We were both quiet on the way to my house. He pulled into the alley in the back of my house and parked next to my garage. "It was a very nice dinner, Clint. Thank you."

"Sure. I better walk you to the door. It's way too dark in your backyard. When we talked about it, I thought you were getting a security light."

"It's on my list." Well, it sort of was. I thought of it now and then.

We got out of the car, and Clint left it running, which eliminated the awkward moment of wondering whether to invite him in or not. We reached the back door—safely, I might add—and my keys were in my hand ready to unlock it. I turned around and faced Clint. "Thanks again."

"You're welcome. Maybe we can do it again sometime." He leaned in, and as his face came closer, it felt like everything was happening in slow motion. When his warm lips finally closed over mine, it took my breath away, and when the kiss ended, the most embarrassing gasping sound came out of me. It was so loud it even gave Clint a start. His body tensed, and his hands tightened on my arms. "Are you all right?"

I nodded, mortified beyond words, and went into my house, grateful there were no backyard beacons shining on my ruby red face.

13

The next morning I woke up early, trying to remember if I was supposed to work or not. Pinky and I took turns covering for each other on Sundays. Neither shop was overly busy, but they were profitable enough to warrant keeping them open. Brew Ha-Ha was busier in the morning, and Curio Finds had the bulk of the afternoon business. We also kept shorter hours, from 8:00 a.m. to 3:00 p.m., instead of 7:00 a.m. to 6:00 p.m.

The upsetting week had thrown me off kilter, and it took me a minute to figure out it was Pinky's Sunday. I stretched and smiled, thankful Molly's ghost had not invaded my dreams. But then I remembered my awful-sounding gasp after Clint kissed me. Why had my body betrayed me like that? I had to think it was for the best, really. Just because Clint was the most talented kisser who'd ever shared that skill with me, that did not mean we should have a personal relationship.

The ringing phone surprised me, and I rolled over and picked it up from its holder. "Good morning."

"Morning, Camryn, it's Emmy."

I sensed anxiety in her voice and sat up straight, waiting for the next shoe to drop. "Emmy, what is it?"

"Well, you know the police found something here that they say is poison, so my neighbor Lester came over to help me try to figure out where it could have been hidden. I thought I'd see what things had been disturbed or were missing."

"Did you find something?"

"Yes, I finally did. A box that had come from my husband's shop is gone. It was on a shelf in the garage. I surely couldn't understand why they would have taken that. And then I realized that must be where whoever is trying to frame me put the cyanide."

Emmy believed someone was guilty of planting the evidence, but who in Brooks Landing knew of her past? And even if they did, they'd have a lot of dots to connect to come up with a scheme in a very short period of time.

"Emmy, how about I come over to your house and we talk about it?" I'd check with Mark to see if I could tell her what was in the box with the cyanide.

"That would be nice, Camryn. You and Lester are the two I trust the most here in Brooks Landing."

"Thanks."

When we hung up, I phoned Mark and asked him what Emmy was allowed to know. "It's evidence that will be used in court. Her attorney will have access to all the information, so there should be no problem. Clint probably told her about it when he questioned her, but you can double-check with him."

I would not be doing that. "Okay, I appreciate it. So, what are your plans for the day?"

"Working, but it's my Friday so I have the next three off."

"Sounds good, Mark. I'll let you get back to it."

I wanted to get to Emmy's as soon as possible, so I condensed my morning routine to brushing my hair and teeth and pulling on jeans and a sweatshirt.

Emmy opened her front door before I rang the bell. Lester was standing beside her, and it struck me that they were a very nice-looking couple. They both had snow-colored hair and intelligent eyes. "Distinctive" was the word I'd have used to describe them. "Come in, Camryn. I didn't expect you so soon. We're having a cup of tea, if you'd like some."

"Thanks." We went into the kitchen where their cups were waiting. A decorative teapot from a bygone era was in the center of the table. Emmy got a cup out of the cupboard for me. We all sat down, and Emmy poured tea into my cup. It was an herbal blend, and I took a decent whiff but detected no smell of almonds. Not that I was paranoid; it was only a precaution.

"Emmy, if it's all right, I'd like to go back to when you were arrested and Assistant Chief Lonsbury questioned you."

"What do you want to know?" She set her cup in her saucer.

"Did he tell you where they found the evidence?"

"Yes, he said it was in the garage, but he didn't go into specifics. That's why I thought to look there. And now I know it must have been in a box from my husband's shop."

"What else was in it?"

She shook her head. "I don't know. I hadn't looked through the boxes yet. My husband was a carpenter by trade and rented a warehouse space for his tools and supplies. He had a little shop inside of it where he did different projects, woodworking, mostly small items like birdhouses to give to friends, things like that."

"Did he use glass in his projects or make anything out of glass?"

"Well, not that I know of . . . Wait a minute." She looked from Lester to me. "Let me back up here a minute. When I was in jail for my husband's death, his friend Darwin asked me what I wanted to do with all his tools and supplies. There was no reason to keep renting the warehouse, so I asked if he'd mind selling or giving away everything except maybe what he was working on in his little shop."

Emmy got up, went to the living room, then came back holding a glass ornament in the shape of a Christmas tree. It was intricately etched on both sides. "After I was acquitted, Darwin came over to my home and gave me this. It was on my husband's workbench. It even has my name on it."

"It's beautiful. So your husband also did glass etching?"

"Not that I knew about until then. I think it was supposed to be my Christmas present. He was always working on something."

"He must have had a big assortment of tools," I said.

"Hold up here," Lester interrupted. "Glass etching, you say?"

Emmy and I both turned to him.

"I seem to remember one of my clients years ago telling me about this glass and metal etching hobby of his where he used cyanide something or other. He gave it up after he got sick and nearly died. He wasn't wearing safety glasses and splashed a drop in his eye. Lucky for him he got medical help right away."

"Oh my Lord, that's awful. Howard never told me he worked with cyanide. Maybe so I wouldn't worry. His shop was his sanctuary, and I didn't pry until he showed me his finished products. Lester, you said he could have used cyanide to etch the glass on this ornament?" She held it up.

"It seems like a good possibility from what I know," he said.

Emmy frowned and thought a minute. "Howard came home that day, said he wasn't feeling well, and collapsed. He had a cut on his arm. I remember looking at it and thinking that it didn't look bad enough to make him pass out. I thought he had been out on a job, but he could have been at the warehouse. Our house was just a couple of blocks from there.

"I called nine-one-one, but it was too late. Of course I thought he'd had a heart attack, but the medical examiner suspected cyanide. He had smelled an almond-like odor on Howard. I surely hadn't smelled any such thing."

I interrupted. "You couldn't smell it?"

She shook her head then went on. "The police looked at my husband's job log and mapped out where he had been that day. There was no mention of being at the warehouse, and there wouldn't have been. Howard only recorded his paying jobs. The police eventually determined I'd done it because I had access to chemicals at the hardware store. And there was a twelve-bottle case missing from the store's inventory."

"Really?"

"The owners of the hardware store didn't suspect me until Howard was poisoned. And the other thing they looked at was Howard's very large life insurance policy. We'd had our ups and downs over the years, but I loved him with all my heart."

I reached over and put my hand on hers. "If Howard had been using cyanide and splashed it on his cut, that might have been what caused his death. You need to tell your story to the police."

Lester nodded. "And they should be able to tell whether the cyanide that was in your garage—if it was your husband's—is the same stuff that killed Molly. I watch those forensics shows, and they solve cases similar to that every now and again," Lester said.

I felt a ray of hope for Emmy. "Lester's right. There must be different grades of the poison. Is it okay if I call Mark?"

Tears formed in Emmy's eyes, and she nodded.

I phoned Mark, and he arrived a few minutes later. His sidekick Clint wasn't far behind him. Emmy's story trumped any personal embarrassment I felt when his eyes met mine. The two officers listened intently and wrote down the details of what Emmy now surmised had happened to her husband. She showed them the ornament at the story's climax.

"If what you're telling us turns out to be true, that would explain why there were no fingerprints on the cyanide bottle. He would have been wearing gloves if he was working with that chemical. I figured the killer wore them to hide her—or his—prints," Clint said.

Emmy shook her head. "When my husband died, I had no idea how he could have been poisoned. I guess we still don't know what happened for sure. I was an easy one for the police to blame."

Clint pursed his lips. "We'll make sure all the tests we need are run right away. And when the results come in, hopefully you can get your life back."

The look Emmy sent him said that wasn't possible. But then she and Lester caught and held each other's eyes, and it seemed to me things were looking up for both of them.

I got home late morning and found the note I'd left myself on the kitchen counter, reminding me to find out what I could about Will Dalton's buddy. Before I dove into the search, I checked in with Pinky. She said she was doing fine managing the shops, no problem. We had made a pact that if it was an unusually busy day, one of us could call the other one in. It had happened a couple times over the past few months.

I grabbed a protein bar as a late breakfast treat then went into the spare bedroom that also served as my office. I opened the laptop and followed Susan's instructions. They worked like a charm, and I navigated through the site in no time. I typed Will's friend's address in the property search line, and in seconds I had the information. The house was owned by Bryan George.

Next, I looked up the law firm Will Dalton worked for, Turner and Marshall. I knew it was one of the top ones in the Twin Cities area and learned it was the fourteenth largest with 63 lawyers. The largest one had 254, and next largest was close behind with 251. I did a search of the firm's attorneys and found something that got my attention. Congratulations were in order for Bryan George, who had made partner on Thursday, November 13. He thanked his mentor, William Dalton, for the recommendation. November 13. That was two days after Molly died and the day before her service. Given those circumstances, it seemed in poor taste to post his promotion at that particular time, whether it was scheduled or not. They should have held off for a week or two out of respect for Will Dalton.

Emmy phoned when I was logging off the computer. "Camryn, there is something I keep forgetting to tell you about that day, the day Molly and I started at your shops. The day she died."

My heart rate picked up a beat, hoping she'd remembered something about a man who acted strange or out of place. "What is it?"

"I need to apologize to you and to Pinky. And I can't tell you how much I wish I could tell Molly that I'm very, very sorry."

"Sorry for what?"

"For being so crabby. I was not myself that day at all, and I'm not sure why. I took it out on Molly, and the only reason I can think of is I was afraid she'd do well and I would fail. I felt insecure and worried I'd do something wrong like break one of your precious pieces."

No, Ramona Zimmer had done that instead. And she had yet to apologize or at least pay for the snow globe. "Emmy, we were all nervous about how it would go, and that might have made things tenser than they should have been. It's not necessary, but I accept your apology."

"Thank you, Camryn. I'll talk to Pinky, too."

"She'd like that."

After we disconnected, I phoned Irene Ryland to ask her about writing a letter to Troy. "Cami, I took to heart what you said yesterday and wrote the letter this morning. I wrote

'Urgent' and included my return address on the envelope. And what I said in the letter is about Molly, so it is urgent."

"Yes, it is. Thank you for doing that. I'll run over now and pick it up then drop it off at the post office. If it's collected tonight, or even first thing in the morning, it'll be in St. Paul by Tuesday morning for sure."

"You don't have to do that. I can mail it."

"I was going to go out, anyway, so it's no problem, really." I wasn't being completely honest with Irene, but I had thought about stopping by the shops.

"All right."

With the letter safely mailed, I stopped in to see Pinky. A few customers were sitting at her front counter, and she was wiping off tables in her back area. No one was browsing in Curio Finds. "Cami, what are you doing here?" she said when she saw me. "And no offense, but you never wear jeans to work."

I glanced down then shrugged. "It's my day off." Actually, I had been so preoccupied with the day's events I hadn't even remembered what I was wearing. "Did Emmy call you?"

"Emmy? No, why? Or maybe I don't want to know."

"No, it's good. It looks like she's going to be cleared of both murders."

She threw the towel on her shoulder. "Get out of here. A miracle happen or what?"

"I'm sure she feels like it did." I gave her a rundown of the morning and the new information the police now had to work with.

"That is just crazy. She had to be accused of a second

murder so she could be cleared of the first one. Well, maybe the first wasn't a murder after all," Pinky said.

"I guess. So should we offer her the job back?"

Pinky waved her arms around in the air. "Holy moly, I can't even think about that right now."

I nodded. "I get that. To let you know, I'm going to ask my dad if he can work for me Tuesday afternoon, maybe see if Erin can come in, too."

"Your dad? What are you planning?"

"I'm helping Irene Ryland out."

Pinky left it at that. "Well, it seems like your dad is getting more comfortable leaving your mom from time to time."

"And she may want to come along with him. It does her good to get out for a few hours." I knew how much it lifted her spirits, and she was getting a little stronger every day.

When I asked Dad if he could fill in for me, my parents decided they'd both mind the shop Tuesday afternoon. If Mom got too tired, Dad would run her home. I looked around my house, not interested in doing any of the things that needed to be done, but finally coaxed myself into doing some cleaning. Then I sorted through the mail I'd ignored all week.

That afternoon, I got a frozen dinner out of the freezer for a late lunch/early dinner. It wasn't the best lasagna by any stretch of the imagination, but it wasn't the worst, either. I ate it quickly, thinking about the letter Irene had written and wondering if Troy would take the bait. As I threw the paper container away, I noticed a penny on the counter. "Where did you come from?" I said, then I picked it up and carried it to the blue and brown ceramic dish on the coffee table. As I dropped it in it, I nodded at the penny. "Between pennies from heaven, lights turning themselves off and on, and ghosts talking to me in my dreams, I wonder if I should seriously consider taking a long vacation, somewhere warm."

I got to the shop a little before nine on Tuesday morning so I could get some bookwork done before Curio Finds opened. Pinky waved me over. "Clint said to call when you got in. He said you weren't answering your cell phone."

"Oh." I pulled it out of my purse and saw I'd missed his call. "I must have been in the shower when he called. Thanks." When I phoned him, I got good and better news.

"Camryn, the results on the contents of the envelope came back. No trace of a poison. Just a letter and some money. Are you at home?"

A letter and some money? "No, I'm at work."

"All right, I'll be down there shortly."

"Well?" Pinky nosed her face close to mine.

"Clint's bringing me a letter and money, minus any poison. The envelope from Ramona."

"Wonders never cease."

Clint came by about ten minutes later. I was matching credit card receipts with the totals from the card company. He walked up to the counter carrying the envelope like it contained gold. When he gave it to me, I opened it up and withdrew the folded page. A crisp one-hundred dollar bill fell out and dropped on the counter. My face must have registered surprise, because Clint said, "The letter explains that."

I read it out loud. "'Camryn, I'm the one who broke your Marilyn Monroe snow globe, and I'm sorry. But when I spotted you in the shop, I noticed you were wearing the same outfit you had on that day you were with my husband. That snow globe was sitting on the shelf in front of me, and I can't explain it, but I picked it up and dropped it. I heard it break, but I was too upset to do anything except leave. I am sorry and hope this covers its replacement.'" I looked up at Clint. "I think a hundred more than covers it."

Clint lifted a shoulder. "I'll have to defer to you on that one. Our fear that the envelope contained poison has been alleviated, in any case. It seems Senator Zimmer did not intend to harm you, after all, and I see no reason to charge her with petty misdemeanor criminal damage to property."

"No, she has enough problems, between her husband and . . . other things." No need to tattletale about her male houseguest or explain why I was spying on Ramona in the first place. "I was right about one thing, though. She saw Molly from the back and thought it was me."

"That's what she meant?" He shook his head. "Molly. But at least this envelope mystery is wrapped up, and that's good." Then he stood there like he had more to say.

I finally broke the silence. "Thank you."

Clint nodded then left. Apparently he wasn't ready to share whatever was on his mind. The figure of Marilyn Monroe, the one from the broken snow globe, was lying on the counter next to the cash register. I picked it up and looked it over. "Well, Ms. Monroe, we can probably buy two more of you with the amount of cool cash Ramona left. Dad may know where to look."

Pinky came into Curio Finds carrying a newspaper and looked around. "I heard Clint leave, so I'm hoping you're talking to yourself and not a ghost."

I held up the figurine. "No, just wondering where to find another Monroe snow globe. Ramona gave me a hundred bucks for damages." I picked up the bill with my other hand and waved it.

"As well she should have. Good. And speaking of Senator Zimmer, there is something you need to see. I was about to throw out the Sunday edition when I spotted this." Pinky opened the paper and spread it on the checkout counter.

What I saw made my mouth drop open. "You have got to be kidding me." There, front and center, was a picture of Ramona Zimmer and her brother Randy Arthur. *Her brother?* He was the man I'd seen carrying a suitcase into her house. The man I'd seen hugging her before catching a taxi. The man who had recently returned from five years of mission work in the Congo. The brother I'd heard about but had never met.

The article in the *Minneapolis Star Tribune* went on about Randy's ventures for the past twenty years, working with underprivileged people and helping in various ways. When I finished reading, I folded it up and handed it back to Pinky. "Wow," I said. It was my turn to eat a big piece of humble pie. First, I worried that Ramona had tried to poison me. Twice. Then I convinced myself she was having an affair, thinking it was to spite her wandering husband. I looked at Pinky. "Pinch me."

"Pinch you? You really want me to?"

"No, but I deserve it. I was ready to believe the worst about someone I trusted and cared about for a long time."

Pinky gave me a gentle pinch in the arm.

It didn't hurt, but I said, "Ouch."

"Ramona Zimmer turned her back on you when she should have believed you. Who can blame you for doubting her?"

I was nervous the rest of the morning. Ramona Zimmer's strange behavior had led me to the wrong conclusions. I thought awful things about her and what her anger might have led her to do. Peter's actions had hurt her career; there was no doubt about that. I felt badly she was blind to that, but it was up to her to wake up and see things as they really were.

The other thing keeping me on edge was wondering if Troy Ryland was the actual renter of the P.O. box. And if so, would he get a text message from the post office about the letter and then go pick it up? I hoped Irene Ryland was right when she said Troy was a night owl and that we'd be safe getting to the post office after noon. One o'clock seemed like a reasonable time. The post office lobby was open until 6:00 p.m., so that meant it was possible we'd have to wait five hours for him. And he might not show up at all.

I took my cell phone off the charger then went into Brew Ha-Ha for something to do for the last few minutes before my parents relieved me. Pinky was washing cups and had splashed some drops of water on her face. She lifted her bony shoulder and used her shirt to swipe the side of her cheek dry.

"Holy moly, Cami, you seem jumpy."

"It's just been a nerve-racking week. And we still don't know who killed Molly."

"It's been tough, all right. Did Molly's ghost stop talking about her killers in your dreams?"

"Yes, for the last couple of nights, anyway. And I'd like to keep it that way."

"I'm with you on that."

"Hello!" I heard Dad call out from Curio Finds.

"We're in here," I yelled back.

Mom and Dad were all smiles when they walked through the archway and greeted us.

"So where is it you have to go?" Dad said.

"Just helping Irene Ryland take care of things. No biggie, but she just wasn't sure how long it would take. I may not be back by quitting time, so I hope that's not a problem."

"Of course it's not. You take all the time Irene needs," Mom said.

I didn't like keeping our real mission a secret, but people tended to overreact sometimes. And something told me this might be one of those times. I scooted out of there before anyone asked me more questions. It was possible I'd cave and confess what Irene and I hoped to accomplish on our fact-finding project before our mission even got under way.

I rene was ready and giddy—or close to it—with the prospect of uncovering the whereabouts of the man who had taken a sizable sum of money from her and bilked her daughter out of thousands upon thousands more. Her disguise brought a smile to my face. She looked like a wealthy socialite who was trying to hide her aging face from the world. She had on her fur coat, knee-high black boots, a reddish auburn wig with too much hair for her small face, and big sunglasses that effectively covered much of what the wig didn't. With the collar of her coat touching her jawline, all that was visible was her chin, lips, the tip of her nose, and a bit of her cheeks.

"I hope I look all right," Irene said.

"Oh my goodness, you look great. I would never have recognized you."

I helped her into my car, and we were on the road to St. Paul with a common goal. We had programmed each other's numbers in our cell phone contacts so we'd be prepared to call each other if the need arose.

"Cami, I need to thank you again for letting me tag along. Molly was desperate and did a terrible thing, killing her stepfather. With Troy it's a different story. I was wrong when I panicked and gave him money to keep quiet about the crime. But then it got worse and worse."

Molly, Irene, Troy. They were all victims and criminals at the same time because a man had abused his stepdaughter. "We'll do our best to help the police locate Troy. The first step is to prove he really is the one who's getting mail at the address listed in someone else's name."

took the downtown exit off I-94 and drove to Fifth Street East, but then I discovered the entrance was on Robert Street and dropped Irene off there. There was no parking there, but I was lucky enough to find a spot on Fifth, a half block away. The catch was it was in front of a thirty-minute meter. I dropped coins in it knowing I'd have to add more every half hour.

Irene was waiting for me near the entrance and pointed. "The post-office boxes are over there."

The area was L shaped, and I was surprised it wasn't much bigger than the one in Brooks Landing. There was a retail area behind double glass doors where clerks were waiting on a few customers. The wall in front of us was covered with mailboxes. They continued around the corner and were in size order, from small to large.

"Okay, we'll want to find the one Troy is renting, then we'll decide where to hang out and keep watch. And let's hope and pray we don't get kicked out for loitering." Although there seemed to be a number of other people who were doing just that.

"Oh my, I didn't consider that possibility."

"We may have to change our strategies as we go along, especially if it gets to be hours of waiting. Why don't you stay here and I'll go find the box so we know exactly where it is."

"All right."

"Keep your cell phone handy, in case."

"It's in my pocket, and I'll call to alert you if I see Troy."

"Great, and remember to snap a picture if you can."

She nodded. "I practiced how to do that at home so I wouldn't look like I was taking a picture."

"Very good, Irene. I wish I had thought of that."

I headed over to the section with the boxes and located the right one around the corner. When I was headed back to join Irene, my phone rang. "He's here," was all Irene said before the phone went dead.

I still had the phone to my ear when a man I recognized rounded the corner and almost ran into me. It was the man who'd been into our shops and acted so strangely, looking around without uttering a word. That was Troy? My face must have registered disbelief or fear or uncertainty or all three, because that's how I felt.

His eyes opened wide when they landed on my face and he placed who I was. He didn't know was why I was there, for a few seconds, anyway. And if I had been smoother, he may have chalked it up to coincidence. I pulled the phone from my ear and hit the camera icon then tried to act like I was dialing a number when I snapped a picture. He didn't buy it. He lunged for my phone, but I stuck it in my coat pocket before he snatched it out of my hand.

"Give that to me," he said and threw his arms around me.

"If you don't let me go, I'll scream for someone to call the police."

I said the magic scare word—"police"—and he dropped his arms, turned tail, and took off. As I watched him run, all of a sudden Irene was there standing in his path. And then she risked life and limb by doing something I would never have predicted. Just before Troy reached her, she turned and bent over. He didn't have time to react, much less dodge her, and tripped. He did a nose dive across Irene's back, somersaulted, and landed on his backside.

He lay there for a while like he was trying to come to his wits. It was long enough for Irene to stand up, regain her balance, direct her phone at his face, and snap a picture. And long enough for a number of people to close in on him and ask if he was okay. But not long enough to get law enforcement there, even if I'd thought to dial 911. I'd hung back with the gathering crowd, gawking in stunned surprise.

Troy finally rolled over on his stomach and pushed

himself to his feet. He took off running, full speed. It was then I yelled, "Help! Did anyone call nine-one-one?" I got a bunch of head shakes and shrugs. I had a little trouble getting my phone out of my pocket with my shaking, sweating hand, but I managed.

"I did. I called nine-one-one," Irene told me.

"It looks like he got away," a man in the crowd said.

"What did he do?" a woman asked.

"He stole something," I said as I took Irene's arm and guided her away from the people and any further questions.

Two St. Paul Police officers were there a minute later, and Irene flagged them down. "What's the complaint?" the younger male officer asked.

Irene went through the whole litany of who Troy Ryland was and the crimes he'd committed. She explained how we were hoping to discover whether it was really him renting the box under a false name. Irene showed the officers the photo on her phone.

The older officer took the phone from her hands, studied it, and nodded. "Yeah, we got an attempt to locate, apprehend, and detain on Troy Ryland. Can you send this photo to my phone since it's the real deal?"

"Will you do it?" Irene asked.

"With your permission, sure," he said, and he completed the task in no time. He handed the phone back to Irene. "We'll need your names, birthdates, and addresses to complete our reports."

We spent some time with the officers, answering their questions. When they'd finished, the older officer shook his head at Irene and me. "I want you both to think twice before you do anything like this again. And then don't do it."

I nodded, agreeing in theory, anyway. Irene said, "Yes, Officer." She gave them the impression she had put me up to the whole thing. I was about to clear up the misconception when Irene put her arm in mine and guided me away from them.

When we were back in my car, I noticed the meter had run out. Irene removed her sunglasses and let out a big breath of air. "My heart is still thumping a little bit."

"Irene, not that I ever wanted you in harm's way like that, but the way you tripped Troy was amazing."

"I didn't know how else to stop him. I have been filled with so much anger at Troy for too many years. And if it turns out he poisoned Molly, I don't know how I'll go on."

I reached over and gave her hand a light squeeze, then I started the engine and we were on our way back to Brooks Landing. "You know, Irene, now that the police know the name Troy has been using—to get the post-office box at least—they should be able to find him."

"When I leaned over and took his picture, he didn't even notice that. And I know he didn't recognize me."

"That's a good thing. He seemed pretty anxious to get out of there, that's for sure."

14

I dropped Irene off at her house, surprised it wasn't quite three o'clock. I headed to the shops so Mom and Dad could go home. What I hadn't expected when I walked into Curio Finds was the stern look on my Mom's face and the sterner look on my Dad's. "What?"

Mom filled me in. "Assistant Chief Clinton Lonsbury stopped by a few minutes ago, hoping to catch you. And he seemed upset."

"More than seemed; he was downright steaming," Dad said.

My earlier thought about people overreacting came back to haunt me. "Did he say why?"

"He said he needed to talk to you about the shenanigans you and Irene Ryland pulled today," Mom said.

"Shenanigans?"

"That's what he said," Dad confirmed. "He wants you to call him."

Pinky picked that moment to poke her head in our shop. "Cami, you're here." She took in the picture my parents and I must have presented. "I take it you got the message to call you know who."

I nodded then looked at my parents. "Thank you for filling in for me. Feel free to take off."

"I think we'll hang around until after you talk to our assistant chief, make sure everything is okay," Dad said.

Great, just great. Well, they'd find out sooner or later. "All right." I glanced over at Pinky.

She lifted her hands. "I have nowhere to be anytime soon."

I used the shop phone and dialed Clint's number. "It's Camryn."

"I see you're calling from your shop. I'll be right there," he said and hung up.

"Clint's on his way," I announced to the snoopers, then I switched subjects. "So how has business been today?"

"It came in waves," Mom said.

The bell on Pinky's door dinged. "Oh sure, now I get customers," she said quietly. Dad followed her, probably to offer his help.

"Clint is an intense man at times, isn't he?" Mom said.

"Yes, he is." Most of the time, it seemed to me. Mom and I studied each other a minute. "I meant to tell you earlier that you are looking better all the time, Mom."

"Thank you, Cami. I feel pretty good. A little tired, maybe, but I have the rest of the day to laze around before I go to bed." She smiled, appreciating her own dry sense of humor.

I gave her a hug, grateful for her steadfast love and

support. It was at that moment Clint walked into Curio Finds. As I stepped back, he nodded at Mom then stared at me. "Have a minute, Camryn?"

"Yes, maybe even two."

Mom thought that was worth a grin; Clint did not. "Do you want to go into the back room?"

"No, it's all right. Mom can listen in." The truth was, I figured Clint would temper his response with her being there.

And I think he tried to for a second or so. "Camryn, what in tarnation were you and Irene Ryland thinking when you went to St. Paul looking for Troy Ryland? He's a known felon and potentially dangerous."

Mom's smile turned upside down. "What is Clint talking about, Cami?"

Clint didn't appear to hear her. "Imagine my surprise when I got a call from Sergeant Morse detailing all the drama at the downtown post office this afternoon."

"What drama?" Mom asked.

Dad and Pinky both crept into Curio Finds. Clint's voice carried well, even when he tried to keep it low.

I held up my hands. "Okay. It's true, Irene and I went on a little mission, hoping to find out if Troy Ryland was still around. And it turns out his post-office box was rented under a false name. We had no intention of getting close to him. I thought it would be a giant place, but it wasn't at all.

"Irene and I planned to position ourselves so we could get a picture of him to show the police. That's all. And then he saw me, and I sort of panicked and tried to take his picture. And he recognized me because he had been in our shops."

I turned to Pinky, who was standing with her arms across

her chest. "Pinky, you know the guy who came in the other day, the one who was acting strange?"

Pinky half shrugged. She hadn't seen him.

I left out the details about my little scuffle with Troy. "Anyway, he started to run away, and Irene tripped him and snapped his picture with her phone before he took off. The police came and took our statements and are looking for Troy. We—and Irene, especially—got the answer we were hoping for. Troy is still the holder of that P.O. box."

"You're saying the end justified the means?" Clint said.

"All I'm saying is Irene will be very relieved when Troy Ryland is arrested."

Pinky moved in close to me, put her arm around my waist, and came to my defense. "What's done is done. And we'll all feel better when they catch that hoodlum, right?"

Clint didn't agree with her, but he didn't say he disagreed either.

climbed into bed that night mulling over the day. In retrospect, staking out the St. Paul Post Office in search of Troy Ryland was not the smartest thing I had ever done. If I had to do over again, I would not have involved Irene. I'd have asked my friend Mark to come with me instead.

I was completely caught off guard when Troy recognized me. My sense of panic caused me to do something dumb. Irene had kept her wits about her and come through with flying colors. Ultimately, though, we had uncovered valuable information to help the police. *Yes, Clint, I didn't admit it to you in person, but I'm convinced the end did justify the means.*

Troy would likely be arrested soon, and Irene would have the satisfaction of knowing that. I fell asleep with a deep sense of relief. Molly paid me another ghostly dream visit a few hours later. It shouldn't have been surprising, since I thought about her most of my waking hours.

She was different—calmer, not quite as distressed as she'd been in her prior visits. I was in Curio Finds with Irene when Molly suddenly appeared. Irene didn't seem to see or hear Molly when she said, "The killers were here. Did you see them?" The killers? I looked around, but Irene was the only other person there. Molly brushed her hand on her mother's shoulder, smiled, and disappeared. Irene hadn't noticed a thing.

When I woke up, I wasn't quite as alarmed as I'd been the other times. Either I was getting used to the ethereal Molly visiting me in my sleep, or I was comforted knowing I wasn't alone with her and a bunch of people I couldn't identify. Irene was there with me, too.

I rolled over and pulled the covers up to my ears. *Molly, the police are after Troy. It's just a question of time before they find him.* I smiled into my pillow. It wasn't bad enough that I talked to myself and my deceased parents; I'd also fallen into the habit of trying to send telepathic messages to the spirit of Molly Dalton.

On Wednesday morning, Pinky called me early. "Cami, I can't stand it anymore. I noticed a light in your shop, and it's that bathroom light again. I thought the electrician fixed it."

I sat up and rubbed my eyelids so I could open them all

the way. "He said there was nothing to fix. What in the world is going on with that thing?"

"I think it must be Molly's ghost. One of my customers was talking about that yesterday, and Erin said the same thing on the night Molly died. When people die suddenly like that their spirits stick around because they don't know they're dead."

"Let's not get into that again, Pink." I got up and headed to the bathroom. "I'll be down there in a little bit."

Pinky raised her hands when I walked into her shop. "The light went off right after I talked to you. If it's not Molly, then it's got to be the wiring."

"If it happens again, we'll get Allen back to do another check."

A group of coffee seekers came in and put an end to our conversation. I went into Curio Finds, hung up my coat and purse, then peeked in the bathroom before I went back to help Pinky with orders. When the rush was over, I was on my way back to Curio Finds when my eyes fell on a shiny penny lying on the floor by Pinky's service counter. I bent over and picked it up then asked the two young women standing nearby, "Did either one of you drop this?"

One of them said, "It's yours." She pointed at the penny I was holding between my pointer finger and thumb. "Hey, you got a heads-up."

I smiled and stuck the penny in my pocket. A heads-up? I hadn't heard that phrase in reference to finding pennies before. My birth mother had recited to me more than once the old ditty, "Find a penny, pick it up, and all the day you'll have good luck." For some reason my young mind had latched onto the phrase like it was my own. But the more I tossed the two phrases around in my mind, "heads-up" made more sense given the experiences I'd had.

I assembled a stack of paperwork and was able to work on that and pay bills between customers. When I'd sealed some envelopes, I discovered I was down to my last few stamps. There were no customers in either shop, so it was a good time to run the errand. I grabbed my coat and purse and stuck my head in the archway between our shops. "Hey, Pinky, I've got to run up to the post office. I'll be back in a few."

She was writing something on a notepad and gave me a quick look. "'Kay."

The post office wasn't far, but the temperature was in the low thirties, and I decided to drive instead of walk. On my way back I was about to turn left on the street that led to the back parking lot when I noticed a familiar car pulling up to the curb across from our shops. It looked like the same one I had followed to Plymouth, the one belonging to Bryan George. Instead of turning, I pulled over and parked not quite a block away. Will Dalton got out of the passenger side and headed across the street toward Brew Ha-Ha's door. That could not be good. I had on a knitted cap and pulled it lower so my cheeks were partially covered. I got out of the car, crossed the street, and walked fast and furiously to my shop door.

I heard Will Dalton's voice in Pinky's shop and moved to the archway to listen. "I heard your employee bailed out of jail and went to talk to the Brooks Landing Police. They indicated there might not be enough evidence against Emaline Andersohn after all. Be assured I am not going to let this rest.

The poisoned coffee came from here, and if the police dismiss the criminal charges, I will pursue civil action."

I stepped into Brew Ha-Ha, ready to defend Pinky, but Will Dalton was already headed out the door. Pinky's face was white, and her mouth was open as she watched him leave. Then she pointed and ran halfway to the door. "That's him!"

"Who?"

"That guy standing by the Porsche. He's the one who was in the shop the day Molly died, the one that asked about the blonde."

"*What?*"

"He's getting in his car now. And Will Dalton is getting in with him."

"Dear Lord. Call Mark or Clint or any cop. I'm going to see where they're going. We'll talk about what Dalton said later."

"Cami—"

I didn't hear the rest of her words. I rushed out my shop door and was heading north on the sidewalk before Mr. George pulled onto the street. I prayed he didn't spot me in his rearview mirror. And when he started driving away, I crossed the street as fast as my legs would carry me. I climbed in my car, glad I'd forgotten to turn the ignition off. It was warmed up and ready to go. Two cars fell in between the Porsche and mine, a good separation. Mr. George went south then turned west and drove to the golf course, the same one Clint and I had eaten at Saturday night. One of the cars had turned off, and with only the one between us, I held back a bit as George turned onto the golf course drive then into the main parking lot.

I drove straight to the back parking lot, thinking it was

nothing less than serendipity or divine intervention that Clint and I had used the back entrance on Saturday. I wouldn't have known it was there otherwise. My cell phone rang as I was turning off the ignition. I wrestled it out of my coat pocket and saw it was Pinky. "Cami, I left messages for both Clint and Mark."

"Thanks, Pinky. When they call back, tell them I'm at the golf course restaurant. I followed the Porsche here. You know what? I'll call them myself." After we hung up, I phoned Clint, and when it went straight to voicemail, I told him where I was and why. Then I headed into the clubhouse. I crept up the steps until I could see into the bar area where a handful of people were eating. Will Dalton and Bryan George were not among them. There was a hostess at the top of the steps, and I willed myself to be casual when I said, "Hi, I'm looking for the two men that came in a minute ago."

"Oh yes, I'll show you to their table."

"No, that's okay. Just point me in the right direction."

"All right, well, they requested to be in the small dining room to discuss some business. It's normally not open for lunch." It was the one Clint and I had eaten in, and unless they were sitting by the door, I figured I could slip in unseen.

"Sure, that makes sense. Thanks." I turned and headed to the short hallway that led to the room. One of the glass double doors was closed, and the other was slightly ajar. I couldn't see the men from there. I remembered the wait station area on the immediate right, went through the door, and quietly slipped into it. There were two open pass-through windows for the waiters to use.

I unbuttoned my coat, went down on my knees, and crept

to the openings. The men were sitting next to each other at a table two rows away. It was angled so they could both see out the large south windows that overlooked the golf course. They had their backs to the wait station. Even though it was dark in the area, I stayed to the side of the opening so they wouldn't see me if they happened to turn around. I remembered my cell phone, took it out, and turned it to silent.

Bryan George was talking, and the first thing I heard was, ". . . very smoothly."

Will Dalton reached over and gave Bryan George a slap on the back. "That's an understatement. It was nothing less than ingenious. Why I married Molly in the first place is beyond me."

Oh my gosh. I lifted up my phone and found the video record icon. I set it on the counter by the opening, praying they didn't notice. As it turned out, they were too preoccupied with their disgusting discussion.

"We all have a lapse in judgment when it comes to women at least once in our lives. So be careful with that hot little red-haired beauty you keep close at hand."

"Tiffany's a nice diversion and not a bad assistant. But I think it's about time for her to move on."

"That's wise. Now that you're a widower, she might start seeing wedding bells."

"That won't happen. Been there, done that."

"Molly was a real fool to think she could divorce you. And you're right about what you said earlier; she probably would have gotten half your money," Bryan said.

"Molly played me for a fool, no question. First she wanted a baby, then when I made sure that didn't happen, she wanted fertility treatments, and then she wanted to adopt. The last straw was when I stumbled across the bill from her divorce attorney," Will said.

"She had no clue that she was the one who helped us pull together the perfect murder. When she told you that she and Emaline Andersohn were going to be working together, everything fell into place."

They'd known Emmy was Emaline Andersohn before Molly died and had used the information for their wicked plans. Dear Lord.

Will chuckled then said, "It was the ideal setup, and Andersohn was the perfect dupe for the Podunk cops here. I did not expect her to bail out of jail, however."

Bryan shook his head. "No. Don't worry, we'll figure out a way to seal her fate, make sure she's convicted of the crime. She's old so what does it matter? The two of us have a lot of living ahead of us."

"I picked the right man when I picked you for the job, Bryan."

"Offering me partner in the firm was the right incentive, Will."

"And meanwhile, the cyanide is safely hidden until we need it as evidence against our prime suspect?" Will said.

"It's in the lockbox of my trunk, at the ready."

Will and Bryan were Molly's killers. I had to call 911. My heart started pounding so loudly, I thought they'd hear it for sure. I had to get out of there while the getting was good. I reached for my phone, but my hand wasn't working right and it slipped out. The noise was enough to alert the men.

"Someone here?" I heard Will say.

I plastered my back against the wall, hoping they wouldn't see me as I slid my way to the exit door. But they beat me to it and blocked my path. The three of us were at a staring standoff for what seemed like an eternity when Will finally said, "What in the hell are you doing here?"

"Um, well, it's lunchtime." I dropped my phone in my coat pocket.

Bryan reached for my arm, but I turned and he missed. "What are you hiding?"

The look on my face must have given me away. "Hiding?"

"How long have you been here?" Bryan said.

"Not long."

"You're lying," Will said.

I tried sidestepping away from him, but he was faster and grabbed hold of my arm. Then Bryan grabbed the other. "You were in the wrong place at the wrong time, but we've got a solution for that, right, Bryan?"

Bryan lips twisted into a sneer. "Yes, we do. A solution at the ready."

At the ready. His words burned into my brain. He was talking about the cyanide; they were planning to poison me. We were in a public place, and there was no way they could kidnap me without being seen or heard. I'd scream at the top of my lungs. As soon as I found my voice.

"Grab a napkin to gag her," Will said and tightened his hold on me. It was now or never. I threw myself back against the glass door, prepared for the worst. It wasn't latched, and it pushed open with enough force to bounce against the wall. When I fell, Will lost his balance and stumbled. The door caught him on the side of the head.

I rolled to my feet surprisingly fast and rushed toward the lobby yelling, "Call nine-one-one! It's an emergency and we need the police!"

"We're here." Mark and Clint came running toward me. A number of people filled in behind them but stopped at the end of the short hallway. I pointed at the dining room where Will Dalton and Bryan George were standing. Will was rubbing his head and looking a little stunned. Bryan's eyes were darting every which way.

"They did it. They killed Molly. I heard them talking about it and recorded them." The words tumbled out.

"You little—" Will started. But before he finished, Mark grabbed him, turned him around, and handcuffed him.

Why Bryan George tried to push his way past us is beyond me, but Clint had him on the ground and his hands cuffed behind his back in seconds. Then he guided him to his feet. Bryan George and Will Dalton exchanged one last look.

Clint threw a glance at the growing crowd. "Show is over, folks. It's time to get back to your own business." When the people all turned and were walking away, he zeroed in on me. "Meet us at the station."

There was a lump in my throat, and I nodded. After Clint and Mark left with their prisoners, I hurried down the steps and out the back way before anyone stopped me to ask questions. Safely in my car, I reached in my pocket for my phone, and my fingers touched a penny I'd dropped in there at some point. I needed a heads-up today, that was for sure. I sucked in a big breath then released it as I pulled the phone out. It was still recording. I stopped it, sat for another minute, then called Pinky with the news.

Pinky coughed then cleared her throat. "Cami, oh my gosh, Cami. Will Dalton is one evil man."

"He is, and so is his friend. I have to go the police station, and I don't know how long I'll be there."

"No worries here."

"Give my folks a call if you need help; maybe they can come in for a while."

"We'll see. Cami, they are going to totally freak out about this."

The police department receptionist directed me to wait in Clint's office. The minutes ticked by slowly until Clint finally joined me. "You can relax, Camryn. I have calmed down and will not be giving you the same lecture I gave you yesterday, because I would obviously just be wasting my breath. That being said, I have to say thank you—for following your instincts and for your quick thinking, recording the conversation of those two hoodlums. Well done." He held out his hand. "Can I have your phone, please?"

It was cradled in my hand. It seemed like the safest place to keep it. I gave it to Clint without saying a word.

"Did you listen to the recording?" Clint asked, and I shook my head. Hearing their conversation once was enough. "I'll send it to the computer here and save it on a few flash drives for backup evidence. And I'll need to put your phone in evidence."

"Really? Is that necessary?"

"Until I hear differently from the county attorney. A smart lawyer might argue we altered the recording."

It was a small sacrifice if it helped put Molly's killers away. "All right."

"Neither one of those men will talk, which I expected. They lawyered up, and it might take a while for the attorneys in their firm to track down the best of the best to defend them."

"If the lawyers in their firm were smart, they would put as much distance as they possibly could between themselves and those animals."

Clint nodded once, found the recording he needed, and finished his task.

15

Two days after Will Dalton and Bryan George had been locked up in the Buffalo County Jail, we got the news that the St. Paul Police had tracked down Troy Ryland at his girlfriend's house. He was transported to Buffalo County, booked into jail, and would be appearing before a judge the next court day.

Pinky and I had decided to have a little impromptu gathering at Brew Ha-Ha when we closed up shop Saturday night. Erin offered to bring wine, and Pinky and I made food. We invited the people we felt needed to debrief with us. Irene Ryland, Emmy Andersohn and her friend Lester, my parents, Erin, Mark, and Clint.

"Why didn't you invite Ramona Zimmer, Cami?" Erin said before the others got there. She waited for my reaction then added, "Kidding."

Pinky frowned. "Erin."

"Believe it or not, she called me this morning and apologized for breaking the snow globe and running off." Pinky and Erin exchanged a look I couldn't read. "What?" I said.

"Nothing," Erin said.

I let it go. "Anyway, we talked for a while. I don't think things are going that great for her and Peter. It wouldn't surprise me if Peter takes off in search of greener pastures soon." And maybe she was starting to realize I was not to blame after all.

"I think that's the best thing that could happen," Pinky said.

The rest of our guests arrived in the next few minutes, and we hashed and rehashed the events of the past week and a half. Erin and Mark opened the bottles and poured wine for everyone. When we all had a glass in our hands, I lifted mine up. "Here's to Molly, who left us too soon, and to the police who put the bad guys behind bars." The tinkling sound of glasses filled the room.

"And here's to our brave friend, Cami, who—" Pinky started.

I waved my hand and smiled. "I don't think the police officers here want to get into all that again."

A few people snickered, and even Clint smiled.

"No, I think we should toast you, Cami. You believed me when not everyone else did." Emmy raised her glass.

Irene did the same. "Yes, and you showed you cared by doing something about it. Now my Molly can rest in peace." Clint had spoken with the county attorney who'd assured him the case against Irene Ryland was very weak, and they were dropping the charges. There was no physical proof

Molly had been responsible for her stepfather's death. What Irene relayed to the police—what her daughter had told her she'd done—was considered "hearsay" evidence, and not admissible in court.

I had tears in my eyes as we clinked our glasses again.

Irene raised her hand. "Oh, and I have a proper service sct for Molly next Tuesday evening, and you are all invited."

I took Irene's hand in mine and nodded.

Pinky disappeared then returned with her hands behind her back. Erin moved in next to her, and they stood in front of me with smiles on their faces. "What's going on?" I said.

Pinky brought her arms back around, and in her right hand was a snow globe. She held it up for everyone to see then handed it to me. The figure of Marilyn Monroe was standing in the center. "Ta-da! Here you go. Erin made it for you, and I helped by sneaking the figure off your counter this afternoon."

I hadn't noticed it was missing. "Pinky, Erin, I love it."

"And that's what gave us the idea to put Marilyn back in a snow globe. We knew how much you admired the original one," Erin said.

I shook the globe and watched the snow settle around Marilyn Monroe's feet. "I am really impressed—it looks professional."

Erin shrugged. "I had fun learning how to make them last month at the class you and Pinky held here."

"And you're good at making them, too," Pinky said.

Mom and Dad moved in closer. "If we have any more mishaps and break a snow globe, it looks like Erin is the one to call," Dad said.

I gave Erin and Pinky each a warm hug. "Thank you." I

passed the snow globe around so everyone could take a closer look. Emmy held it the longest, and I imagined she was working through the unpleasant memory of Ramona Zimmer breaking the original one.

"Excuse me a minute." I walked into Curio Finds carrying the snow globe and my wineglass. The light was on in the bathroom, but for once I didn't care. I held up my glass and whispered, "I'm sorry if I was ever unkind to you, Molly. We'll miss you." As I took a sip, the bathroom light went off. I took one last drink, shut the bathroom door, set my new snow globe on the checkout counter, and rejoined my family and friends in Brew Ha-Ha.

QUICK AND EASY
SNOW GLOBES

....

SUPPLIES

• A clean jar: baby food, jelly, pint, or any size

• Waterproof glue

• Distilled water

• Glycerin, for thickening

• Glitter

• Small figures, depending on your scene: animals, characters, vehicles, toys, trees, etc.

Pick the jar size to fit your scene. Using waterproof glue, such as Gorilla, attach your figure to the inside of the dry jar lid. Fill the jar with distilled water to the neck of the jar. Add 1-2 tablespoons of glycerin. A larger jar will require more. The more glycerin you add, the thicker the water will get, and the slower the glitter will settle. But too much may cause the glitter to float. Add the amount of glitter to your liking. Larger pieces of glitter will have a different effect than very fine glitter. Attach the lid to the jar. Add or pour off water as needed. If you use a baby food or other jar without a tight seal, put a bead of glue around the edge of the lid before attaching. Then screw on the lid, give your globe a shake, and enjoy.